"I am really taken by this story. The characterization is great . . . I love the style/voice. It was great to be able to read Jillian's and now Jack's [scene]. They each have their own distinct voices . . . It's apparent that the writing voice is well crafted and is really enjoyable to read. The dialogue is really fun."

—Industry professional final judge

"Engaging and the premise is great! I enjoyed the family dynamics, the dialogue, and action. Jack is sexy and affable—so hot!"

—*New York Times* bestselling author Cheyenne McCray

"I loved everything about the premise, the catchy names for the businesses, and especially the chemistry between Jack and Jillian. The story, the structure, the concept, the hero and heroine—give me a fan! It's amazing, without them even being in the same place when they reunite. I love the secondary characters!"

—*New York Times* bestselling author Erin Quinn

GIGI TEMPLETON

Text copyright © 2024 by Gigi Templeton
All rights reserved.

Published by Montlake, Seattle

www.apub.com

Amazon, the Amazon logo, and Montlake are trademarks of Amazon.com, Inc., or its affiliates.

ISBN-13: 9781662517877 (paperback)
ISBN-13: 9781662517884 (digital)

Cover design by Letitia Hasser
Cover photography by Wander Aguiar Photography
Cover image: © Pic Media Aus / Shutterstock

Printed in the United States of America

This is for fans of 'cuein', grillin', and smokin' who like a little extra spice in their lives!

Chapter One

"Great podcast this morning," said Mindy Vonn over the phone, in lieu of a hello.

No shocker there. Jillian Parks's überefficient producer didn't chit-chat much. Mindy was mindful of Jillian's quiet life in a sleepy Seattle neighborhood where everyone was engrossed in their own doings and didn't hang over the hedges to yak her ear off. The perfect setting for a reclusive insomniac who recorded her foodie podcast, wrote her blog, and sent out her newsletter—all titled *I'll Bite*—from her basement at three o'clock in the morning.

Also where Jillian created her spicy dry rubs and hot sauces in her certified kitchen. Her latest line had just been released, and sales for her Hotter Than Haba products were nice. Just not through the roof. As evidenced by the dozen—not *dozens of*—outgoing packages she was placing in the secured bin on her front porch for USPS pickup when Mindy called midmorning.

"Didn't know much about hatch chilies until today," her producer added.

"An underrated pepper, in my opinion. I've created successful hybrids with it." As was the case with most of the chilies she grew in her greenhouse. "I'll be featuring more of these particular fusions this week."

Jillian closed the lid on the storage container and rolled her utility cart back into the house.

"Looking forward to it," Mindy said. "Now . . ."

Jillian drew up short.

She shut the door and locked it.

"Now . . . *what*?" The change in Mindy's intonation worried her.

For good cause.

"I'm going to throw you for a loop."

So typical of Mindy to not sugarcoat anything.

Jillian adjusted her AirPods, like that might alter the course of this discussion.

No such luck.

"There's this dreamy Texas rancher," Mindy said, diving right in. "Our age, with his own YouTube BBQ channel. I want you to check him out."

Panic skittered through Jillian.

"Uh, no," she immediately responded.

"Just listen before you get judgy."

"I'm already feeling the hives coming on."

"Less sass, more acceptance, please."

"Are you trying to set me up on a date?" Something Jillian was *so* not ready for.

"Could be."

"Oh, my God."

"Relax." Mindy plunged forth. "Business first. Hear me out."

Jillian zipped her lips. *Business* being the operative word here. She was all for new marketing strategies—as long as they didn't stretch her boundaries.

"He also live streams on multiple social media platforms against a sensational backdrop, and he's collected a substantive number of subscribers. He's a champion pitmaster—I have no idea what that is, but it sounds sexy and rugged and virile. He has a huge family who helps to put on his show. His views are soaring, and it's not only due to his content. If you get my meaning."

Hands down, that was the longest Mindy Vonn discourse Jillian had ever heard.

That wasn't why Jillian sank into a chair in her living room as a thought penetrated her apprehension and tickled the back of her brain.

"Dreamy Texas rancher. Our age," she murmured. "Huge family. Champion pitmaster."

"Did a parrot join this conversation?"

Jillian ignored the joke. "Tall, dark, and devastatingly handsome? Sparkling blue eyes?"

"Mm-hmm. He puts the *yum* in my yummy. I'd gobble him up if I could lose ten pounds first—and dare to show him all my naked glory."

"You don't need to lose ten pounds," Jillian said. She didn't even need to lose five.

"Neither here nor there," Mindy stated in her clipped tone. "Point being, he's reviewing your latest line on his show today. And you're going to surprise him by calling in."

"Oh, hell, no!"

Undeterred, Mindy didn't miss a beat. "His producer, Garrett Jameson, contacted me on the down-low. Mm-hmm. He claims you know this culinary cowboy from college, and the two of you are going to reunite after an entire decade. *So* perfect."

Jillian's jaw dropped.

"No vid," Mindy assured her, filling the silence. "Strictly a call-in sitch. You'll tell his audience all about your peppery goodness, while he grills up whatever it is he's planning to grill up. Dazzling repartee will ensue, along with some harmless flirting, sending his stats into the stratosphere—and nabbing you a slew of fans. And customers. It's pure genius." She was really getting into this.

But . . .

"Whoa, wait. Pump the brakes." Jillian sprang to her feet. "Who *is* this guy?"

It couldn't be—

"Jack Reed, owner of the TRIPLE R: Reed River Ranch," Mindy proclaimed with a flourish.

Jillian could barely breathe.

"And. Get. This." Dramatic pause. "His ranch is in Serrano, Texas. Serrano! Like the pepper! How fated is *that*?"

Too much so.

That was *precisely* what Jillian had told Jack when they'd met during their second semester at Seattle Pacific University.

She had an instant "of all the gin joints in all the towns" moment. But they weren't talking gin. They were talking chilies.

She plopped into her chair again, her pulse pounding as a past she'd left in the rearview mirror now flashed before her eyes.

"Oh, Mindy . . . I can't. I truly *cannot*."

Jillian couldn't pull in a proper stream of air at the mere mention of Jack Reed.

How would she actually *speak* with him?

The guy who'd been her first . . . *everything*.

Her first love.

Her first time.

Her first heartbreak.

"This will be fantastic," Mindy asserted, not knowing the full extent of this fresh wave of anxiety. "Garrett said Jack lit up when he realized you were the owner of Hotter Than Haba. The timing is terrific with his show this week. He also has a big Memorial Day celebration coming up. Chances are, we'll get mentions there too." She was quite pleased.

Jillian, however, reeled from this shock wave rippling through her universe.

"Mindy," she said on a distressed exhale. "There's history you can't begin to fathom."

"Making it even more spectacular. Everyone loves a reunion, Jillian. Toss in food and family, and *bam*! Insta-win!"

Could it be that simple?

Jillian wanted to protest further. But Mindy was right about a potential insta-win. And Jack didn't know Jillian had fallen for him. Nor did he ever have to know.

A few dates, followed by sexy kisses under a tall tree outside her dorm, and one night in her room when his hand under her sweater had led to so much more . . . those were instances she'd had to sweep under the rug upon his jarring departure from campus following his dad's stroke their freshman year.

He'd left her with one parting line.

Don't ever think I didn't want more time with you, darlin'.

Words Jillian had never forgotten, despite having to move on from Jack Reed.

"It'll be a light and breezy convo," Mindy promised. "A saucy promotional event. Ha. See what I did there?"

"You amuse yourself, don't you?"

"I really do."

Jillian gnawed her lip. She couldn't deny she was tempted. She and Jack excelled at light and breezy conversation. At least, they had, once upon a time.

Unfortunately, her heart was a bit darker these days, the aftermath of a traumatic trampling incident at a concert six years ago that had delivered yet another painful blow—an emotional and physical one that had almost wiped out her entire existence. And which had destroyed the future she'd dreamed of.

In one fell swoop, she'd lost her fiancé and the baby she hadn't even known she'd been carrying. Had almost lost her own life.

A soul-crushing catastrophe on so many levels.

Something else Jack didn't need to know.

She stood and started to pace once more, her seven-month-old rescued Maltese, Ollie, gazing up at her. If he could crook a brow at her erratic behavior, she was certain he would.

"This is easy PR, Jillian," Mindy prodded.

Jillian mulled over this wild corkscrew, assessing what damage one call-in to Jack's show could possibly do.

If they failed to launch with the banter Mindy and Garrett were aiming for, they could flip the commentary on its side and turn the call into a quick "Hey, hey! Hope all's well with you!" Then Jillian would dole out her marketing spiels, and . . . they'd move on from each other. Again.

Not the end of the world, right?

Sure, reconnecting with Jack after all these years would crack open a sealed sorrow, another lost dream of hers.

Yet she couldn't deny the enticement of this spontaneous reunion. Or the necessity of it.

"Fine, I'll do it." The words tumbled from her parted lips, unbidden. For all the right *business* reasons, but also because kismet and some innate enthusiasm she couldn't grasp spurred her on. All wrapped around Jack Reed.

"Fabulous," Mindy said. "Look at his channel. I just emailed you the link. He has a website too. You're on in an hour."

"An *hour*?" Jillian gasped and felt the color drain from her face.

The panic returned. Full force.

Of course it did.

"Mindy—"

"I'll Zoom with you in the background the whole time. Just chill."

"*Chill?* Oh, my God, how can you say that? I have to do something with my hair! I need makeup and—"

"It's a *phone call*," Mindy reminded her. "He can't see you, Jillian. You can be in your SpongeBob SquarePants pajamas with curlers in your hair, or a lacy nightie, and *none would be the wiser*. I mean . . . except for me. You know, because of the Zoom."

She glanced down at her tan yoga pants and matching jacket. "We're all good there."

And Mindy was right—it didn't matter that Jillian's caramel-colored beachy waves were pulled into a disastrous ponytail and she wore only lip balm.

"I'll cue you," Mindy told her. "Now . . . go prep." She dropped off. Jillian blinked. Once. Twice.

Several minutes ticked by while she remained stalled out, rooted to the floor, still freaked. Ollie held vigil at her feet, head cocked to the side, looking perplexed.

"I know, I know," she said. "Forward movement is key to our recovery." She'd had to teach her neglected and malnourished pup that when she'd adopted him, convincing him that his forever home was a safe haven from all he'd endured in his short life. Just as her isolation had served as a respite to help her heal and regroup.

Making it advantageous that Jillian had found Mindy and was able to work with her remotely.

With her producer's voice echoing in her head, Jillian latched on to her personal goals. Her professional ones as well. She shook her hands out at her sides. Inhaled. *Too shallow.* Exhaled. *Too harsh.* She tried again, for a deeper, smoother effect.

It's just a phone call.

She urged herself into action, doing her best to reconcile the bizarre mixture of exhilaration and nervous energy dancing along her spine. She homed in on the outrageous notion of her and Jack circling back to each other. The probability seemed so slim. Except for his barbecue obsession and her pepper fetish. The fact that she was originally from the Southwest, too, hailing from Arizona. And they'd both enjoyed cooking with their dads. Jillian had also lost hers at a young age, fifteen. A bighearted man who'd called her Jills.

Also not to be discounted was the way she'd recalled everything about Jack Reed, simply because someone had said his name, after all this time.

Somehow, Jillian's heart rate slowed, and the air pushing from her lungs wasn't quite so agitated. Recalling that infectious grin of his and his natural charm made the shock wave dissipate.

You can do this.

As long as their producers knew what *they* were doing . . .

Jillian took Ollie to the basement and fed him treats from a baggie she kept in the drawer of her desk, positioned off to the side and laden with her laptops and podcasting equipment. She grabbed her notes from the clipboards in wire baskets on the credenza behind it and reviewed her sales pitches, hoping she could spew forth information on autopilot if she got lost in blue-eyed, dark-haired rancher dreaminess.

Too bad Mindy had made those references. They were stuck in Jillian's head.

"He's just a cowboy. Like any other cowboy," she said to herself. While knowing that was an absolute understatement.

She used the remote to turn on the flat-screen mounted over the fireplace. All she had to do was tap in the key words "Jack Reed BBQ," and there was his banner and logo, with a photo of him.

"Whoa," she whispered. "That's just *too* much man before noon." The rekindled embers crackled through her veins.

Good God was he gorgeous. Like melt-her-off-her-chair gorgeous.

Mindy chimed in on the computer, and that was the only thing to snap Jillian out of a brief waltz down memory lane, where Jack was teasing her about her less than stellar mathematical skills. He'd invited her to join his study group anyway.

"Now I know why I did so poorly in that accounting class," she muttered. "Too busy lusting after the hunky cowboy quarterback." Which could be her downfall today.

She connected with Mindy, who asked, "How are you doing?"

"Not as calm as I'd like to report," Jillian confessed, falling just shy of admitting her insides sizzled and popped and there was a sudden, long-lost sensation that now prickled between her legs.

"Deep breaths," Mindy encouraged.

"Been doing that."

The live cast started. And there was Jack. Devastatingly handsome Jack.

"He's able to live stream on more than this platform, with an encoder," Mindy informed her, "so I'll follow along on Facebook to see what the reactions to that feed look like. Let him do his intro, then dial in. I texted the number his producer gave me."

"Sure," Jillian absently said, preoccupied by the image on her TV. Ten years after she'd met Jack Reed, he was more strapping than ever. A mountain of a man a woman inherently wanted to climb.

And still so damn charismatic as he greeted his audience in his sexy southern drawl.

"Welcome to the TRIPLE R, my friends. I'm Barbecue Jack. Reed, that is, but sometimes I do add the Daniels." He chuckled, his stunning irises warm and scintillating. "We're grillin', 'cuein', and smokin', and yes, there is a difference. Most importantly, what does every prime cut of meat deserve? The right spice." His expression turned pointed, yet remained provocative, riveting. "I'm ready to *Rub It In*. Are you?"

Oh, sweet Jesus.

Jillian's inner thighs went up in flames. She crossed her legs, like that'd help.

Nothing is going to help, Jills.

The man had a scorching appeal that could incinerate her to pure ash. That fast.

She reached for the water bottle she kept on her desk. And nearly drained it.

Mindy cleared her throat as her prompt, and Jillian forced herself to hit the connect button on her cell, yet again wondering if she'd have a breath with which to speak.

From behind the scenes of Jack's show, a voice—Garrett Jameson's?—said, "We have a special guest on the phone for you, Jack."

His head whipped back. So, he really wasn't expecting her. Or any call-in, for that matter.

"Is it my birthday, and no one told me?"

"Nope. But you can thank me later for the gift."

"All right, I'll play along. Who might we have on the line, Garrett?"

Jillian stood. Miracle of all miracles, her knees didn't knock together.

She found her voice from the depths of her soul and managed to say, "Hey, there, Jack. This is the owner of Hotter Than Haba. I hear through the grapevine that you remember me from college." She let out a quavering laugh—tossing all hope of sounding cool and composed out the window.

His eyes twinkled.

"Jillian Parks," he said. So simple, so casual.

Yet there was nothing simple or casual about the way he stared into the camera, as though he was talking only to her . . . like no one else existed.

How she wanted that to be true. She might not be so nervous.

Doubtful.

She quashed the thought.

"How the heck are you, Jack?"

"Doin' just fine, thank you." With a slight shake of his head, he added, "I cannot escape you this week, and I'm darn glad for it."

"Cosmic intervention, I guess."

"More like we've been set up, darlin'."

Oh, with his low, intimate timbre and the *darlin'* that nearly had her swooning as the embers turned to a roaring heat that blazed through her.

Another thing Jillian hadn't forgotten about Jack was the commanding and yet somehow soothing presence he exuded. She'd just buried all the stimulating influences in the back of her brain. Where they refused to stay, as of this moment.

Every fiber of her being buzzed radiantly.

Though she strove for nonchalance to mesh with his laid-back demeanor. She'd have to put extra effort into keeping up with the dialogue. A challenge, what with her heart hammering and her palms sweating. "Seems apropos. You are reviewing my sauces and rubs, right?"

"Happy to do so."

"Your producer invited me on the show. I hope you don't mind, Jack."

He didn't respond, as if trying to wrap his arms around this bizarre twist.

She was blown away too.

He raised his hands in the air, in surrender, and said, "I can't think of a better surprise, truth be told." He continued to stare into the camera, his searing gaze turning her blood molten. "Welcome to my show, darlin'."

"It's an honor to be here."

"Honor's all mine." He beamed. "This is my lucky day, barbecuin' with an old friend. One as pretty as you, honey, is just icin' on that cake nobody made for me."

She sucked in a breath, at the same time Mindy murmured, "Oh, my . . ."

Jillian shot her a wide-eyed look.

"My bad," Mindy whispered and pressed a finger to her lips. "I'll mute."

"You still on the line, Jillian?"

"Still here, Jack. Just dealing with some distracting feedback."

He chuckled again. "I know how that goes. Got a whole family on the opposite side of my counter, giving me first-base-coach hand signals. Can't for the life of me read a one of 'em."

"They're *all* there?"

"Well, not all. But enough. Mom and my nephew Hunt are in charge of supplies and inventory. His twin, Ale, handles social media, TikToks, Reels, all the stuff that makes my head spin. My cousin Avery preps food with me. My sister—"

"Um, Jack . . . ?"

"Yeah, darlin'?"

"Sorry to interrupt," Jillian tentatively ventured, "but, uh . . . holy cow."

She stared at one.

"Beg your pardon?" he asked, perplexed.

"Literally," she said. "You've got a cow wandering into your frame, Jack." She pointed, not that he could see the gesture.

Yet he glanced behind him. His attention returned to the camera. He grinned.

And by "grinned," he basically set the world on fire. It was both devilish and electrifying.

Jillian propped her hip against her desk to steady herself. Her teeth sank into her bottom lip to hold back the sigh threatening to give her away.

Damn, but the man was hotter than her own habaneros.

Jack broke into her punny thoughts, saying, "Darlin', that's just Bessie comin' to check things out."

"Looking for one of her friends in your smoker?"

His laugh was much heartier this time. "Shhh . . . don't go gettin' me in trouble with Ol' Bessie. She likes to follow me around. Think she's got a crush on me." He winked.

Jillian's stomach flipped.

Oh, geez.

Who wouldn't have a crush on him?

Here was the full-on justification for choosing him as her first lover.

Jillian rounded her desk and dropped into her chair before her knees buckled.

"Someone hand me a rope, please," Jack called out.

He accepted the offering from a crewmember and knotted the end, forming a lasso.

"Y'all'll excuse me for a moment?" He turned away, walked a few paces, and slipped the loop onto Bessie's neck, as efficient as could be.

He passed the opposite round of the rope to a gentleman on a horse meandering by, to lead the cow from the set.

"That," Jack said as he faced the camera once more, but hitched his thumb over a broad shoulder, "is Mateo Martinez, my brother-in-law and the slickest buyer of livestock at auction."

Mateo tipped his hat, then disappeared from the frame.

Jack went to the apron sink in the corner of the enormous L-shaped outdoor kitchen to wash his hands. A rectangular cowboy grill accompanied the cooking facility on the open portion of the L, the base of which was encased in the same cultured stone. A long grate hung over the flames on thick chains, and Jillian could practically smell charcoal and mesquite wood chips wafting under her nose.

While he dried his hands and then squirted sanitizer on them, Jack suggested, "Maybe you can tell us about your spices and sauces, honey."

In her mind, she remained his captive audience of one. Of course she knew that wasn't the case in reality, what with Mindy showing her stats and all the like and love emoji floating over her phone screen as she watched live on Facebook.

"Sure, Jack." Unfortunately, he left her with little oxygen in her lungs. As a diversionary tactic, she asked, "First, what do you have fired up?"

"Glad you asked. I've had a Texas shoulder clod in my offset, goin' on sixteen hours now."

Bingo! *This* would pull her from all thoughts sexy and seductive. "What's your rub?"

His gaze smoldered as he said, "I do like that you speak my language, Jillian Parks."

So much for pulling her from all thoughts sexy and seductive. She yearned to hear *him* speak an alternate language to *her* . . . a very dirty one.

But she shook that naughty rumination from her head as Jack continued.

"So here's what this mammoth slab of beef looks like, naked."

Another member of his crew set an oversize sheet pan on the counter in front of Jack.

"Darlin', meet the clod and my cousin, Avery Reed. Two separate entities, mind you."

The cousin had the same thick, almost onyx hair and muscular build as Jack and a comfortable expression for the collective audiences.

"Hope you can tell the difference between me and the clod," Avery deadpanned.

Jillian wasn't sure if her brain blipped out over the word *naked—do not go there!*—or if she'd barreled into lust-filled territory with yet another too-attractive, enigmatic Reed.

Thank God this wasn't her show, and she wasn't on screen with these men.

"Avery's also the bunkhouse grill master," Jack shared. "Almost as talented as me, but I'm a few awards up on him."

Avery gave a half snort and told her, "Don't you go believin' any of that, Miss Jillian. No one treats a porterhouse with more TLC than me."

"I'm sure that's true," she replied.

As Jillian nearly smacked her forehead over her sudden lack of ingenuity, Avery went off to retrieve the finished meat from the smoker. He set it on the adjacent counter, tented it with foil, then stepped out of view.

Jack explained, "This is the mother of all beef shoulders. Sixteen glorious pounds. If you're lookin' to go big instead of goin' home, this is the cut you want." He reached under the workstation for a tray holding divided seasonings in an assortment of colorful southwestern bowls. "There's no cause for barbecue sauce or fancy dousing here. Straightforward spices are all ya need for a hint of heat. I'm startin' with coarse salt and ground black and white peppercorns." He began preparing the new portion as the cooked one rested. "Here's where you really wanna rub it in," he instructed as he all but caressed the slab in slow strokes, with a touch of pressure.

Jillian fell further under his spell, well aware the man's hands knew their way around a woman's body in the most sinful way. Add to that his deep tone, and desire taunted her like it hadn't in years.

Jack said, "The key here is to be thorough. Cover every inch, don't miss a single spot. Be generous. Be gentle. Be genuine. It's a concentrated effort that yields maximum results."

She suppressed a moan.

No, this wasn't Massage 101 and yet . . . it kind of was.

Now she wondered if *he* remembered what it'd been like to have his hands on *her* . . .

Sparing a glance at her computer screen, Jillian found Mindy all but drooling. And it had nothing to do with the food.

No great mystery now why Jack Reed had so many viewers.

Even Jillian was lost in the flexing of his powerful forearms as he continued to work in the spices, the sinew exposed because his button-down had short sleeves. Which hugged his biceps.

Jills . . . Snap. Out. Of. It!

She jumped to her feet again. "So, Jack, what's your special ingredient?"

"Because you know I have one." He flashed the dazzling smile that lit his beautiful blue eyes and now had flame emoji flying over Mindy's simultaneous stream.

"You can stick with what I'm currently doin'," Jack said, "or incorporate a little zest. What I did with the beef we just pulled from the offset was sprinkle some of Hotter Than Haba's smoky chipotle meco chili powder onto the meat and kneaded it in with the S&P. We're gonna find out in a few minutes if we get the enticing, though not overwhelming, kick we're striving for from slow-cooked, traditional Caribbean or Mexican barbacoa. After all, the clod does speak for itself." He wagged a brow for effect.

Jillian felt it all the way to her toes.

"For this particular slab I'm preppin'," Jack resumed his commentary, "I'm gonna try Jillian's cayenne pepper blend that has top secret spices she may . . . or may not . . . reveal to us today."

"Perhaps I should hold a few cards close to the vest," she teased. "So you'll invite me back, Jack."

"Strategic of you, darlin'. Now I recall why I wanted you in my study group when you clearly did not excel at numbers."

"Hey, my hybrids sizzle in Scoville heat units. Those are the numbers that matter the most."

"I do get your point." He completed his task, and Avery stepped in to take the clod to the smoker while Jack washed his hands again.

As he leaned forward to rinse his tanned skin, Jillian—and every other woman smart enough to be watching his show—got a tempting glimpse of the inner swells of his pecs.

Absolute overkill. His chest strained against his pewter-colored shirt. As did his cut abs. That taut material and his inky jeans didn't hide the fact that the man was chiseled to perfection. Even his squared jawline and cheeks were rugged and sculpted.

His dark hair was intentionally messy. Jillian itched to run her fingers through the lush-looking strands and tame them a bit.

Conversely . . .

Why tame a man who emitted raw masculinity and evocative sensuality? Jack Reed was a breed unto himself, and that was why it'd taken less than a semester for her to become enamored with him.

Honestly, it'd been more like twenty minutes.

Though that was moot.

Jack carved his smoked beef shoulder. The outside of the large piece had the right char to it, while the juicy inside appeared tender and tasty.

"You have a winner there, Jack," she told him. He had the process nailed.

He snatched a thin slice and popped it into his mouth, giving a nod. He said, "That's bringing home the flavor. Excellent undertones with the meco, Jilly." He paused, seemed to do a mental rewind, then amended, "Jillian."

She was also derailed as more memories surged forth. But she got back on track just as fast. "Your fans know we've met before, Jack. So . . . I had a nickname."

She shot for levity, though she didn't miss the trill that tinged her voice over him recalling the friendlier moniker—and letting it slip from lips she'd enjoyed kissing.

"You also had a penchant for peppers. Used to grow them in your dorm room windowsill."

Ah, so she wasn't the only one battling recollections of their brief time together . . .

"Let's talk about your hybrid with Trinidad's Moruga scorpion," he continued, "which I used on a wild king salmon filet, and the sweet habanero for the chicken wings."

Food, Jills. Focus on the food.

They discussed her exclusive creations as he pulled the fish and wings from their respective grills and showed them off.

Jack sampled the salmon first and blurted, "Son of a gun! *That's the stuff!*"

"Feeling the heat, Jack?" she asked, a bit flirty.

"There's a full-on fiesta happening in my mouth, darlin'. I'm tasting a fiery palette of flavors that'd be great on their own but are sensational all melded together. Whoa!"

He went into a more detailed description as a blond boy swooped in, dumped a fistful of forks on the rim of the fish platter, and passed it around for the crew to try, the main camera temporarily panning to capture the reactions—all thumbs-up responses.

Jack moved on to the chicken, and his eyes nearly rolled into the back of his head as he said, "Have mercy, darlin'."

"That's not my job, Jack. I want to take you straight to the edge."

By the wicked look he threw her way, she half expected him to inquire if she was still on the subject of sauces.

Am I?

He said, "I'm gonna savor this for a couple seconds, then I'll need some milk."

"The secret to eating spicy peppers is *not* to reach for a glass of water." For his audience's benefit, while he drank, she expounded, "The temperature intensifies because you're swishing the capsaicin around in your mouth. Dairy, as Jack said, alcohol—though not beer, it's water-based—olive oil, or peanut butter will put out the fire. Or carbs, like rice and bread."

"This is the jam," he assured her. "Do they give Pulitzer Prizes for hybrid chilies?"

"No clue," she said with a smile. "But I'm glad they meet your approval."

"And then some. Y'all have to try this," he told his production people and his audience. "You might want some dressin' for dunkin', though. This is a real scorcher. And use wet naps. Don't go rubbin' your eyes with this sauce on your fingers."

The kid slipped in to snatch the wings and make the rounds.

Jack said, "When you're done, Hunt, bring me more of that salmon."

"It's long gone, Uncle Jack. And Uncle Garrett says time's up."

Jack whistled under his breath. "That segment flew by much too fast. Feels like we were just gettin' started."

"I appreciate you letting me hijack your show today, Jack."

"Honey, you can come back anytime." He winked, his signature move.

Jillian's heart skipped a beat. Hell, she didn't even need the scorpion hybrid to get her pulse racing and her adrenaline pumping. Jack Reed did that all on his own.

She should be as surprised to have this response to him as he was to her invading his feed. Yet her innate reaction, after all she'd been through, proved the man's potency.

"Sooo, same time next year, with another new line?" she asked.

"You can count on it, darlin'."

Remorse and a tinge of emotion over *that being that* crept around the fringes of her psyche. But this had been an impromptu, one-off reunion. And she couldn't ignore that they were a million miles apart, in every way.

She concluded with, "Nice chatting with you, Jack, and meeting your family. I hope your viewers enjoyed the cooking and the conversation." She gave her website address and promo snippets, then bid everyone adieu.

Jack seemed to work a bit harder at his jovial wrap-up, transitioning to dialogue that was less singularly intimate and more widely interactive. Still engaging, but . . . he did appear to be experiencing the same disappointment. Minutes later, his outro and credits rolled.

Mindy unmuted herself.

"Well," she remarked. "Isn't he the *cream* in your cream puff?"

"That is downright, deliciously dirty." Jillian laughed.

"Admit you liked the jolt to the system."

"I cannot lie."

And Jillian knew she wouldn't be returning Jack Reed to the far recesses of her mind.

He'd be another *first* for her—the first man she fantasized about in six years.

Chapter Two

"If you were a soccer shoe, where would you be?" asked eleven-year-old Hunter the following morning.

Jack glanced up from the baker's rack sitting on the enormous kitchen island, where his chorizo-and-cheese corn bread biscuits were cooling. He squeezed a dollop of his cilantro-lime crema on their tops as his nephew hobbled farther into the room, wearing only the one cleat.

"Preferably on your other foot?"

"Right?" Hunter quipped, his hands in the air to accompany a shrug.

Jack took advantage and placed the rack on a sheet pan that he balanced on the boy's upturned palms. "Take these to the table," he instructed. "Be careful."

Hunter's fraternal twin, Alejandro, raced in a heartbeat later, nearly slamming into his brother, who called out, "Hey, watch it!" Hunter kept his eye on the prize, though, and made it to his destination, not dropping a single biscuit.

Maintaining his own trajectory, Alejandro declared, "Uncle Jack, you have to see this comment about your last show!"

For the moment, Jack ignored the mini tablet he waved in the air and said, "No running in the house, junior. Your nana catches you—or you knock over one of her vases—there's gonna be hell to pay."

"I know, I know!" Alejandro took a breath, then proclaimed on the exhale, "Uncle Jack, you're not supposed to swear, but look!" He shook his hand to indicate the electronic device he clutched.

"Hold it still, or I can't read it, Ale," Jack told him as he reached for a plate lined with paper towels to drain the hash browns once removed from the skillets. The thinly sliced potatoes, edges perfectly golden and crisp, snapped in the oil.

With notable exasperation, Ale twisted his wrist so the screen faced him, and he announced, "'Texas rancher and award-winning grill master Jack Reed should be nominated for a YouTube award in a new category, Most Charismatic.'" He stumbled over the last word. But he eagerly resumed. "'Can't stop watching him! Totally addictive!'" Alejandro, whose dark hair and deep blue eyes ran in the family, said, "She writes for *BBQ Weekly* magazine, Uncle Jack! *BBQ Weekly!*"

"Lemme see that." Jack's curiosity soared. He was secretly devouring reviews of his and Jillian's unexpected mash-up. So far, responses were positive because they'd sparked from the get-go.

He took the tablet from his nephew and finished the statement. Almost. "'Displaying his wit and wisdom every week on his YouTube channel, *Rub It In*, Rancher Reed is the ultimate in BBQ mastery and visual stimula—' Oh, good grief." He rolled his eyes. So. Not about Jillian.

He passed the device back to his nephew. Who rounded out the online post with, "'PS, ladies, he's single!'"

"How on earth would she know that?" Jack asked as he started huevos rancheros in a few cast irons already heating up on the combination stove/griddle/grill.

"I included it in your bio on your website." Wyatt Martinez, Jack's eldest sister, flashed him a sassy look as she breezed in and went straight to the refrigerator to collect the pitchers of orange juice and milk. She gave them to Ale to take to the breakfast table that sat twelve, then began brewing coffee for the freestanding urn.

"I have a website?" Jack inquired with a crooked brow.

"You do now. Ale and I developed the pages that went live last week," she informed him. "Your inaugural Memorial Day Weekend BBQ Bash will put you on the map, Jack. Push you beyond grassroots fame, even more so than your two-minute cooking segment every week on the local network."

"Do I *want* to be on the map?" he countered as he cracked eggs.

"You want more views and subscribers, right? That equates to greater monetization."

"True fact," he conceded. "Though . . ." Glancing at Wyatt over his shoulder, Jack further questioned, "What does my marital status have to do with . . . anything?"

"Oh, please." Wyatt gave a feisty sigh.

She and Hunter were the blonds of the family. Wyatt was thirty-one, two years older than Jack. She possessed enough energy to account for rambunctious twins, a husband who spent time on the road for auctions and other ranch business, a part-time marketing career, co-coaching Hunter's team, and helping to manage the organized chaos around the house. Which exhausted Jack, just thinking about it all.

Before she could answer, their mother, Brett Reed, marched into the room. A full head shorter than Wyatt but also a dynamo.

"Never hurts to advertise the goods," she told Jack with a mischievous smile. She tousled Ale's thick strands, though Jack was certain his nephew had no clue as to his nana's insinuation.

"It's not a *dating* app, Mom," Jack grumbled, not even wanting to go in that direction, in theory or in reality. He also had way too much on his hands. The TRIPLE R was his coveted legacy and always a top priority—as was his family.

"You joined a dating app?" asked Garrett as he entered from the garage door on the far side of the room, two boxes stacked in his arms.

He was a lifelong family friend, and the younger boys considered him an uncle. He met up with everyone at the island as Jack transferred pancakes to a platter.

"Don't we wish," Wyatt teased as she set the table with an eclectic assortment of mismatched dishes. She'd leave extras on the counter, along with to-go containers, for those who came and went in the morning, like Chance Reed, their cousin and the foreman of the ranch. Chance could smell a home-cooked meal from a thousand paces.

"Who signed up for a dating app?" He kept the inquisition going as he came through the opened doors off the courtyard and patio. "Aunt Brett?"

She swatted Chance's arm. "Never, ever would I."

Despite her levity, they all knew that answer was set in stone. She'd given her heart to one man and one man only. Unfortunately, that man's heart had given out on him.

The very reason Jack had left college after his first year and returned to the ranch.

Tragically ironic. He'd gone to Seattle Pacific University on a football scholarship, dreaming of playing pro for a few years to build a nest egg for the ranch and relieve some of the fiscal burden on his dad.

In that vein, he'd also wanted a degree in economics, knowing the TRIPLE R would be his responsibility someday. That day came much quicker than anticipated, and he'd fumbled through the early years until he'd discovered that his YouTube channel, other multimedia platforms, and the associated affiliate programs rapidly filled in gaps better than any drawn-out "budget reforecasting."

So . . . yeah. Maybe he did want to be *on the map*.

"I'm not claimin' you're a lonesome dove," his sister told him. "But ya kinda are."

He smirked. "How can I be a lonesome *anything* with all these mouths to feed?"

Though there was no denying his love life was lackluster—and speaking of the *lust* part, there'd not been much of that going on either. He was more focused on finances than flirting.

With the exception of . . .

"I don't suppose anybody's gonna mention the fire in Jack's eyes when Miss Jillian Parks called into his show," Garrett said.

"We don't know she's a *Miss*," Jack retorted. Though in every steamy thought he'd had of her last night, she was. "Y'all get this food on the table before it goes cold." He plated the huevos rancheros and bacon, then dumped his crown jewel, roasted southwestern potatoes with sautéed red onions and bell peppers, into a serving bowl.

Garrett hefted his boxes once more and carted them over, propping them on an empty chair, then pulling one out for Brett and one for Wyatt. The seat at the head of the table was never occupied. That had belonged to Jack's dad. And always would.

"What'd you bring us, Garrett?" he asked.

"Overnight delivery, compliments of Jillian."

Shit.

Jack would never escape this woman he couldn't have.

"Another batch of her dry rubs and sauces," Garrett announced, "since you plowed through them yesterday."

"Holy hotness." Wyatt fanned her face with a hand. "Where is my husband at a time like this?"

"Cup not running over with *this* brood?" Jack inclined his head at Ale. Jutted his chin toward Hunt. Again, both boys oblivious to the context.

"Just sayin'," she mocked.

Garrett passed a box of products to Chance. "Take these to Avery. The bunkhouse cowboys'll get a kick out of the heat level."

"Literally," Chance quipped.

While everyone gushed over Jillian's spicy hybrids, Jack had to force more fiery thoughts of her from his mind. No easy feat. Even before she'd dropped into his feed, she'd drifted through his subconscious from time to time. Okay, more than that.

"This woman is a true connoisseur," Garrett continued. "And you scored big time with that collaboration, Jack."

Ale showed his Reels and pics. Wyatt went crazy over the analytics she'd gathered. Brett kept shooting Jack sly smiles, like she knew his mind wasn't on data and social media responses but on Jillian Parks—and his mom was right.

He didn't have to be face to face with Jillian, didn't have to be in the same room with her, to feel a sucker punch to his gut. Just hearing her voice and the smile in it, picking up on the exuberance in her tone, had him recalling dozens of conversations and so many moments when he'd just wanted everyone in the study group or the library or their class to fade into the background.

Granted, it'd been painful not to *see* her when they'd been talking. A deep-seated longing had gripped him fiercely from the second she'd joined the show, and he'd craved a visual interaction.

At the same time, he'd been even more attuned to the hitches of her breaths, her soft sighs, and her delicate laughs when he was just listening to her, not being distracted by how damn pretty she was.

If Wyatt and his mother and the rest of his family were wondering why he didn't have his mind on settling down with a woman, Jack could assert it had less to do with him not having time for a social life and more to do with the fact that an intense yearning in his core was more powerful than "settling." It had to be appeased. Or left alone.

He couldn't ignore the particular longing he'd had for Jillian, couldn't manufacture it with someone else. So maybe that was the answer to his own question about the importance of his marital status.

Being in a relationship just for the sake of being in a relationship was not what Jack Reed was about.

"She's also just put out a cookbook." Garrett grabbed a hardback from the other package he'd brought with him.

Brett snatched the book and said, "That cover is *gorgeous*. Wyatt, look at this spectacular table setting."

"Good grief, all of her dishes match!" She studied the photo, then glimpsed at her brother. "Gee, Jack. She's awful strikin'." Wyatt turned the cover toward him.

There was that physical jarring deep within him again.

This time, it spawned a new idea for Jack.

He took the cookbook from Wyatt and flipped back the cover, shuffling through the pages, a thought rattling around in his head.

He could envision this side dish or that salad paired with one of his specialty meats or seafood entrées.

Also, the numbers from Wyatt and the others didn't lie. The audiences had truly gotten into the unexpected reunion and had responded fantastically to his and Jillian's balanced contrast.

All this had him thinking the two of them might have tapped into a dual marketing strategy that would benefit them both.

And, yeah, Jack also had an ulterior motive. Banking on the fact that she truly might be single because she still went by Parks, Jack wanted more time with her.

He glanced up at Garrett and said, "I have an even bigger idea, with Jillian."

"As spectacularly as it went yesterday . . ." Garrett grinned. "I'm all ears, Jack."

"Let's hope Jillian will be too."

He kept his thoughts private for a moment, churning over them.

Until Garrett prodded, "Yeeessss?"

Jack chuckled. "I'm just piecin' this together."

"Somehow, I think you've hammered it out. Let's hear it."

Jack closed the book, resting his forearms on the cover, his hands stacked just below Jillian's vivacious smile. He speared Garrett with an intent expression and said, "We have the staff and the resources, without pulling directly from the holiday BBQ party, to put on a similar production. Adding a few extra shows to our schedule is what I mean. Ahead of Memorial Day."

Garrett's gaze narrowed. "It's a bit of a time crunch. But not impossible."

"We don't want to put the big soiree in jeopardy. However . . ." This spontaneous add-on initiative of his might prove lucrative. "My

26

analytics outweigh hers. So I can't believe Jillian would pass on this kind of free publicity."

"Tell me what you've got in mind, Jack."

He gave a decisive nod.

And said, "Live, in-person cooking segments with Jillian. Here at the ranch."

◆ ◆ ◆

"I was allowed to rebroadcast the audio from Jack's show as bonus content incorporated into your episodes this week," Mindy said in her hasty tone over speakerphone. "That, in addition to the subscribers you picked up from the live stream, has more than tripled your social media numbers."

"Even better, orders for my products have exploded," Jillian informed her. "I could use a temporary assistant or two to help me get them packaged and shipped."

She thought of the teenage sisters at the end of the block who walked dogs for cash and had offered their services to Jillian when she'd adopted Ollie six months ago.

"Your orders will continue to be off the charts."

Jillian's brow quirked. "What makes you so sure?"

"Something exciting has cropped up. Another 'can't refuse' opportunity."

"Oh?"

"Garrett contacted me again. Mm-hmm."

"Is there an infatuation going on here?" Jillian mused.

"I don't know. You tell me." She waited.

Jillian was certain they were no longer talking about Mindy and Garrett.

"I, uh . . . umm . . ." Jillian stumbled over the words.

"'Nuff said. I already drew my own conclusion. You've been talking barbecue for days now, and I'm guessing you're having a fantasy or two that would turn my cheeks red."

"Mindy!" Jillian gaped.

Though, in truth, she *had* run through that one semester she'd shared with Jack.

As a rule, Jillian didn't dwell in the past—a survival tool that had helped her through her recovery process. She'd had to shut the door on her previous existence in order to form her new one.

Yet she'd found herself wondering how different her life would be today if Jack had stayed in school. If they'd remained a couple. If she'd never met Scott, a man she'd had so much in common with. He was into horticulture and planting roots, literally. He'd wanted a family as much as she had. In Seattle. They'd gotten engaged, and then she'd gone to that concert with him.

Where her whole life had been upended.

Which had led her right back to thoughts of Jack. And, yes, they had turned a bit wicked.

"I will confess to recalling our one and only night between the sheets," she said.

"Which makes this next proposal so decadent. I'm recommending you say yes before you even hear my pitch."

"Yeah . . . but, no." Jillian laughed a bit uneasily. "I'm not a 'sight unseen' buyer."

"Well, we didn't steer you wrong with the live stream, did we? You and Jack are the opposite poles that flip and attract each other. Sheer. Magnetism."

Jillian's stomach fluttered. An affliction that occurred every time she thought of Jack Reed.

To borrow a Mindy-ism, though, *Neither here nor there.*

Because Jack wasn't here, and she wasn't there.

Her producer interrupted her wistful sigh by saying, "This new concept came directly from Jack. Well, through Garrett, but it's Jack's brainchild."

As was her habit, Jillian started scratching her arm through one long sleeve, like hives were about to cover every inch of her. Though these hives were only imaginary.

She'd been thrust back into lusting after Jack, and that was difficult to reconcile when she hadn't felt even the faintest hint of desire in years—and was now getting zapped around every corner.

Something to consider. Yet she'd bite on this line. She couldn't resist.

"Spill the beans," she told Mindy.

"That is very close to being spot on. Here's the sitch: Jack enjoyed reconnecting with you, and both your audiences vibed on your flirty banter, so he's wanting to do four more shows, in advance of the bash he's hosting for the holiday weekend. He's interested in whipping up several of the recipes from your cookbook. *With you.*"

"Huh." The itching vanished. She settled back in her chair, nodding her head despite her and Mindy being on a regular phone call, not Zoom. "I always believed he was fabulously clever."

"Thought you'd dig this. However, there is one fat fly in the ointment that's going to push your boundaries."

Jillian sat forward.

Mindy ripped the Band-Aid off. "He wants to film the segments at his ranch. Not with split screens but with the two of you live and in person. *Together.*"

Her eyes popped. "That's impossible!"

"It's perfect," Mindy countered. "So buck up and let me tell Garrett you'll do it."

"I will not!" She shoved out of her chair for the ritual pacing she did when her nerves were tweaked.

Having gone through endless physical and psychological therapy sessions, she'd reached the resurfacing and reclamation portion of her recovery process. And though she suffered from ochlo-enochlophobia, an intense fear of crowds and mobs, she attempted to make a distinction between what had become a habitual reaction to certain scenarios versus what was a true trigger.

At the moment . . . she was at a loss.

"These are very straightforward and effective promotional activities," Mindy further contended. "Four shows, that's all. And it's not as though you don't know this man."

"There are sooo many other factors involved, Mindy."

"Of course. I thought of them all," she said. "His ranch is a contained environment, Jillian. You won't be out and about, mixing and mingling with a throng of people."

"Oh, my God . . ." Her breaths accelerated.

"Jillian," Mindy iterated with emphasis, "opportunities such as this do not grow on trees. And you self-pubbed your cookbook, with no one other than yourself to market it. That is what you excel at with your product line, yes. But if you don't get the word out for this additional venture and get your face in front of readers, you're not going to have any."

She flattened a hand to her roiling stomach and mumbled, "I'm going to be sick."

"No, you're not," Mindy insisted in the tough-love tone she only used on Jillian when necessary. "You're going to do this. And when you're done, you're going to thank Jack for the invitation, Garrett for producing, and me for pushing you out the damn door."

She flopped into her chair. Sucked in long streams of air. Did her absolute best to latch on to reasonable thoughts.

Mindy added, "The two of you were magic together. Tell me you didn't enjoy the joint venture, that you didn't get a thrill out of having a partner in crime, a change from your one-woman podcast."

The corner of her mouth quivered in an emotional half smile as Jillian thought of how she and Jack had slid into a groove. Easy peasy.

The enticement of the man was undeniable.

Yet . . .

That didn't automatically trump a phobia. Or insomnia. She'd been plagued with such insidious nightmares that she'd not wanted to close her eyes. Ever.

With help from sleeping pills—because there were also horrific screams to distance herself from—she'd managed to retrain her body to rest. Though six years later, Jillian still experienced flashes of that night in a packed auditorium, where a fire had broken out alongside the stage, and everything had gone up in flames *so fast*. She'd been trampled under the feet of stampeding concertgoers as she'd helped a young woman who'd fallen on the concrete stairs. To this day, she could still feel the pressure and weight of terrified people climbing over her.

Those were her prevalent issues.

Still . . .

As Mindy had pointed out, this wasn't a "live in front of a studio audience" scenario. It was a "live on social media" one.

Night and day.

"Ugh," she murmured. "Damned if I do. Damned if I don't."

"Jillian, you're set up for this trip. You have portable recording equipment, and you can tend to your peppers before you leave."

"Yes, but—"

"I know you have an automated irrigation system in the greenhouse as well as an app to monitor growing conditions."

"Sure, though—"

"And speaking of apps," Mindy interjected, "I'll book you into motels with exterior rooms and you can check in and open your door from your phone—never even entering a lobby. Use drive-throughs for meals. Find quiet gas stations to pee when needed."

"You've figured this all out."

"This is your *livelihood*, Jillian."

One she clung to.

She'd rebuilt from a shaky foundation up. She couldn't let all that fall by the wayside when she had this new marketing prospect to consider. Even if it meant she'd have to interact with at least a few people along the way and at the ranch, she could do that.

Circumstances were circumstances, good or bad. Joyful or painful. Sometimes the only control you had over them was how you emerged on the other side. How you processed that pain.

And since Jillian was trying to free herself from certain habits and emerge *successful* on the other side . . .

Her eyelids squeezed shut to hold back the sting of tears. Her stomach knotted.

You can do this, Jills. It's part of the reclamation and reintegration process.

You have *to do this.*

Her lids snapped open.

Fucking fuck.

On a broken breath, she said, "I'm in."

◆　◆　◆

"How did I even agree to this?" Jillian mumbled as she plugged in the access code at the wrought iron gates she had to crane her neck to see the top of through her windshield.

"TRIPLE R" was stamped into the intricate scrolls elevated above the two arms that opened toward her, to welcome her in.

A bit more excessive than she'd anticipated, setting her pulse racing.

She drove her SUV along the winding, hard-packed dirt road, lined by lush grass and mature trees, fields of bluebonnets. Offshoot trails to the left led to several outbuildings and a maze of corrals.

She climbed the gentle slope and crested the rim, the scenery even more stunning as she took in the rolling hills in the distance and a river winding through the backdrop, where more trees lined the periphery.

Jillian was used to the greenery of Seattle, what with the regular rainfall. But this was different. This was another world, so vast and striking she had trouble keeping her eyes on the road as she took it all in.

Gravel now crunched under her tires as she approached a circular drive that featured a gorgeous fountain. On the right were stables. On the left was a house and, a hundred feet away, a mammoth three-story abode, resembling a ski lodge for all its smooth river rock and rounded-beam accents.

Her attention drifted back to the stables, two corrals along one side and a series of others on the opposite. The dual enclosures were currently occupied by a single horse that paced with notable anxiety. One had a visitor. A tall, strapping cowboy, dressed all in black, including his hat and boots.

"And there he is." She bit back a moan. Warranted, but not something that would help her as she navigated this alternate universe.

Jillian rolled to a stop, cut the engine, and slipped from the driver's seat. She let Ollie out of his soft carrier on the floor of the passenger side and set him on the ground to tinkle, while she strolled to the end of the vehicle and leaned against it, watching Jack circle the front of the horse, murmuring to him. Jillian couldn't hear the words.

He had a rope in his hand, and every time he inched in, the horse balked and snorted.

Her breath caught.

Jack eased in from varying angles, reaching out with his free hand to touch the horse's neck, nose, or flank. The horse was having none of it. And reared up.

Jillian gasped.

Jack jumped out of the way, though his hat fell to the ground. He spoke in a low tone again as he dropped the rope, somehow soothing the animal. Talking him out of perceiving Jack as a threat.

After a couple of minutes, he snatched up the rope and his hat, plopping the latter on his head and hanging the former on the outside of the gate before he moved a heavy metal latch into place and secured the bottom with a lock he depressed with his foot. The stable door opened to the corral, and a ranch hand tended to feeding and watering the horse, not getting too close.

Jack turned and gave a casual lifting of his chin in acknowledgment of Jillian's presence. He removed his gloves and stuffed them in his back pocket as he crossed the gravel to where she stood, a bit in shock, but not so much that she hadn't whisked Ollie into her arms, as though the horse's hooves might come down on him.

A protective instinct.

Jack's dangerous extracurricular activity made her shudder. But she and Ollie weren't in harm's way, so she told herself to stay the course.

"Hey, there," Jack greeted her as she fought for a stream of air—not just due to the slight scare with the horse but also the man, in general.

Once again, he wore a short-sleeved shirt, straining against his thick biceps, with pearl snaps that were undone enough for her to get another stellar glimpse of his pecs. The front hem was tucked behind a large belt buckle that proclaimed he was a champion pitmaster. She'd thought only gods of the rodeo arena sported prestigious buckles, but apparently it was an accolade bestowed from the BBQ circuit he'd been involved with when his dad was alive.

Jack had not dressed like this at SPU. Thank God. She'd found it difficult enough not to drool over him in jeans and T-shirts under heavy jackets—not to mention his football uniform. Him looking full-on cowboy now had heat flaring low in her stomach, spreading outward, downward.

Not at all helpful to her plight.

She tried not to stare. Too hard.

Lucky for her, Jack's attention was on Jillian's vehicle. "You're right on time." His gaze slid to her license plate, and he added, "You drove from Washington?"

"I don't fly," she told him. "Packed airports and cramped planes are . . . not my thing."

And Mindy providing real-time traffic updates the entire way kept Jillian from getting stuck in any jams. Above and beyond the call of duty, but Mindy vowed they were in this together, and Jillian was grateful for the camaraderie as she entered uncharted territory.

Jack whistled and said, "Darlin', you must be exhausted."

She didn't bother informing him she was accustomed to endless "awake" hours.

"I made the appropriate overnight stops along the way. Took me four days to get to Austin. Another three hours later, and here I am."

"I could've sent someone for you to do the drivin'," he said as he scratched his nape, the gesture further flexing his biceps.

Better get used to that, girlfriend.

He was sexy as hell. Towering over her, virility rolling off him in waves, if that was even possible. No denying she sensed it.

His blue eyes were warm and shimmering, so that even the vibrant Texas sky couldn't compete with those entrancing irises. His grin didn't waver. Like he truly was pleased to have her here.

Though he said, "I didn't mean to put you out, Jillian."

"Oh, gosh, no!" she blurted. "I'm the one invading your turf. Again."

And the wild tumble her belly took reminded her she was severely out of her element.

Except . . .

Jack was standing a proper distance from her, not swooping in for an exuberant bear hug but also not appearing uncomfortable about the physical gap. He was cool, mellow, like he'd been with the riled horse.

For a moment, Jillian wondered if Mindy had discussed with Garrett, who would have discussed with Jack, that she was wary of being crowded.

Jillian had been up front about her ochlo-enochlophobia from the time she'd hired Mindy. Given they weren't even in the same state, Jillian hadn't worried about them spending extensive time together in her basement, producing the podcasts. Jillian did her thing in the wee hours, and Mindy edited and released episodes during the day.

If Mindy had explained Jillian's reclusive tendencies to Garrett, it would have been done out of kindness—and to safeguard Jillian. So she didn't mind if the word had been passed around. She knew it'd be a blanket statement made by Mindy, without the horrific details, including Jillian's hospitalization and lengthy rehabilitation. The fact that Scott had abandoned her only a week in, unable to deal with all of Jillian's surgeries and her induced coma. Not to mention their loss and his guilt. Mindy didn't deem that to be anyone's business other than Jillian's, and Jillian appreciated that she respected her privacy.

As Jillian contemplated this, Jack took a step closer, though he maintained a decent span between them. He indicated the puppy in her arms with a finger. "This must be Ollie."

"Mindy said you wouldn't mind me bringing him along."

Their producers had made the arrangements, keeping everything on a professional level.

Jack told her, "Not at all. In fact, the nephews have been buggin' for a dog, and this is a good chance for them to experience the responsibility involved."

"I'll warn you," she said with a smile, "he's super low maintenance, can hardly be bothered to bark. So I'm not sure you'll be able to count him as an experiment."

"It'll be entertainin', anyway. And, wow, he's a tiny thing."

"Yeah, the runt. He was rescued from a puppy mill where he was caged with his litter. He learned to keep to himself, the surveillance cameras from a police operation showed. He stayed out of the way of the others when they were climbing over each other to get closer to the mom for feeding." Another connection that bonded Jillian and her dog. "He wasn't yet weaned when I adopted him. I fixed him formula in a doll bottle until he started to lap mushy food from a bowl."

A more amusing thought pushed out the less desirable ones.

She smirked at the recollection of feeding Ollie in the beginning.

"By 'mushy,'" she told Jack, "I mean it was going in and coming out the same way." She grimaced.

Jack laughed, though not at a decibel to disturb Ollie as he rested his chin in the crook of Jillian's arm, completely content. "That's a valuable point the boys'll need to know."

"Made for messy times," she confessed. "But it was worth it."

"He clearly trusts you."

"We share the same vibe," she simply said.

A curious expression flickered in Jack's eyes. He didn't prod, though. "I really am happy you're both here. We've got the guesthouse all set up, just down the way. I'll grab the key from the main house and meet you there. Drive on over. There's a designated parking spot for you."

Her gaze roved the immediate area, with eight or so trucks and cars lined up. "Looks like you've got company."

"This is nothin'. Mom and Wyatt are in town, and the kids are at school." It being Monday. "But we have a lot of doin's and the right people to do 'em," he replied. "Don't you worry about all that. There's regular work to tend to, and then there's prepping for the Memorial Day weekend."

"Right," she said. "Mindy told me about the shindig you have planned. Sounds eventful."

"You can come back for the festivities," he offered. "The family and the fans would get a kick out of you joinin' in."

The sparkle in his eyes almost had Jillian saying she'd love to.

But what was she thinking? She was on a two-week excursion in the middle of the release of her new products, and the only way she was swinging this adventure was that she'd packaged her immediate orders and had put them in the bin on her front porch for pickup. She hadn't had time to train the teens to help her while she was gone; therefore, she'd filled foldable storage carriers and stacked them in the massive cargo space of her SUV so she'd have inventory on hand to send out as more orders came in.

"I only have so many supplies with me, and then I'll need to get back home to work. Also . . ."

She hedged a moment or two, giving more consideration as to whether she should be the one to put her anxiety on the table, regardless of anything Mindy might have said.

Having her condition out in the open would aid her in not feeling so awkward about her paranoia of people surrounding her, closing in on her.

Conversely . . . it was one thing for Mindy to touch on the subject, out of goodwill. But for Jillian to bring it up—that could incite questions she wasn't quite ready to answer. Questions that went far beyond coping strategies. Root causes were their own triggers, even when describing them after the fact.

Yet Jack was just one person, not a crazed mob. And he certainly wasn't pressing in on her. The truth was, she liked that he was just close enough that she could smell his cologne. An earthy, sandalwood-tinged scent that teased her senses.

However, the mere thought of horses clopping down on her, or God forbid Ollie, kept her hyperaware that anything could happen here, including traumatic flashbacks and nightmares.

A double-edged sword, for sure.

As was Jack's furrowed brow as he queried, "*Also*, what?"

Chapter Three

Jillian pulled in a deep breath. Let it out slowly.

There was a tranquil air about the man. In this instance, a contradiction to his palpable charisma. That made him multifaceted and intriguing.

His changes in disposition when he'd read the dynamics of a room or the study group had enthralled her. Even the synergy coursing between the two of them. He was perceptive and reactionary to the people around him.

The very reason she trusted him, enough to share from her own lips, "I don't do so well in large groups, Jack."

"I will surely keep that in mind, darlin'."

Emotion burned up her throat as Jillian's internal struggle continued.

"I'm grateful for your hospitality and for your understanding. I'm looking forward to us cooking together."

"Who would've thought we ever would?" he mused, lightening the mood. "After all this time. And . . . pleasure's all mine, Jilly," he told her in his seductive tone and tipped his hat.

Jillian suspected she wouldn't breathe properly again until she was back in Seattle. Even that was debatable.

"I'll grab the keys to the guesthouse," he said, "and meet you there. Get you unloaded."

"I brought equipment to do my podcast too."

"Plenty of room for that. Go on over."

She resumed her position behind the wheel, Ollie in her lap. Gentleman that he was, Jack closed the door for her. She curved around the fountain and returned to the more modest home, though as she pulled into the private drive, *modest* really wasn't the term she'd use. The yard was richly carpeted with neatly trimmed grass. Bushy-topped trees provided ample shade. A fancy bistro dinette sat under an umbrella of leaves, and a babbling brook ran along the perimeter, with rapids that sent serene sounds through her opened window.

She exited the vehicle and inspected the deck, with a gas grill, a round table, and chairs for six, plus two chaise lounges with thick cushions.

Minutes later, Jack came jogging from the main house. He passed through her gate, saying, "I had the yard fenced in for Ollie."

"That was nice of you, thanks." Did the man think of everything? "The mutt doesn't really go anywhere without me, but he'll like the freedom to roam. Supervised." Jack bounded up the steps, and she added, "You know, I could have waited for you and given you a ride."

"Darlin', I always need the exercise. I'm not a man who skips meals."

Her gaze flitted over him. She mumbled, "Or workouts."

Jack wagged a brow. "Go ahead and express if you like what you see, darlin'."

"Jack." She swatted at him. "Don't make me blush."

"If I recall right, Jilly, you always did that quite beautifully."

"Oh, with the charm," she jested as she fanned her face. Though in truth, she wasn't mocking him. "Really, Jack, you're too much."

"I happen to think I'm the perfect amount of *much*, honey. Unfortunately . . ." He gave a shrug and contended, "My opinion of myself holds very little weight around here."

"Somehow, I find that hard to believe."

He chuckled, a deep rumbling sound that caused her nerve endings to ignite.

Good God . . . her entire existence had just capsized once again with this impromptu trip, yet it wasn't peppers and recipes and burgeoning sales she was preoccupied with.

It was Jack Reed.

He reached into his pocket and extracted a key chain with one key dangling from it. He pushed through the door, then set the ring on a slim entryway table. "All yours."

He did an about-face and went to her SUV to collect her bags and boxes, piling everything on the porch as she took a few moments to rise above the hot flashes he caused. Then she stepped into the house to survey the surroundings, finding she felt right at home.

Her first inclination, of course, was to scout the kitchen, which was spacious and well appointed. She checked out the six-burner stove and the double oven. She crossed to the dining table along the far wall of windows—an out-of-the-way location with a fantastic view of a side yard and more trees.

She moved in the direction of the living room space, her fingers trailing the top of a plush L-shaped sectional that faced a tall hearth, the mantel of which was decorated with candles and knickknacks. An armoire in the corner likely concealed a TV and stereo system. A short hallway led to the bedrooms and bathroom.

Jack came in with his hands full and said, "The spare room has a fold-up bed that converts into a desk, so you can spread out for your podcasting and store your inventory."

"Excellent, thanks."

He ducked in there to drop off his current load before returning for more. On this next pass, she followed him down the corridor, then beyond to the bigger suite, and set her Rollaboard next to the window seat.

When she joined him out front again, he suggested, "Why don't you unpack? If you want to decompress after your drive, take your time. Come up to the house for lunch if you'd like. By the way, the linen's straight out of the washer and dryer, which are right off the bathroom.

Your fridge and pantry are stocked. Help yourself to anything. If you're missin' something, you can snag whatever you need from the kitchen up at the house or ask Avery. He's got all sorts of cowboy classics in his cupboards—which, bein' on the ranch, you might be inspired to cook with."

"Like baked beans and camp bread?" she quipped.

"Flaky, southern-style biscuits in a buried dutch oven are more his jam, but the possibility does exist."

"Jack . . . all this trouble you're going to—"

"No trouble at all, darlin'," he said in a tone that sounded genuine. "You're doin' me a favor with these shows."

"We're doing each other a favor," she pointed out. "This is all for publicity."

He stared into her eyes for several suspended seconds. Stealing her breath. Making her damn near forget her name.

Jack's head dipped. His lips were mere inches from her temple as he murmured, "Is it, now?"

He stepped back. Gave her a mischievous grin.

While Jillian reeled, and her heart almost stopped.

Granted, she hadn't expected hers and Jack's chemistry to change. Not that it was a foregone conclusion that an overwhelming sense of awareness would remain between two people years down the road and with all this distance between them. But when it was innate and palpable . . . Yes. It could be deemed a foregone conclusion.

That wasn't the current issue she tripped over, though.

Something poignant struck Jillian—like a lightning bolt that jolted her to the core.

It occurred to her that she hadn't felt a breath on her skin in years that wasn't Ollie's.

Her dentist and hygienist wore masks, as did other health-care professionals during annual wellness appointments. And Jillian always checked in via text from her SUV in the parking lot, where she remained until she was alerted it was her turn for an exam, thus avoiding a populated waiting room.

But the crucial point being . . . no human had been in such close proximity to her that she felt the gentle wisp of air on her cheek.

Heat crept up her neck. A gnawing ache inside her, which was becoming all too familiar where Jack was concerned, had her shifting from one foot to the other in an absolute worthless attempt to stymie the insistent pulsating at the heart of her.

In an overkill–Marilyn Monroe voice—she had no idea where *that* came from—she told him, "Mindy says everyone loves a reunion. One of the reasons we had such a great response from viewers."

His gaze bore into her as he mused, "I'm not discountin' the trope, mind you. But . . . don't you think it really had more to do with our personal connection? And you weren't even on screen or on site with me."

Jillian's heart still stammered. Her chest rose and fell. Quickly. That did not go unnoticed by Jack, as his irises now deepened in color.

"Audiences do like when cohosts gel," she commented.

"The word you're looking for is *spark*, Jilly." His expression turned roguish. Keeping every fiber of her being humming like a live wire.

"Admittedly, I used to thrive on our repartee," she said. "I didn't realize how much I'd missed it until that call-in."

Perhaps that had been the ultimate inspiration for her to leave her secure sanctuary.

She added, "I always did like that we can say almost anything to each other—and flirt at will. I mean—" A new thought dawned on her, knitting her brows. "Oh, crap, Jack. I know you're not married. I saw your bio on your website. But is there someone who wouldn't be too thrilled that this comes naturally to us? I don't want to get you in hot water."

He gave a self-deprecating half snort. "Darlin', I can't be held responsible for what's on my website; that's all Wyatt's doin'. But the fact is . . . I haven't had time for dating. I've got a ranch and a show to run. I don't hang in town, even at Luke's joint, hopin' some sweet thing's gonna bat her lashes at me."

He shook his head. Rolled his eyes.

Interesting response. Like perhaps Wyatt's mention of his marital status in his bio was a source of contention—but he recognized his sister's goodwill. A complexity for him.

More than that, on the one hand, Jillian felt a modicum of relief that he wasn't romantically entangled.

On the other hand, she couldn't dismiss the sting of the solitary existence they both experienced.

Though, circling back to that first hand . . .

She smiled. And said, "Good to know I'm not stepping on toes."

"Not at all. I'm basically fixated on finances," he confessed. "So, yeah, this publicity is crucial to me. However . . ." His voice trailed off for a moment. His jaw worked. Then he added, "I can't help but think there's a bit of fate at play here. Once again."

Jillian drew in a breath.

He asked, "You get that, too, right? Or . . ." He was the one to turn contemplative as he flipped *her* question in her direction. "Is there someone on your end who wouldn't be too thrilled that this comes naturally to us?"

Oh, God, as if.

Her stomach wrenched.

The agony over a broken engagement skittered through her, but the emotion was almost immediately overshadowed by the way Jack stared so intently at her.

"I don't date either. I pretty much keep to myself, Jack."

"Hmm." He appeared to mull this over—but couldn't land on anything conclusive. "Fair enough, Jillian. I won't ride ya on it."

"I appreciate that, cowboy."

His grin returned, crinkling the light lines around his eyes, which hinted at long days in the sun and likely late nights poring over receipts and balance sheets.

"What I do," he gently asserted, "is lend an ear whenever it's needed."

He winked.

"Oh, geez." She sighed dreamily. "I should request that you dial down the magnetism. I'd regret it, though."

This seemed to please him. "Duly noted, darlin'. Now how about I get out of your hair so you can get settled in. Lunch'll be ready whenever you are. Bring Ollie along. My nephew will get a kick out of his name—Ollie and Ale. This dog will not be starved for attention, I promise you that."

"He never is, and it's precisely what he prefers. He has a few tricks up his sleeve to ensure he's the life of the party."

"I don't doubt it. He's damn cute."

"He's well aware."

Jack headed to the door. Over his shoulder, he said, "You'll both like it here. Just keep in mind that when we invite someone to the ranch, they're instant family."

A daunting statement. For so many reasons.

She understood it was meant to be a friendly one. And were she the old Jillian, it would have been that straightforward. However, there were convoluted connotations connected to the sentiment for the new Jillian. The word *family* elicited images of holiday gatherings and summer festivities. Events Jillian couldn't fathom partaking in, not only due to her unease around crowds, but also because she'd had a vision of her own family plotted out, with Scott. Regardless, she forced herself not to hyperventilate over all of this.

Left to her own devices, she glanced about and decided she felt neither confined nor pressed in on. Jillian was still jittery about her overall surroundings, though, so she didn't unpack. Didn't remove anything from her suitcase other than a pair of jeans and a fitted tank top in navy with a matching cardigan. From another bag, she retrieved her ankle boots. She freshened up in the bathroom.

After snatching the key ring and a baggie of treats for Ollie, she set off with him, enjoying the balmy breeze, the mountain air, the scenic walk to the main house.

Jillian looked forward to working with Jack. What prickled her nerves was that they had a parking lot here. A graveled one that was set back from the circular drive, where there were now a dozen vehicles lined up.

Causing her to stall out on the welcome mat on the porch.

Of course she was going to extrapolate that each vehicle could hold two or three people. More than that. What sort of busy environment was she about to walk into? How many of Jack's friends, family members, and employees might be milling about?

Her heartbeats ratcheted up several notches. Her palms turned clammy.

She didn't even raise her hand toward the doorbell. Well . . . at that . . . there wasn't one. A knocker, yes, but it appeared to be more of a novelty than a manner with which to announce one's presence. Especially given the size of this place.

She glanced down at Ollie and said, "I might have let nostalgia and delusions of soaring subscribers get the best of me. This doesn't at all seem like a good idea and—"

The twelve-foot-tall door swung open.

"Holy Moses!" An attractive salt-and-pepper-haired man balancing a wooden crate on his lifted thigh, so as to free one hand, started at the unexpected visitor. He hastily recovered and said, "Miss Jillian! What a pleasure. Garrett Jameson. I'd shake your hand, but as you can see, mine are full." He had to grip both handles of the heavy crate as it threatened to topple over.

"It's nice to meet you," she said, collecting herself as well. "Thank you so much for all you've done to pull this venture together—and for allowing me on Jack's show previously."

"Are you kidding? I can't tell you how glad I was that you agreed—to all of this. Now please forgive me, but I'm runnin' late. Gotta get these outdoor speakers to the technician to repair them, or we're gonna be buyin' new ones, after that hellacious storm we had last week. Blew 'em clean off the columns they were mounted to."

"Yikes! Don't let us stand in your way," she said and moved aside.

"No, no. Ladies—and puppies—first," he joked. Then gestured with a slight jerk of his chin for her to enter. "Jack's in the kitchen. He's the only one in there. All the way to the back, past the dining room and to the right. Can't miss it."

"I'll follow my nose," she said. "Better yet, Ollie's."

Garrett laughed. "For future reference, no need to use that knocker. No one'll hear it. If you have the code to get on the property, you're one of us. Just come on in." He grinned, then hurried off.

Jillian shut the door behind him. Pulled in several breaths. Willed her pulse to slow.

"Come on, Toto," she said to her dog. "Let's go see the Wizard about some food."

She shook out her hands and squared her shoulders. Then they were on their way again.

They passed through a foyer with a round table bearing a floral arrangement in a pretty pottery vase below an antler chandelier. Jillian entered the cavernous great room boasting large windows and an exposed-rafter ceiling, three stories high.

Split railings encompassed the upper-level mezzanines. Several sitting areas were arranged around two fireplaces, with lots of accent tables, as well as lamps that provided a soft amber illumination.

The hardwood flooring was polished to a lustrous sheen, and there were rugs in varying sizes and shapes in rich sienna and gold, with southwestern patterns.

Ollie scampered along behind her, and she felt the need to pick him up and carry him so he didn't scratch the floor. Not that she anticipated he would with his trimmed nails, but the place was so immaculate, she didn't dare risk marring anything.

She passed the staircase with a gleaming banister and steps and traveled a long hallway with doors on either side. She reached the opening to a magnificent dining room with a hearty mahogany table featuring artisan-crafted legs and high-back upholstered chairs.

Seating for sixteen, dear Lord!

She whispered, "A small village could live here."

She feared it might. That caused the ominous sense of tiny spiders crawling under her skin.

Farther down the hall, she rounded a corner and caught the hint of peach cobbler baking in an oven, the decadent scent instantly chasing away menacing thoughts.

As Ollie's nose twitched, she sniggered at how accurate she'd been with Garrett.

"I'm going to gain the ten pounds Mindy thinks she needs to lose," she murmured. "And will savor every single calorie."

She walked under another oversize opening and voilà . . . the kitchen. Which looked more like a quaint Mexican restaurant for all its commercial-grade appliances and the huge island. Another massive table, this one accommodating twelve. Three different hutches—one for dishes; one for spices, staple ingredients, and cookbooks; one for family memorabilia.

And then . . .

There was the cowboy.

Jillian's gaze unabashedly roved his backside since he couldn't see her do it. Those broad shoulders of his gave way to muscles that damn near stretched the bounds of his shirt. He had a tapered waist, and Jillian was certain his obliques were elongated with toned sinew to match the rest of him. His jeans molded to his ass—and his powerful thighs.

Good Lord, that really was *a lot* of man.

"Enjoyin' the view, darlin'?"

Oh, crap. Busted.

Humor laced Jack's tone as he added, "Take your time. No need to rush."

"Ha, ha." She shot for levity, though she knew her face was beet red. Luckily, he still had his back to her.

Given that the floor was tiled, Jillian set Ollie down and worked on normal airflow. When she straightened, Jack was turning to her with a bowl of water in his hand.

"You don't miss a thing, do you?" she asked.

For the moment, he ignored the pup's provision, staying in the vein of Jillian checking him out.

"Heard your heels clickin'—then not. Felt your gaze on me," he said with a wicked smile.

"Humph," she mumbled.

Jack snickered. Then his attention shifted to Ollie, and he told the pup, "Bad news, I don't have actual dog food."

"No worries." Jillian yanked the bag from her pocket. "I'm prepared."

"Excellent." Jack set the bowl over by the table, and Ollie went straight to it.

"You have a friend for life," she said.

"Nothin' to it. I'm all about the essentials."

Jillian really couldn't deny he was effortless to be with, even with the zings flying between them. More of her consternation melted away as she wandered over to the collapsed patio doors and admired the outdoor seating, the kitchen setup Jack utilized for his live streams, and the lawn beyond, the wide knoll gradually descending to the river and the tree line.

"Hell of a ranch you have here, Jack," she said as she strolled toward the island. "And a fantastic infrastructure for your show. By the way, I'm convinced the majority of your fans are of the female persuasion."

He pulled out a rawhide saddle stool for her and then rounded the island. "What would make you think that, darlin'?"

"Cowboys are sexy, Jack. One who cooks . . . well."

What more did she need to say?

"Ah . . . so you think I'm sexy?" He grinned. Spectacularly.

"I was making a generalization."

"Sure you were, darlin'." He retrieved their lunch from the fridge. Sparing a quick glance at her, he teased, "But you do think I'm sexy, right?"

Her cheeks flushed again. "I didn't take you for the type to fish for compliments."

"Well, honey, a man likes to know where he stands, especially with a woman who looks like you."

Butterflies took flight in her belly. "So out of the frying pan and into the fire," she muttered. Loud enough for him to hear.

"For the moment," he said with an impish glint in his eyes, "there's no fryin' pan."

Rather, he delivered double-deckers piled high with deli meat, veggies, and thick slices of cheese.

"Um, Jack? Dagwood called. He wants his sandwiches back."

"Aren't you adorable," he lobbed her way. "Can't read a cookbook on an empty stomach, Jilly."

"True. We'll never narrow down our choices."

"And we'll find ourselves cookin' up a feast in the middle of the day."

"Good point."

Though that sounded like fun. She could envision an impromptu food fest out back for the workers, perhaps with Avery's help.

The only thing she couldn't picture in the portrait was her. Jillian and Ollie would be off to the side once everything was prepped and pulled off the grill. Worse, she saw herself inching toward the patio doors, putting distance between her and the feeding frenzy.

A depressing image, given how accommodating Jack was. And she didn't doubt for a second that he only hired the best help and had a fantastic family.

That last word still wreaked havoc on her psyche, but she was able to override her anxiety as Jack continued, in a somewhat professional tone, which amused her.

"We only have one hour per segment," he informed her. "Twice as long as our last snippet, sure. But we're not just coverin' the entrée for these pieces. I figure we should select three sides to accompany each main course. One of those could be a bread or a dessert."

"I have appetizers, salads, and side dishes included in my cookbook. I don't bake, so no breads. No desserts. You seriously do not want to let me near a standing mixer or a baking sheet. Mass devastation will ensue—like an F5 tornado blew through here leaving flour, eggshells, and milk splattered everywhere."

He grinned again. "I do appreciate that warning. We have a house-keeper who'll be delighted we're not heapin' on kitchen duties to her day. We clean up after ourselves in here. Well, mostly Mom, because the rest of us are off to perform other tasks. But . . . yeah. So. I'll be certain to steer you clear of the mixer."

"Piece of cake," she joked. "I'm smelling a peach cobbler I know is going to rock my world."

"Making it in a dutch oven. My great-grandmother's recipe. Usually done outdoors, over indirect heatin', like coals. But comes out just as good in the house."

Jillian's gaze narrowed. "Do you even need me?"

He was about to answer, but Garrett returned and took advantage of the break in conversation.

"Jack, I've got a flat. Looks like I ran over a nail. Got the truck up on the stand but discovered my spare's low too. Mac McGovern can't make it out this way for a few hours with a replacement."

"Take mine. Fob's on the rack."

"Thanks. I'll be back later. Miss Jillian." He gave her a courteous nod.

"Nice to see you again, Garrett."

He made a hasty exit.

Jack asked, "Where were we?"

"Sides to coincide with the entrées."

"Right, so, let's choose the proteins and then—"

"I'm just sayin'—" came a new voice.

"And I'm just counterin'—" came another.

"If the two of you could make up your minds—" and a third.

The three men who'd cut Jack off barreled through the opened patio doorway, all talking at once. Loud.

Jillian hopped off her stool and crossed to the table, where Ollie was lapping water.

Jack was on the move as well, shifting from behind the island to intercept the trio. "Y'all are yammerin' at each other—are ya hearing a single word?"

"I'm trying to convince these two yahoos that—"

"Hold that thought," Jack interjected. "First, introductions need to be made." To Jillian, he said, "This is Mateo, my brother-in-law."

"Ol' Bessie's wrangler," she remarked, praying her tone wasn't as high-pitched as it sounded to her own ears from the sudden invasion.

"Pleased to meet you, ma'am." Mateo made to lunge toward her, presumably to shake hands, but Jack blocked his trajectory.

"And this is Avery," he continued, minimizing the deflection, which Jillian appreciated.

The cousin said, "Your photo does not do you justice, Miss Jillian."

"That's very sweet. You're the bunkhouse cook, right? I'd lay odds you make a mean Stetson chopped salad."

Another diversionary tactic for her. Shift attention to someone else.

He said, "Damn straight, I do. Pardon my French. Arugula and fire-roasted corn, red bell peppers, and tomatoes. Pearl couscous, pepitas, and dried currants. Though," he turned introspective and mused, "the cowboys prefer it when I swap the pepitas for black beans. And the couscous for rice. And the—"

"She gets the idea," Jack interrupted. "This, darlin'," he said of the other ridiculously attractive man, "is Chance Reed. Also my cousin and foreman of the ranch."

Chance gave a low whistle and said, "Geez, Jack, she's much too beautiful for you."

Jillian laughed in spite of herself and said, "A girl can only take so much flattery."

"And I'm the one dishin' it out, so why don't you boys be on your way?" Jack told them, more so than suggested.

A tad territorial.

Interesting.

He'd not been possessive in college.

She found it exhilarating now. And that helped to kick her anxiety to the curb.

"Chance and I have heifers to discuss," Mateo said. "If I could just get a word in edgewise."

"You let me know how that works out for you." Jack smirked. A borderline lethal-to-her-heart expression that kept Jillian's pulse soaring.

Mateo and Chance trailed after Garrett.

Avery was still gazing at Jillian, looking a bit lost.

Jack cleared his throat to prompt him.

Avery grumbled to himself, "I'm here *why*, exactly . . . ?" His purpose hit him, and his gaze fell to the travel mug in his hand. "Oh, fuck, yeah!" He winced, then said, "No offense, Miss Jillian."

"None taken," she avowed. "I speak French too. And just Jillian is fine."

He nodded and grinned, then announced, "I need creamer. Those cowboys in the bunkhouse razzed me about my sugar-free hazelnut, and then they went and drank it all."

He made a beeline for the fridge, located what he was searching for, and poured a splash into his mug before replacing the lid. He put away the creamer, then said, "I'm outta here." He touched the brim of his hat and disappeared through the patio doors, just as two other men came through them.

Also chatting incessantly.

Jillian scooped up Ollie, and she realized it wasn't just instinctive protection for him but also a comfort for her.

Jack remained the buffer so no one could get near her spot by the table.

He held up his hands and said, "Guys, what the everlastin' . . . ?"

Both halted their argument.

Jack told Jillian, "This is Tucker Swanson, our main cameraman."

"Oh! Fabulous to meet you!" Jillian injected enthusiasm into her voice, which masked the trepidation inside her over all this hustle and bustle. And voices. So many voices, when she was only accustomed to hearing hers while monologuing to Ollie. Or Mindy's, more so of late.

"And this is George, the gardener," Jack further expounded, about the older gentleman.

"I prefer landscape architect," George corrected, punctuating the point with a raised hand and the tips of two fingers pressed to the pad of his thumb. "If you don't mind."

Jack chortled and replied, "My mistake. Landscape architect, darlin'," he amended.

"I'd say 'artist,'" Jillian stated. "The grounds are sensational."

"Well, I do have a crew," he said.

"You should all be commended."

"Now what's this all about?" Jack asked.

"We have to rip out the bougainvillea," Tucker lamented. "Both of them. I can't get the full set and the patio in my frame with all those blooms in my way. We need a wide angle for the BBQ bash, and it's not happening with flowers blockin' my view."

To which George responded, "Miss Brett planted those herself when she moved in here. They are her pride and joy. Why do you think I spend so much time pruning and shaping them?"

"That's a fact," Jack concurred. "So, *no* to rippin' out the bougainvillea. Find different angles, Tuck. Do somethin'—*anything*—'cuz my mama's plants aren't gonna be victims of our live streams, no matter how much we need the revenue."

Now both men lifted their hands in the air in surrender. Mumbled *fine* and turned around to leave.

Meanwhile . . .

Jack's head dropped, and he shook it.

Jillian set the puppy on the tile. In a delicate tone, she said, "Jack . . ."

He whirled around to her. "Don't you rely on your podcast for monetization?"

"And my subscription-based newsletter."

"Same with my channel. Runnin' a ranch this size takes substantial capital, Jilly. I don't mind puttin' in the work and the hours. I just have to get more and more creative every year, particularly when cattle prices dip or some disease runs through a portion of my herd."

"I didn't know."

"Not your concern, darlin'," he answered. Though she could see plenty weighed heavy on his mind.

Jillian took a few more deep breaths to steady herself. There was a lot going on here that she struggled with. And Jack's business was Jack's business.

One thing she couldn't do, however, was pretend this wasn't tumultuous for *her*.

She told him, "I'm really not comfortable with all this activity."

"I've gathered." His gaze softened.

"I'm just not used to . . . I . . . Jack . . ." She sighed with frustration, directed at herself. She wanted to project a confident, pulled-together persona. But she was far from that. "I live the most peaceful, almost silent, existence in Seattle. I just encountered seven people, including you, in an hour. I don't see, let alone speak with seven people *in a week*. I'm a text and an email kind of girl."

The panic started to overflow. She scratched her arm. Then her neck. Feeling those hypothetical hives.

She said, "I love the concept of us collaborating. And I'm looking forward to watching your inaugural Memorial Day festivities. But I'm not capable of following through on this prelude event. I'm so sorry, Jack. I know how much effort you put into the guesthouse for me and

Ollie, and I'm so grateful. Beyond grateful. It's just that . . . I don't . . . do . . . all of this . . ."

She swirled her index finger to indicate the kitchen, the mammoth house, the entire ranch.

"Jillian." He planted a hand on his waist. And pragmatically said, "You don't have to deal with 'all of this.'" He mimicked her gesture with his other hand. "We can shoot in the guesthouse, away from the commotion. We can keep the crew to a minimum—Garrett, Tuck, and, of course, Ollie."

She grimaced, with a touch of amusement.

He went on. "Okay, we do have to let Hunt in on it too. He's my self-appointed assistant, and I can't let him down. Plus, Ale for social media. That's it. Wyatt can track analytics remotely, and Mom'll come in later to help clean the set."

Jillian sank into a chair. "I don't want to let anyone down either, Jack. Or push your production people aside."

He strode toward her and knelt on one knee. His fingers almost skated along her sleeve as he gazed up at her, but he drew his hand back.

Adding to her dismay because she wanted to feel his touch. Despite that notion coming with some serious internal conflict as it pertained to physically isolating herself.

"You have to do what's right by you, Jilly. If this isn't it . . ."

He groaned. Stood. And paced. Like he agonized over his desire to crowd her, to get closer to her . . . but sensed it'd throw her off her game.

Not that she had a game. This was the reality she lived, and he seemed to grasp that. And even though it went against the grain for him to back off when he wished to surge forward, he took the high road for her. Every time.

Jillian could not discount that. Found it incredibly endearing. He was empathetic and supportive, rewiring his own thought processes and instincts to mesh more with hers.

Truly a hero in her book.

Which had tears pricking the backs of her eyes.

Hell, him forsaking the perfect angle for his BBQ bash to save his mother's prized plants had her heart swelling.

She let out a long sigh.

He had no qualms over figuring out how to knock this venture out of the park. Jillian had to step up to the plate too.

So she tamped down her panic and said, "Jack, I want to do this." She got to her feet again. "I honestly do."

It was her absolute truth. She didn't want to reload all her things into the SUV and drive off into the sunset on her very first day.

Nor did she want to leave Jack holding the bag for a cohosted series of shows he'd promised his audiences.

Yet . . . he didn't appear convinced of her stance.

"We can't do this at the expense of your mental health, Jillian." He stared at her with an earnest expression on his rugged face. "Whatever's distressin' you, darlin', it's not worth allowing it to escalate if this is beyond your comfort zone."

She tapped her toe on the floor, a little impatient with herself, feeling a bit foolish. Though her accelerated pulse assured her she wasn't being melodramatic.

"I don't mean to be difficult," she murmured. Nor could she deny that powering through was to hers—and Jack's—advantage. "This is an amazing plan. Not an opportunity either of us should squander. I need the publicity, too, or my cookbook is going to die on the vine, since I refuse to do any live demos and signings. I've even passed up offers for home and garden shows. I can't afford to flake out on this. And I for sure don't want to. I can take a Xanax."

"Jillian. I don't want to be the catalyst that—"

"It can help to counter the amygdala effect I suffer from."

His gaze narrowed. "Always knew you were too smart for me. I'll bite. What's an amygdala?"

She caught herself by surprise as she laughed at his "I'll bite" comment. He'd used that phrase frequently in college, and Jillian now wondered if she'd subconsciously named her marketing vehicles after his terminology.

Hmm . . . yet another curious tidbit . . .

But a different quandary for a different time.

She explained, "We have almond-shaped sensors on either side of our brain, in our temporal lobes. One registers and records negative experiences; the other, positive ones. Repetitive negative and positive reactions in routine situations are logged and can activate memories that 'set the mood' and generate a response before you even walk into that familiar situation."

His expression turned quizzical. "Are you telling me that every time I meet with my banker, whether I'm in the black or creepin' toward the red, I break out in a sweat for a reason?"

"Your right hemisphere trips the negative emotion. So you automatically fear or assume the worst, whether or not that's truly the case. Even if you *know* that's not the case. Those minuscule radars are that sensitive and that precise."

He fell silent for several seconds, giving this due consideration. Then he said, "Seems to me, darlin', that 'reprogramming' can change a negative to a positive."

"Yes, that is correct," she agreed with some apprehension. Because it was a tricky coin toss.

Though not for Jack Reed. He clapped his hands together and said, "I have a proposal."

"Seems like you always do," she retorted—with relief.

His exuberance was contagious. On the spot, Jillian swore to herself that she'd put substantial effort into being open to and accepting of any alternative he drummed up. Fascinated enough by his quick resolve that she found herself breathing a bit easier. Relatively speaking, considering how he affected her.

Jack extracted a couple of to-go containers from a cupboard, boxed their sandwiches, and put them in a soft-sided cooler he found in a pantry. He threw in individual bags of chips and napkins. He found a smaller bowl for Ollie. Included a few bottled waters with the stash.

"What are you up to, Jack?" she queried with a smile.

He flashed his electrifying grin in return. Then slung the strap of the cooler over his shoulder and grabbed her cookbook, which had a notepad and a pen sitting on top.

He told her, "Bring that package of sticky flags so we can attach them to the recipes we select. We're goin' on a picnic, darlin'. Follow me."

"I'll bite, indeed," she whispered.

Chapter Four

Jack snagged a folded blanket from the shelving unit on the patio and led Jillian past the synchronized chaos on his outdoor set, where Tucker and George were still fervently conferring. Ranch hands fixed broken lights, cleared away debris, and repaired anything and everything that had fallen victim to the catastrophic winds and golf ball–size hail a week or so after Jack's show that had featured Jillian.

Thank God the local meteorologists predicted smooth sailing up to the holiday barbecue. With any luck, the weather would remain moderate through the weekend.

They crossed the event lawn to the three redwood picnic tables and scattered Adirondack chairs under a grove of trees.

Flower beds were in vibrant bloom, scenting the air—though it was the faint hint of Jillian's perfume that stuck in his nose. And enticed him.

Everything about the woman enticed him. Her long legs and shapely hips. The caramel-colored curls that flowed over her shoulders. Her tawny eyes and sultry voice.

Lord, with the sultry, breathy voice . . . a man could get lost in that alone.

Along with the provocative sway of those hips. The dip of her waist and the full swells of her breasts. Okay, and yeah, she had an ass his hands itched to palm, to squeeze, as he pumped into her with her legs wrapped around him while he elicited soft moans from her.

Jack could recall her whimpers and her whispering his name when he'd made love to her, despite it being ten years ago. He'd known it was her first time. He'd been mindful of that, had put extra effort into slowing things down, exploring her body, discovering what made her gasp or giggle or beg for more.

He'd regretted they'd only shared that intimacy once. Then Wyatt had called. Jack had been on a flight within hours. Chance had flown back to pack up Jack's dorm room and ship his stuff. And while he'd agonized over his father's stroke and the subsequent massive coronary that took him—and he'd been immersed in catching up on weeks' worth of accounting and operational management—he'd had a hell of a time getting over the fact that he and Jillian were not destined to be.

Jack had obligations here, ones he'd been planning for his entire life.

When the dust had settled and he'd found his groove as ranch owner, he did allow further thoughts of Jillian to seep into the cracks and crevices of his mind. Yet he hadn't reached out to her, not after their occasional texts had faded into nonexistence before she'd even graduated.

Family and the ranch came first. It always had. It always would.

Yet now here was Jillian Parks, their two worlds colliding—even if only for a week.

Sure, her presence on the ranch led to him having thoughts and visions of what it might be like if she were to stay awhile longer. Of course he was going to have those thoughts.

They just weren't smart ones to entertain. Not the least bit realistic when she had a life elsewhere.

So Jack attempted his own mental reprogramming.

He set the cooler on a table after Jillian draped a blanket over it, and he started to unpack. She poured water for Ollie. With her help, he hopped onto the low bench, knowing where she intended to light. Wanting to be next to her. Clever pup.

Jack laid out the food and placed the cookbook in the center as he sat opposite her. Not the cozy positioning he'd prefer, but he was trying to keep himself in check.

Jillian fished out the sticky flags she'd stuffed in her pocket and peeled the backing to dump the four packets on the table.

She inhaled and exhaled. A few times.

Then she said, "You know how to set a scene, cowboy. No Xanax required."

"You do what helps you, Jilly."

She spread her arms and told him, "This is one astounding wide-open space, Jack. Therapy on a ranch."

"I do believe this place can be cathartic. I was missin' it more than I realized that year at SPU."

"I can see why."

"Much as I hated leaving Seattle because there were specific reasons I was there, when I came home, I truly felt this was where I was meant to be. Not some big city or a university. And I didn't feel that way just because I suddenly had the weight of the TRIPLE R on my shoulders—it wasn't a forced reaction. It was an understanding that this was and always would be my home. I neither regret nor resent that. I embrace it."

"I can't say that I blame you," she told him. "Miles of green grass, surrounded by rolling hills and grazing cows . . . it's a treasure trove of beauty and serenity."

"We'll just figure out how to maneuver around the multitude of people."

"It's not that I don't want to meet everyone," she assured him. "I just need—"

"For them to be less overwhelming. Not quite so loud and . . . close in proximity?" He groaned. "It's a big order here, Jillian. I won't lie."

"I don't want anyone stressing over my condition, Jack. I just need . . . a balance."

"We'll find it," he promised. "And none'll be the wiser. They'll just think I want you all to myself." He winked.

She tapped two fingers against her lips, as though she were attempting to contain a smile.

"Go on . . . ," he gently encouraged. "Tell me that's another proposal of mine that you like."

Her hand fell to her side. "You seriously are too much."

"And you don't mind me flirtin' with you."

"Mmm . . . no, I do not."

"Good. Now." He passed the pen to her. "How about blue flags for Show One. Green for Show Two. Yellow for Show Three. Purple for Show Four."

There'd be a break in the middle, for Jack to go into town to record his morning segment.

Jillian jotted down a legend. Then she opened her food container and asked, "Really, Jack, how am I supposed to eat this thing? It's like, six inches tall."

"Hey, I once saw you devour three-quarters of a pepperoni pizza during an all-night study session. Don't go actin' all dainty on me, darlin'."

She laughed. He didn't miss that it came more naturally to her now, as though her nerves had settled, since they were alone, with no more noise than the yellow-breasted songbirds, the rustling of leaves in the breeze, and the flow of the rapids from the river.

She said, "I was stress-eating my way through midterms. I majored in marketing to be creative, not to crunch numbers. But those classes were part of the curriculum."

"Gotta gnaw through some gristle to understand profit and loss. You can't say learnin' spreadsheets and pivot tables hasn't helped you with your own company, right?"

"Jack." She pinned him with a sassy expression. "That's what accountants are for."

He chuckled. "Touché, darlin'. Touché."

Jillian smashed down the slice of sandwich and bit into one end. He didn't make fun of her, though he was certainly amused.

They chatted about the first show as they ate.

"You pick the protein," she recommended. "Being the champion pitmaster that you are."

"I'm thinkin' for Day One, let's demonstrate grillin' indoors, since that's where we'll be while the outdoor kitchen's under construction for the bash."

"What's your meat?"

"Rib eyes on a raclette."

She stared at him. "No clue what that is."

"An electric grill that originated in Switzerland but is also hugely popular in France. I have a couple of them. The top generates sufficient heat to sear meat, seafood, poultry, whatever, with eight individual warming trays—like mini frying pans—beneath it for sauces, melted cheeses, sautéed veggies, what have you. Basically, it's a great party platform."

"Huh. Sounds interesting." She seemed to scroll through the database in her brain for potential accompaniments to the rib eyes.

At one point, she pursed her lips, and Jack's gaze dropped to her mouth. Again.

"Stop that," she teased.

"Wasn't doin' anything."

"Aside from eyeing me like I'm the Last Supper?"

"Got mine right here." He took another bite of his sandwich. Washed it down with a swig of water and continued. "You do have a very tempting mouth, darlin'. Took me too damn long to get around to kissin' you."

Her gaze connected with his. Excitement flashed in her glowing irises.

She was breathless for several seconds.

Then she murmured, "Right. About those kisses . . ."

For months, Jillian had fantasized about Jack asking her out on a date. Kissing her at the end of it. Maybe suggesting something more might be transpiring between them after tons of late-night study sessions and a semester in a class she would have found boring AF were it not for the cowboy quarterback shooting her comical grins and suggestive smiles that were more potent than her morning lattes.

Then she'd gotten her wish.

The dates and the "more."

Only to lose Jack to a phone call.

Well, a traumatic medical emergency back home, but she'd been with him when the call had come through from Wyatt, and she'd recognized Jack's instant mental and physical pullback. Like everything that had existed at SPU vaporized in an instant. Including *them*.

A jagged pill to swallow. Even today.

So she skipped over it, saying, "We have endless possibilities with the steak."

"Smooth subject change, Jilly," he scoffed with humor.

"We have work to do, Jack."

He polished off another hunk, then lobbed back, "Sure, but it's fair to say there's some catch-up involved when you haven't seen someone in a decade."

"Pondering a past that can't be changed isn't going to advance the future. My therapist told me that. A golden rule not to forget."

"Oh, there are plenty of things I haven't forgotten. Your eyes and your smile. But also how you leave no stone unturned when you're solving a problem."

"Which will make this particular job a tedious one if we don't concentrate." She gave him a pointed look. Yet she doubted she was convincing him that *she* was trying to be professional. Not when gazing over at him had her melting.

"Nothin' tedious about spendin' the afternoon with you, Jillian Parks."

If he winked, she'd be a goner.

Thank God he spared her and continued with his sandwich.

A full week of sensory overload was going to leave her wilted into oblivion.

And damn it, since he'd mentioned their kiss . . . she couldn't get it out of her mind. Along with the many more that had followed.

A yearning she'd suppressed years ago ribboned through her. Taunting her.

She could say to hell with planning the cooking show and suggest they choose a new tree and pick up where they'd left off.

But what good would that do?

She vacillated over this for a minute or two.

It could help them to return that ill-fated night and the what-ifs to the past, where they belonged—so that she truly was following her therapist's direction. Hell, for all she knew, the chemistry between them *now* was strictly due to verbal flirtation. And there was something to be said for overestimating a rekindled infatuation and having it fall flat.

They could kiss today and feel . . . nothing at all.

She rolled her eyes.

Yeah. Right.

Jack's brow crooked. "What's goin' on inside that pretty head of yours, Jilly?"

She was already under his spell.

She knew it.

He knew it.

And she suspected he was equally entranced.

So, no. There'd be no *feeling nothing at all.*

A startling revelation because, for so very long . . . Jillian truly had felt nothing. She'd shut herself off to the reminder of even the faintest touch. The only way she'd survived a reclusive existence.

Another thing that was significant to process.

At a later time.

For now . . . Jillian told Jack, "I'm thinking we could do romaine boats on the grill." She flipped to the page in her cookbook, surprised by her ability to shift gears and stunned she could even speak. Though she was still having trouble finding her normal voice, not this breathy one.

Jack fought a grin, reading her mind.

She plunged forward. "Along with fajita peppers, sautéed onions and mushrooms, and some sauces, all for the warming trays. Chimichurri, béarnaise, black bean and sesame, red wine and peppercorn—oh! And I have the perfect rub!" she declared—mostly because she was so damn proud of herself for getting back on track. "Ancho chili with a smoky paprika texture. A subtle undertone that doesn't overpower the natural flavor of the beef but hints at a slow-cooked brisket."

"Speaking of, I've got one in the smoker." His eyes widened. "How am I hungry again?"

"Well, you were worried we'd never get through this without cooking a midday feast."

"Yes, but we *just* ate."

She laughed. And moved them along. "We need two more sides. We could do roasted veggies that we finish on the grill with the boats and individual southwestern lobster mac and cheese in the additional raclette pans." She showed him the pages with photos.

"Done and done," Jack said with a flourish.

Jillian flagged the selections in the cookbook.

"Now for the ingredients list," he added.

"Mm, yes, there is that."

She wrote down everything they needed as he read from her recipes. And included a baguette.

Jack said, "Mom and Hunt usually make the trip to the farmers' market, but we'll need plenty of time to prep, so I'll make the run tomorrow while I'm out on other errands."

"It's amazing that your family's so into helping out."

"That's what we do around here. Not just on the ranch but in town, within the county."

"Don't you also have a younger brother and sister?" she asked. "Twins?"

"Luke is the brother. Riley is the sister. And lemme tell ya . . ." He let out an honest-to-God guffaw that was robust—and contagious. Jillian laughed too—and didn't even know why yet. "That Riley's a handful. One thousand percent lightnin' rod. And Luke's voltage ain't much less."

"What do they do?"

"Riley's trying to kick the crap out of Nashville at present."

"A lightning rod named Riley Reed—she sounds like a country music sensation."

"Oh, she's not interested in being a superstar, darlin'." A spark ignited in his blue irises. "Riley Reed can't be bothered with someone tryin' to mold her into somethin' she's not. She doesn't want to be the next *anyone*. She's an original. The girl's got personality to spare and mad songwriting skills to boot. That's her forte."

Jillian whistled under her breath. "Wow, impressive."

"Ehhh, yes and no. She's talented, without doubt. But, again, she wants things her way and her way *only*."

This intrigued Jillian. "Force of nature?" she ventured.

"That would be puttin' it mildly, darlin'." He chuckled, though Jillian didn't miss the tinge of adoration—and admiration—in his tone. He was a proud big brother.

She asked, "What about Luke?"

"The black sheep of the family." He shook his head. "That kid—and I'm being facetious because he's twenty-five—collected a massive jack-pot in a poker tournament the day he turned twenty-one."

"Get. Out."

"True story. Gave a chunk to Mateo to buy a prized bull at auction for breedin', knowing I wouldn't take the money from him. He used the rest to open a cantina in town."

"Mateo accepted the cash?" She found that to be a fascinating tid-bit. Given how Jack minded the P&L statements on the ranch, he likely wasn't pleased with these two working around him.

Yet he admitted, "They both knew we needed the bull, darlin'."

"Gotcha."

"Nature of the beast," Jack murmured. Then more solidly stated, "My dad used to gripe that his dignity could get in the way of issue resolution. I try to learn from him. This particular lesson is not a simple reconciliation in my mind, but when you own a ranch such as this, you do what has to be done. And be damn grateful you're surrounded by people who comprehend your stance, who also care about what's prudent, what the bottom line is. For all concerned."

"That's . . ." Jillian was at a loss for words. Emotion swept through her, somewhat unidentifiable, yet poignant, nonetheless.

She grasped the precariousness of operating a generational ranch. Anyone who read financial news reports was aware that the cattle industry had been in peril for decades. But Jack Reed and his people were resourceful. And determined to continue their way of life.

Even Luke seemed sensitive to this.

Thus, she concluded, "Luke's not into ranching but supports the cause. And the foodie gene runs in the family, so he has his own kitchen, in town."

"Yes and yes. A damn good cantina, by the way. I'll take you there. It's—"

"Oh, umm . . ." Her brows scrunched from an instant zap of dread. "Thing is, Jack, I don't eat out. I haven't set foot in a restaurant in years."

Jack appeared astonished as his head snapped back and he regarded her for several seconds, as though attempting to process that statement. Like . . . it simply didn't compute.

He slowly verified, "At all?"

"If I can't get it via a delivery service or my personal courier—or at a drive-through during this excursion—I'm missing out on it."

"Jillian—"

"Jack. To be frank"—she wrangled the elephant in the room—"I'm basically a shut-in. I mean, other than twice-daily walks with Ollie, trips to the mailbox, and setting out and collecting packages on my porch. I have a greenhouse and the internet. Amazon Prime, Jack. There's a mechanic in my neighborhood who services my SUV every month, to ensure it's running okay, and even takes it for a spin to keep all the fluids moving, whatever that means. He spent an exorbitant amount of time confirming the vehicle was up to snuff for this journey."

Jack stared at her, stumped. Eventually, he said, "But, Jilly, you used to be—"

"I know what I used to be," she assured him. "I'm not the same now."

Their gazes locked for a few moments. Then he glanced away, as though searching for an explanation written on a tree trunk or drifting on a sliver of a cloud overhead.

Finally, he glanced back at her. And averred, "But you *are* the same."

"Think about that," she challenged with a level look. "Do a mental comparison. I know what you *want* to see, Jack. What you want to remember. I see and remember things about you too. But right now . . . I'm looking at someone I want to get to know in *this* new lifetime, in this place. Do you understand what I'm saying?"

"I never did tell you too much about the ranch."

"Sound bites," she agreed. "Names and some memories. I thought it was fabulous and fated that you were from Serrano and I love peppers. But we had school to worry about, to focus on."

"More irony for Jack Reed," he mumbled. "I went to school for a pro career and an education. Not to meet a girl I had to force myself not to ask out every time I was near her—until I couldn't *not* ask you out."

She nodded. "We were two ships passing in the night."

"I don't want to believe that," he said.

"But it's our truth," she replied. "I found your affinity for numbers to be sexy as hell, despite my lack of an attention span for them. Yet we meshed in so many ways. At the end of the day, though . . ." Emotion crept in on her. "You had this whole other world that you'd someday return to."

"Sooner than I ever thought."

A lump swelled in her throat.

They'd both had dreams. They'd both been thrown curveballs.

The plus side was that they'd learned to assimilate, to recover, to move forward.

That was what Jillian coveted. A positive.

"You did what was necessary," she offered. "You fulfilled a familial obligation. This is your destiny, Jack."

"Yes, it is," he said.

"I respect that. Further . . . I realize I'm still not fully enlightened. Lots of moving parts to this particular universe. I'm used to constants, not variables."

"Careful, Jilly," he warned with affection, "you might wander into a mathematical equation."

She laughed softly. Swallowed that lump down. "Be sure to push me through the right door, so I don't embarrass myself. Too much."

"You always managed to find your way." He pressed his hands to his thighs as his head dropped for a moment. Then lifted as he added, "I'm not fully enlightened either. About you. But I catch glimpses of a deeper laugh. A more exuberant smile. Like old times. And . . . you came all the way out here. I can tell that took guts. A recluse on my property, that's unfathomable. And yet, here you are. Maybe that's why I felt you were the same. You hated crunching numbers, but you tackled the class anyway."

Once more, they gazed at each other across the table.

"You were skittish earlier," he commented, "but only in a crowd. So—"

"Of *four*, Jack?" she reasoned.

"Well, you're doin' just fine now, darlin'. We'll figure it out," he said. "Whatever makes you comfortable for the live streams and distancing yourself, overall. That's what's most important, Jillian. That you can breathe here."

She confessed, "Jack, I have quickly discovered breathing's not an option when I'm around you."

He winked. "Good to know, Jilly. Good to know."

Chapter Five

After lunch and their research, Jack walked Jillian and Ollie to the guesthouse by way of the side yard and then the graveled drive.

"You didn't have to escort us," she said.

"Well, I didn't want you to get lost, darlin'."

"Ha. I think you were concerned that if we went near the house, someone might grab you and tell you the whole damn patio has to be rebuilt."

"Lord have mercy." He let out a low groan. "That is not as big a stretch of the imagination as you might think, after that near tornado we had."

"Then you should get back there and make sure those gorgeous rosebushes I saw aren't also yanked out of the ground for the sake of Tucker's 'view.'"

"You're just pourin' salt on the wound, honey."

She smiled. Leaned in and whispered, "Better than cayenne, Jack."

"Talk about bein' too much," he chuckled. "Go on and get your work done, darlin'. I have my own to tend to. Feel free to come for dinner. Though . . ." He gave a shrug as he caught himself. "Know there will be plenty in attendance."

She nodded. "Thanks for the warning. Little much for me. I saw the size of your dining room."

His teeth ground for a moment. Jack couldn't imagine someone dining alone when they had family and friends nearby. And even though these weren't people Jillian knew, he didn't doubt she'd get along well with everyone. They'd enjoy her company too.

It was a bit of an awkward situation. He didn't feel comfortable just dropping her off and returning to the house. She was his guest and also . . . he wanted more time with her. All the time he could get.

But Jillian's own comfort level was more important than his. So he didn't cajole her, difficult as it was not to attempt to coax her to join them. This was a battle he'd be waging every day while she was here, he was sure.

Not something he could put on Jillian. He had to accept this was *his* issue to reconcile. And one more flashing beacon of how dissimilar their lives—and their personalities—were.

Opposites might attract.

Didn't mean they were meant to be.

"Well," he said, now that he'd depressed the hell out of himself. "If there's anything you need, just let me know. Better yet . . . I'm happy to cook for you."

He couldn't resist offering.

"Something tells me your hands are full, Jack. And when you said the kitchen was stocked, you were not kidding." She laughed, as though to break the tension permeating the air. "I'm all set. Plus, I have emails to get through and transactions to follow up on. New episodes to record since I'm about out of the ones I prerecorded for Mindy to edit and release while I was on the road."

"Right. You've got an enterprise to run. From here. I won't interfere with that."

She gazed up at him. Opened her mouth to speak, but no words came out.

"You know how I meant that to sound," he said in a low tone.

She smiled to reassure him. "Yes—that you're not sulking. And I appreciate that you understand I can't just be on vacation this week. Not in the middle of a launch."

"Then I'll take my solace in knowing sales are booming for you."

"I wouldn't go *that* far," she joked. "Though, following these segments we have planned . . . maybe." She touched his arm. And added, "Don't worry about me, cowboy. I take care of myself."

Ah, wasn't that a golden nugget to seize, for a man who couldn't help taking care of everyone else?

He was reticent to leave her. But had no choice. He wouldn't smother her.

Jack returned to the main house. His office was on the ground floor. He settled in his big chair before a large mahogany desk, positioned at an angle to capture the fireplace and seating on one side and the big picture window looking out on the stables where Jack trained his horses on the other side.

There were bills to reconcile and inventories to approve. A dozen other operational and strategic tactics to work through.

When he'd pared down the pile in his inboxes, he headed to the kitchen.

Chance retrieved the baked potatoes from the double oven and followed Brett and Wyatt into the dining room, the women carrying the place settings. Garrett and Tuck collected all the condiments that were needed. Wyatt returned to retrieve the corn bread, just as Avery came from the courtyard with an oversize baking sheet that he set on the counter.

"Pulled this from the smoker ten minutes ago," he said. "Fully rested."

"Thanks," Jack told him. "Glad we still have some functionality outside right now."

"Need me to slice the meat? Requires just the right thickness," Avery chided.

"No one knows that better than me," Jack shot back. "Don't go hacking up what I've painstakingly tended to."

Avery chortled. "Like watchin' a pot of water to see if it boils. The smoker does most of the work. And you were more preoccupied by your girlfriend than the brisket."

"She is not my girlfriend. She is my cohost. And I assure you, I put ample time in with the wood chips and maintaining the perfect temperature. Now get out of my way. Grab the slaw from the fridge and take it on in."

Avery would have ribbed him more, without doubt. Cousins would be cousins. But he knew Jack still had prep to do.

As he transferred the brisket to a cutting board, Wyatt separated the corn bread and arranged the squares in a towel-lined basket.

"Where is Jillian, anyway?" she asked. "Haven't seen hide nor hair of the woman. I'm dyin' to meet her, Jack!"

He winced.

"She is havin' dinner with us, right?" Wyatt pressed.

Jack knew Avery wasn't going to be the only one to assign the girl-friend label to Jillian, even though it didn't currently apply.

Wouldn't *ever* apply.

Apples and oranges and all that . . .

But Avery had witnessed Jack placing himself between three men and Jillian—and had jumped to the right conclusion. That Jack was protective of her. Territorial.

Wyatt would pick up on that as well.

However, there were circumstances beyond his control that prompted him to say, "Jillian's got podcastin' and orders to fill, plus a puppy to look after. She's uprooted her life for these shows but still has other obligations."

Wyatt's gaze narrowed in a challenging manner.

Jack blew out a breath.

"She doesn't do crowds, Wyatt."

Okay, he hadn't planned on outing Jillian in that way, but when it came to his eldest sister, Jack knew to head off sticky conversations at the pass. Especially given that, when Wyatt *did* see him with Jillian, she'd have the two of them married off in her mind. Just like that.

"All of us in the dining room at one time will stress her out," he continued. "So until she's more amenable to a significant lifestyle change—*if* she's amenable—it's best she follow her usual routine."

"It's just dinner, Jack. And what the heck is she going to eat? Not to mention, it's downright unhospitable of us to leave her fending for herself and dinin' alone!"

Jack loved his sister for numerous reasons. This was one. She couldn't bear the thought of *anyone* being a "lonesome dove," not just him. She'd expressed on several occasions (and in strictest confidence with him) how she worried over their mother not seeking companionship. She grasped the reality of the situation, yes. She understood that some people loved only once. That, however, didn't keep Wyatt from fretting about a void she felt needed to be filled.

She wasn't off the mark, not at all. Jack could attest to there being a missing component in his own life. He sensed it within his mother as well, and that bonded them a bit more. Brett also agonized over how the ranch could weigh him down sometimes. But mostly . . . they seemed to have some secret-society consensus, even if it did cause them some concern. An all-encompassing "it is what it is" acceptance.

He told Wyatt, "The guesthouse does not lack for food and fresh produce. Hunt and Mom saw to that. And I do appreciate that you have Jillian's best interests at heart, and that you're eager to be a gracious hostess."

"I understand my exuberance can be overwhelmin'," she admitted. "I shall endeavor to tone myself down a decibel or two."

"No call for that, she'll get a kick out of you. Just . . . from a reasonable distance at first. Let her acclimate. Might take some time."

"Jack, she's only here for a week."

Not a reminder he needed.

"Regardless," he said, "she's determined to get her feet beneath her. She's a trooper."

Wyatt took the baking sheet to the large apron sink and rinsed off the crumbs from the corn bread, then washed and dried the pan. She grabbed two long marbled platters with handles and side grooves to capture extra juice. She set them on the island so Jack could transfer the slices of brisket.

She asked, "Exactly how attracted are you to this woman?"

"You never did learn to mind your own business."

"Not like any of us have missed the sparkle in your eyes since the moment you realized she owned Hotter Than Haba. Think even the twins caught on to that. So . . . lights your fire?"

"And then some. Let's eat."

◆ ◆ ◆

Jillian processed a full round of orders, confirming receipt of payment and moving those invoices to the next stage—as more of them flowed in. This pleased her, but damn, she only had so many supplies with her.

Her first inclination was to contact the manufacturer of her five-ounce bottles and the burnt-wood holders to send more to her here at the ranch. As well as the labels, tags, and twine, which were color-coordinated to denote specific flavors.

Problem was, she couldn't just whip up extra batches of her sauces. Not without her hybrids and not without a certified kitchen. So she posted a note on her website that announced shipping might be delayed due to a higher demand than usual and organized a new group of sales.

Her progress was interrupted by a video call from Mindy, who cut right to the chase. "Scale of one to five, how's your anxiety?"

"I only get to five?" Jillian countered.

"So that's a middle-of-the-road three."

"Yeah, at the moment. Three's the magic number."

"And the dreamy rancher?" Mindy prompted. "Putting the *giddy* in your giddy-up?"

"I don't even know what that means."

"Neither do I. Sounds cute, though."

"But I don't think it applies."

"Comment still stands. How's the in-person reunion?"

"Considering I'm able to form complete sentences that are coherent, for the most part, I'd say good. A little dicey at times, yes. But good."

"So. Absolute sparkage."

"Absolute." Jillian resisted the urge to sigh.

"Yum. Now, let's talk about Garrett. Deets."

"Tall and brawny, late thirties, full head of hair—distinguished, with threads of gray. Very cowboy-esque, from head to toe. Tiny bit of a clusterfuck, but aren't we all?"

"I beg your pardon?"

"I mean, aside from you."

"Thank you. All right, then." Mindy turned professional again. "All well and lovely to know. What do you need from me?"

"Umm . . ." Jillian racked her brain. And shrugged. "Nothing at present. I'm about to have dinner."

"Then I'll drop. Call me in the morning."

Jillian gave her an earnest look. "Don't stress over me, okay? Jack knows I have 'crowd control' issues. I think we can manage this."

Mindy's expression softened. "You tell him why?"

"Nope."

"Should you?"

Jillian's teeth gnashed. She waved a hand in the air and said, "I suppose it gives context. It's just, well . . . private."

"You don't have to reveal all, Jillian. Give him the gist. So he doesn't mistake your apprehension for anything he's done."

"Oh, shit, I never thought of that. Excellent advice."

"I know. Gotta jet. Tomorrow, it is. Have a fantasy or two. It's healthy."

"Yeah, you too."

They shared a laugh.

Ollie bounced Jillian's way and gazed up at her.

She smiled. "I got you out of my crappy ordeal, so I have that going for me."

His tail wagged.

Then he sat back on his hind legs and spread his front ones wide, giving her his own "king of the world" impersonation.

"What are you, part meerkat? Want some cheese with that ham, little man?"

He yipped.

"Nonstop circus act. They should've warned me at the shelter that you were the court jester."

Of course, at five weeks, scared and starving, he hadn't been.

Thus, Jillian said, "Glad to see you're living your best life, pal."

He came down on all fours, lifted his head, and gazed at her with his soulful, chocolaty eyes.

"I know. Feeding time."

While the pup inhaled his meal, Jillian snatched the to-go container from the fridge. She ate the rest of her sandwich and chips at the table on the deck as the sun set. She sipped her chardonnay. Derived some inner peace from the tranquility and the splashes of crimson, gold, and bloodred orange that painted the sky.

But in the distance, over the sound of the brook, she heard one of the horses neighing and snorting.

She set aside her glass and stood. She told Ollie, "You stay here."

Jillian left the yard and crossed the short drive where her vehicle was parked. She stood under a tall oak and folded her arms over her chest. She watched as Jack worked with the same horse, her muscles bunching, though she willed herself not to get overly panicked. He was clearly skilled. He ebbed and flowed with the animal, moved with it. Until the horse was less unruly and instead only mildly antsy.

Jack left him in this more settled state. He removed his gloves again as he met up with Jillian.

"Looks dangerous," she commented, concern edging her voice.

"Darlin', I've been training horses for a long time. Nothin' to be concerned about." Jack propped a shoulder against the trunk. "We've found ourselves another tree."

"So it would seem . . . ," she mused.

He asked, "How was your dinner?"

"The sandwich that kept giving. I probably could have saved some for breakfast. But it was just too tasty, I couldn't stop eating."

He grinned. "Happy to satisfy you, darlin'."

She felt the innuendo all the way to her soul.

Flirting with the man at nineteen was not the same as flirting with him at twenty-nine. Jillian found that to be exhilarating. Invigorating, even. It'd been forever since she'd experienced above-average dynamism with a man.

She debated her clever comeback—one that skirted the sudden thickening of the air between them . . . or contributed to it.

His gaze smoldered as he murmured, "Ticktock, Jilly."

She shook her head and laughed, this one faint and tenuous. "I swear you can read my mind."

"If that were the case, I'd know precisely how to proceed. But I don't want to be overbearing."

"You're not overbearing, Jack. *Situations* can be overbearing."

"Amygdala," he stated.

"I do admire how you pay attention to the details."

"Tell me more of them," he quietly urged, his fingers slipping into his pockets, thumbs hanging out, as that unassuming disposition took over, quelling some of the charisma he radiated in spades, though not all of it. Just enough so that Jillian could compose herself.

The witty repartee was easy for them. Jillian wasn't so sure how they'd do with a more serious conversation. But what Mindy had said earlier resonated.

She told Jack, "When I look at those horses, I think *trampling*. When I see your herd of cattle stretched along the pasture below the stables, I think *stampede*. Not comforting words for a person who was nearly crushed to death."

He used his elbow to shove him away from the tree and stared down at her more intently. "What's this?"

"I was at a concert at a large venue six years ago. The stage caught fire."

Jillian's eyelids closed for a moment in an attempt to help steady her, but the opposite occurred. She saw visions that still haunted her nightmares, images that had spawned her insomnia, which had been infinitely worse in the beginning, when she couldn't shut out the sights and sounds. Not without sedatives and tranquilizers.

"Jillian," he said as he gently clasped her arm, like he knew she could use a stabilizing hand.

Even the sleeve of her sweater couldn't diminish his natural heat. Or the strength in his fingers. A shiver cascaded down her spine—not related to the tragedy she was revealing. It was Jack's gesture that reverberated within her.

Jillian's initial instinct was to pull away. She'd only been touched on the rarest of occasions since her release from the rehab facility she'd been transferred to after her discharge from the hospital. Jack's tender grip on her might be solely for reassurance, but because it was him, it felt intimate, stimulating.

One more thing to send her off the rails if she wasn't careful.

Her lids fluttered open, but she blinked back the mist covering her eyes.

"There was a gas explosion backstage that rocked the place, and everything went up in a blaze, like a roman candle. Everyone clamored to get out. Climbing over the seats, climbing over each other . . ."

Her breath stuck in her throat at the remembrance.

"Jesus," he mumbled.

"With the mass exodus, the entire audience was pushing its way up the stairs," she told him. "I spotted a girl, maybe seventeen, who'd fallen. A few people tried to help her up as they passed by, but the crowd propelled them forward so that they couldn't get a hold on her. And then she was clinging to the railing and got trapped there."

"Jillian . . . ," he repeated, his entire visage darkening.

"I don't know what compelled me, but I plowed right into that fervor to get to her. She was crying and bleeding. I fell on top of her," Jillian said with jagged breaths. "I didn't know what else to do. She was slight of build and getting squished, and I just thought . . . I'm bigger than her and I can cover her, protect her."

Tears filled Jillian's eyes at the painful recollection. And over how crazed everyone had been as they'd tried to save themselves.

"They all stepped over me. Or on me. *Right on top of me.* People were screaming and kicking . . . I couldn't get us up."

That had been as physically destructive as it had been emotionally harrowing.

"I'd been helpless," she told him, hating that she couldn't erase that memory from her mind—or the feeling of impending disaster and devastation. "The entire scene was hopeless."

She sucked in a quavering breath.

Jack suggested, "Maybe you don't have to tell me more." His voice was raw.

She gave a small shake of her head. "If you at least have the basics, then you won't question why I get spooked."

Clearly, he couldn't dispute that logic. Just held her gaze and let her continue.

"The sprinklers engaged, but all that did was cause everyone to slip and slide. I couldn't maintain a grip on the wet railing. When I tried to push the girl upward or forward with a hand on the concrete step for leverage, someone's foot would land on my fingers. Until they were broken."

Jack opened his mouth again but didn't speak, evidently not having the right words.

In reality, there were no right words. It was such a vivid reliving of something that still seemed so inconceivable, even to her. Yet it *had* happened. And this was the best she could describe the mayhem without going into the grisly details of *feeling* every kick and crunch and brutal jostle. Until she was crying in agony and close to blacking out.

That was not part of this telling that she chose to allow in the forefront of her mind because, for endless horrifying minutes, Jillian had believed she was going to die in that fire. From her injuries, from smoke inhalation, from the flames . . . she wasn't sure. But the melee had been catastrophic. And she'd feared becoming a fatal victim of it, as unconsciousness crept in on her.

"Finally," she told Jack, "a couple burly rugby types created a human barricade at my feet that people had to go around, while their friend pulled me off the girl, who was able to get up and get moving, with his help. The other two got me out and to one of the ambulances that had arrived."

Jillian could practically taste the blood in her mouth, which wasn't there presently, but she'd suffered internal damage that'd had her spitting it up.

"I spent a lengthy period in the hospital. Fractured ribs and vertebrae, a broken wrist and ankle, a concussion, deep bruises that seemed to take an eternity to heal. You'd think I'd been steamrolled."

"That must have been terrifyin'," he said. "Then . . . and reiterating it now."

His low, compassionate tone soothed her. The way it did his horses. So that Jillian found herself gravitating toward him.

She said, "Mindy thought I should give you the overview." There was more to the story, of course. Only a handful of people knew the rest. And that was all who needed to know. "I don't want you to misconstrue any anxiety on my part as something you said or did. It's all me, Jack."

He cringed. "That's not true, darlin'. When you're here, you shouldn't have anything to fear. But now I can understand why all the commotion rattles you."

"I don't dislike any of this, Jack. The ranch is spectacular, and your extended family is wonderful." She smiled despite the disquiet roiling through her and the tears glistening her eyes, which she couldn't control. "Then there's you . . ."

One corner of his mouth twitched. "I'm good at creating a buffer."

"I noticed."

"Well, I didn't want Avery or Chance poachin'."

It was a joke. Sort of. Because she suspected there was some truth behind the jest.

"Darlin', we can work with this. I promise."

That brought more tears to her eyes. She wanted to say she was already too much of a hassle, yet . . . when it came to Jack—and his whole family, she guessed—a complication like this was something they'd accommodate.

Jillian was no martyr. She just didn't want to make things difficult, especially for people so willing to go out of their way for her. But she knew Jack neither lied nor exaggerated when he said they could work with this.

So she nodded in silent concurrence. And said, "They broke the mold with you, cowboy."

"I like to think so, darlin'."

He warmed her heart, even though she knew he was being humorous. "Believe it."

He still held her crooked arm, and her fingertips dipped into the thick sinew of his biceps. He raised his other hand and whisked away the stream on one of her cheeks. "I prefer it when you're blushin', not cryin', Jilly."

"I haven't done much of either the past few years. I've had most of my emotions sufficiently contained."

"So I threw ya for a loop?" he queried, disconcertion fringing his tone.

She sniffled. Was about to say *in every way* but caught herself.

She couldn't overlook the fact that she'd fallen hard for him all those years ago, so fast. She'd kept that to herself, for the most part. Sure, he'd homed in on the mutual attraction. But she hadn't spouted proclamations of a deeper infatuation. Regardless, it really wasn't a surprise she was getting tangled up in his web a decade later.

That thought required careful dissection.

Just not this very second.

She reminded him, "I'm the one who drove out here." She flattened her palm to his abs. "Didn't take too much persuasion from Mindy."

That sentiment lingered between them.

So too did the insinuation that accompanied *her* unexpected, intimate gesture.

Jack's gaze dropped to her mouth, briefly.

Jillian's heart tripped.

He eased her closer as his head bent to hers. "What I can't believe is I've waited ten years to kiss you again. And, honey, I don't want to wait another ten seconds."

His warm lips swept over hers in a whisper of a kiss. A question that she answered with another smile. And a silkier sigh.

Jack grinned, making his dazzling blue irises shimmer.

Then he drew her into a completely different world with kisses that were sensual and seductive. Causing her to lean into him, like a reed bending in a tender breeze. Her fingers curled around the material of his shirt. Her pulse skipped through her veins.

Their bodies weren't fully touching, not melding to each other. And yet she felt the sizzle straight to her core.

She'd been the one to make the move. But he was the one teasing her with his flirty kisses, pulling her from her haunting thoughts. He was damn good at it, subtle and sexy, guiding her into this romantic lane, where she succumbed to the molten sensations he evoked.

Jack took his time, his thumb still brushing away drops on her cheek, while his fingers twined in her plump curls as he held her in place.

A tremor of panic that she might be moving too quickly in this direction vibrated through her, only to be eclipsed by awakening desire as Jack's tongue taunted hers and he deepened the kiss. A slow, intense, provocative one that could last for days and days.

Every fiber of her being came to life.

The man knew what he was doing. And Jillian was . . . lost. Her mind went blissfully blank so that she wasn't obsessing over a past that had been exhumed when it should remain buried.

Though, in a sense, sharing her trauma with Jack was liberating. She wasn't fixated on a previous extrovert becoming an introvert and then being thrust into an extrovert's world—a complete fish out of water scenario. She simply existed. With Jack. In these delicious moments.

Until she was lightheaded and winded.

She dragged her mouth away. Murmured, "Jack . . ." And tried to breathe.

Her fingers grasped his rigid biceps. Her pulse pounded, echoing in her ears.

Jesus. It was just a kiss!

But, no . . . a shiver of awareness affirmed it was much more than that.

"Like ridin' a bike," he whispered as he also seemed to fight for a solid stream of air.

"That was *nothing* like riding a bike," she assured him, feeling the heat burst on her now-dried cheeks. "That was—"

"Not even my best work, darlin'." He winked.

Jillian smiled again. "You're swoon-worthy as is."

"Just gettin' warmed up."

Her insides crackled.

"You'd better get going, cowboy, or we'll be kissing till the cows come home."

He chuckled. So rich and rumbling. "You're amusin', Jilly."

"You're easy to be with, Jack. At the same time . . ."

Highly arousing was the phrase that sat on the tip of her tongue. She bit it back.

"Somewhat irresistible," she said in a playful tone.

"Somewhat?" He snickered. And took the high road. Obviously, he recognized how she needed measured increments versus massive chunks of this ranch experience. And him. "You gonna be okay to stand on your own?" he asked before releasing her.

"Well, there's a sturdy tree right here. I'll lean against it if needed."

His grin crinkled his eyes. "Much as I relish the idea of you watchin' me walk away, it's in my DNA to escort you to your door, darlin'."

"Might I remind you, your backside is as enjoyable to look at as your front."

"I do like your compliments, honey."

"Could be my brain's a little scrambled from that last kiss."

"Just the one?" he asked with a quirked brow.

"I don't want you getting a big head, Jack. Your hats won't fit. And you do wear them well."

"Ah, the spicy chef likes a cowboy," he teased.

Her eyes rolled upward as she attempted to suppress a wide smile. She gazed at the sky as twilight consumed the remnants of sunset and stars began to flicker.

She could stay right here, in this very spot, for an hour or two. Just absorbing Jack's presence.

But Ollie's half-assed "Oof" brought her back to earth. "He's not used to me being out of his sight for this long."

"Let's call it a night, then."

Jack led her toward the yard with a palm faintly pressed to the small of her back, sending a ribbon of delight through her. He opened the gate and ushered her in and up the steps to the deck.

At the door, she turned to him. "Scorching kisses and impeccable manners. Think I won the lottery."

"Mm, you just keep thinkin' that, darlin'."

"Well, I do have the evidence presented before me. Hard to dismiss it."

"There you go," he murmured as his lips skimmed hers once more. "Hittin' all the right notes. Sweet dreams, darlin'."

Jillian stared after him, Ollie at her feet.

When she thought he was out of earshot, she said, "*Sweet*'s not a factor. I'm sweltering from the inside out."

"Me too, darlin'. Me too."

Jillian would have been embarrassed her voice had carried, but . . . she couldn't bring herself to blush.

She couldn't be the only one thinking about that steamy night in her dorm room.

Jack was just being casual with her. Recognizing she was still settling in?

Meanwhile, her thoughts were ricocheting here and there.

Best to keep them under control for now.

She collected her wineglass and her to-go container and took them into the kitchen. Then she collapsed onto the sofa, Ollie lying next to her.

Her lips still tingled from Jack's kisses. Her fingertips grazed her mouth. She savored the lingering sensations, acknowledging and accepting everything she hadn't felt in years.

He'd touched her with caution, though not tentatively. More like he grasped that this was a tremendous step for her.

Of most importance, she suspected that he realized her trusting him held significant weight. Sharing her story, not shying away when he'd steadied her with his hand, and inching toward him of her own accord were akin to recovery milestones.

She thought she should be surprised they'd moved the needle in just one day.

But, once more, she wasn't surprised. Because it was Jack.

And it wasn't *in just one day*.

Seeing him on screen weeks ago had taken her to a different space in her mind, where laughter was how she got through grueling classes and lengthy study sessions. Where lust was inescapable and scintillating. Where it was natural to have both emotional and erotic yearnings. Sexy daydreams.

She'd locked all that away after Scott had left her—until she'd heard Jack Reed's name and it'd pried open a vault of memories. Her *good* memories.

Reprogramming, indeed.

That was precisely what he was doing to her.

Jillian's hand dropped to Ollie's head, and she stroked his fur, then twirled the curl at the end of his ear, which made him snuggle closer to her, his spine glued to her outer thigh.

She told him, "I'd say I made a mistake waiting so long to have an intimate encounter like this with a man, but then again . . ." She blew out a breath. And conceded, "It's not just any man who can ignite that kind of fire."

Her eyelids closed for a moment.

It was a test. Jillian wondered what she'd see this time.

She smiled when it was Jack's face and his glowing irises.

She let the visual work its magic on her, soothing her as much as it stimulated her. So that Jillian could imagine more heated kisses. His hands on her body. Her lips gliding over his skin and all those muscles barely concealed by his shirts.

There was a wealth of hesitation that came with the fantasy—because reality could stymie her progress, have it grinding to a halt in a heartbeat if they missed a gear.

But the thrill rippling through her assured Jillian she had great potential for a true breakthrough.

If only she could get past her anxieties, her fear of the ranch, in general. And her panic when it was more than Jack who was crowding her.

Mere habit over honest trigger, she reminded herself. *Focus on that.*

Well, that and the need to check her incoming orders and process payments.

She should be grateful to have something other than Jack to occupy her mind. But she knew flashes of those sultry kisses would continue to jolt her, leaving her in this giddy state she'd never imagined experiencing again.

All because of a hotter-than-hell cowboy with all the right moves . . .

Chapter Six

Jillian waited until there were fewer vehicles parked at the main house before she left hers the next morning.

She and Ollie had breakfast first. Then she set up her equipment to record her first podcast from the ranch.

She checked the schedule on her clipboard.

"The topic of this morning's episode is . . . ?" she quizzed herself. And answered, "Ah, very cool: *Ten Uses for Jalapeño Fry Sauce That Don't Actually Involve Fries*." A personal favorite.

She read through her notes aloud to warm up her voice and to familiarize herself with the content she'd created a couple of weeks ago. She slipped on her wireless headphones and cued her prerecorded intro.

When that concluded, she said in an energetic tone, "Let's talk secret ingredients that'll really bring the heat, such as my personalized, jala-haba-ancho pepper. Yeah, that's a mouthful, but one you're going to love."

As usual, she referred to her website for her various categories of hybrids, then forged on.

"Once sweated, I marinate the peppers in a fiery pickle juice I've concocted for a fry sauce that'll launch your most mundane recipes into the stratosphere. What *is* fry sauce? So glad you asked! It's a mayo-based condiment, and my quadruple combination delivers a tantalizing tanginess you won't be able to get enough of. How do I know this?" She smiled, for no one's benefit than hers and Ollie's. But it was warranted. "This miracle sauce is one of my bestsellers."

She explained more about the pepper and the sweating process, then discussed the numerous uses for the sauce—like adding it to alfredo pasta, meat loaf, encrusted salmon, and fried chicken—wrapping up with her standard reminder that today's recipes would be on her blog and plugging her new products, including her cookbook.

Then she gave some details of the ranch. "Be sure to check out the pics I've posted on socials. And don't forget to tune in later for Jack Reed's live feed that I'm cohosting with him." She dropped the links.

When she was finished, she texted Mindy to alert her the new file was available for editing.

She loaded up Ollie's treat bag before they made the short trek to the resort-style home up the way.

It felt odd to just walk right in. But she believed Garrett when he said no one would hear her knocking, so she did as he'd recommended.

The place was quiet.

"Hmm," she mumbled. "Not exactly what I expected . . ." She forged on.

Decadent scents wafted on the air, and she tried to dissect them all, particularly the spices. Someone had chorizo nailed, along with red pepper and paprika sausage. Jack, she was sure. And the eggs had been scrambled with hot sauce that smelled similar to her chile de arbol and pequin pepper with roasted garlic. The eggs and sautéed veggies had probably been wrapped in homemade tortillas for breakfast burritos.

Her stomach growled, causing her to laugh. She'd had steel-cut oatmeal and avocado toast. She shouldn't be hungry. But even Ollie was sniffing the air. Good Lord, this family knew how to cook!

"Sorry our regular kitchen in Seattle doesn't have this aroma," she told him. Though the certified one downstairs always emitted fiery fragrances. Just not combined with all these other mouthwatering ingredients.

They rounded the bend off the formal dining room, which was empty, and entered what Jillian referred to as *pequeño restaurante*—little restaurant—making her curious as to what Luke's cantina looked like.

Plates were neatly stacked on the island, all cleared of remnants, save for one platter that held the unfinished food that had been scraped onto it—at that, there wasn't much. Nor was there evidence of leftovers. This family had portion control down as well.

Ollie gave a soft snort of appreciation, and the petite woman at the sink at the far end of the room glanced over her shoulder.

"Jillian Parks," Jillian introduced herself. "And a not-starving-but-will-attempt-to-convince-you-otherwise Ollie."

"Brett Reed. The cleanup-crew-because-I-don't-cook mom. Welcome."

"Thank you. Can I help?"

"I'm not a woman who ever says no to that question." She grinned. Her hair was as dark as Jack's, her eyes just as blue. "Jack went to the farmers' market early and should be back in an hour or so."

"We have an extensive list," Jillian commented. And winced over not having gone with him. But she had a feeling he'd not wanted her to feel pressured to join him. And that was kind of him, because that was exactly what the case would have been, and that would have proved awkward. She needed to assimilate to this dynamic first before she encountered another.

Though she could pull her weight in the interim. She stepped toward the island where the platter sat.

"That cabinet by your foot holds the bins," Brett told her. "The one in front is trash; the other is recycle."

"Got it." Jillian used a serving utensil to push the scraps off the dish and then placed it on the counter next to Brett. She collected one stack of the plates, followed by another, moving them closer to the sink. "Seems as though you've got the short end of the stick here," Jillian quipped.

"Don't go thinkin' that for a minute," Brett said with another smile. "I just rinse most of 'em off and put 'em in the washer. Only Jack's pots and cast irons are left to deal with. The latter's not my specialty, so I leave those for him."

Jillian said, "Yeah, I wouldn't mess with a man's skillets. Especially not a chef of his caliber. I'm guessing they're seasoned just right."

"I've never mastered that, but like his daddy, he knows what yields the best flavors."

"I'm sorry about Mr. Reed," Jillian remarked.

"You can call him Royce. He wasn't interested in the 'Mr.' part. He was a rancher through and through. Well . . . a cowboy at heart, really."

"A man who had pride of ownership. This entire place is amazing. I'm awestruck." She grabbed the pile of linens and asked, "What can I do with these?"

"Laundry room's around the corner, back the way you came."

Jillian located the large facility and dumped in the napkins and the table runner, noting the spots of grease and sauce. That entertained her. The Reeds might be a well-oiled machine in some respects, but they were all fantastically human, as she'd already begun to discern. A family who meshed, who jested, who ebbed and flowed together.

Her spirits sank. This was all Jillian had wanted when she was growing up.

Her father had been so warm and down to earth that she could envision an environment such as this that he headed. The two of them had cooked, cleaned, and created peppers and dry rubs. Spicy dishes. They both would have enjoyed large gatherings every day, not just during holidays.

Her mother . . . ? Not so much. She didn't want to get her hands dirty with dishes or in the garden or even emotionally.

Jillian returned to the kitchen, Ollie trailing behind her. She brought with her the fresh linens folded on top of the dryer and asked Brett, "Okay for me to reset the breakfast table?"

"That'd be wonderful, thank you."

While Jack's mom completed her work, Jillian laid out the spread, including flatware and glasses she found in drawers and cupboards, adding plates from the biggest hutch. Brett let her roam free and get the proverbial lay of the land. She wasn't territorial. She seemed to like the camaraderie.

Brett finished up, setting the oversize platters in a rack so they didn't take up space in the washer.

"That is a fabulous collection." Jillian surveyed the varying sizes with colorful decorations.

"They're terra-cotta ceramics I make and sell at craft shows. I teach a pottery class three times a week. Pots, bowls, dinnerware."

"All the vases in the house are yours as well?"

"Every single one."

"Wow." Jillian was impressed. "You must sell out at your craft shows."

Brett's self-deprecating cringe spoke volumes. "Only because I take just six or seven samples with me. Wyatt thinks I need to load up my display table—and charge more. I don't know . . . I'm not a good judge of what the price points should be for something I enjoyed making."

"It's okay to get paid for your labor of love."

Jillian paused. She considered what Jack had said about needing additional monetization to fill in gaps at the ranch and finding it with his BBQ channel. More than that, he genuinely liked sharing his expertise with others.

She continued. "Being passionate about something and generating income from it because you've put your heart and soul into creating *any* sort of masterpiece is rewarding in a lot of ways—not just as a boon to your bottom line. People value hard work and dedication to a cause. Just thinking about how Jack—"

Jillian's voice fractured as a different sort of emotion seized her.

With a knowing nod, Brett said, "It's easy to see where his devotion lies—and that he's proud of carryin' on a tradition. But times are difficult and then plentiful and then difficult." Her eyes misted. "There are instances where you feel as though what you're passionate about *should* generate income . . . yet circumstances beyond your control prevent that from happening. Do you understand what I'm saying?"

"Yes." Jillian groaned. "Everything the Reeds have established, in every form, is subject to economic fluctuation and other factors. Precisely why your son was smart enough to try to learn all he could to overcome those systemic changes and challenges."

"You and Jack share a commonality," Brett said.

"Business is business, yes. I can't survive without mine. This ranch can't survive without your family's attention to all the details."

Brett dried her hands and then approached Jillian, extending her arm.

Jillian's heart wrenched over how such a simple gesture caught her off guard. But she didn't leave the other woman hanging.

They shook hands.

"It's an absolute pleasure to have you here," Jack's mom told her.

"You're all very hospitable. You've gone to so much trouble . . ."

"Not at all. And please feel free to join us for meals. We behave, for the most part." She winked.

"I see where your son gets his charm."

"Oh, that comes from his daddy. That man . . ." She whistled under her breath. "Took no effort at all for him to sweep me off my feet."

Jillian could relate. And she had no doubt Brett would pick up on the electric undercurrent running between her and Jack when she saw them together. Another thing that wasn't simple to address. Jillian had some pivoting to do in that vein, having already known the sexual tension would flare, just not having any recent experience with all the sparks Jack incited.

"Well," Brett said. "If there's anything you need, any way we can make your stay more comfortable, it'd be an honor on behalf of all of us to help out."

"That's a beautiful thing to say. And please know I'm grateful to hear it."

"You're independent and competent. That's not discounted. It's in our nature to contribute if we can."

"I'm sure. And . . . I'm wondering . . . what if I could assist you with setting up an online store for your pottery?"

Brett gasped.

"No pressure," Jillian was quick to say. "It's just that I know how to package and ship delicate items, and from what I've seen in this house . . . you're sitting on a potential gold mine."

"I keep tellin' her that," Jack said as he came through the garage entrance, along with Garrett.

They each brought in a large box, overflowing with fruits and vegetables that they deposited on the wiped-down island.

"However," Jack said as he moved in close to Jillian, "she's too modest to believe anyone will buy more than somethin' here or there—and at that . . . she's almost givin' the stuff away."

"They're not professional quality that'll go into a catalog, Jack," she lobbed back.

"How long have we been havin' breakfast off of the same sets?" he countered.

"Why you contest me, I will never know." She dismissed him with a wave and went to inspect the boxes.

Garrett told her, "You sell out at your booths, and customers ask for more. But you have no website."

"Oh, dear Lord!" Both of Brett's hands flew in the air now. "Do not say those words in front of Wyatt! I'll end up with a profile pic on a dating app—like Jack!"

"It's not a dating app, Mom! Jesus." Jack shook his head.

Jillian laughed, despite knowing this was an inside joke.

He said, "That bio'll be the death of me, swear to God. I just want to advertise my channel and the BBQ event. Not that I'm single." He let out a strangled sound.

Jillian wasn't particularly thrilled women around the world were well aware of his marital status either. She was suddenly curious as to whether Jack received fan mail.

She fought the urge to roll her eyes. *Of course* the man received fan mail. Marriage proposals, too, she suspected.

Something else to disregard, lest she get too twisted up in his bachelorhood. Jillian was only here for a week. Making it dicey to start anything with Jack Reed, even if it was just sweltering kisses.

"If anyone's interested"—she shot a look toward Brett and gave a nonchalant shrug—"I have extensive knowledge in building online stores. No dating profiles required."

"It's something to consider. Thank you for the offer, Jillian," Brett said. "Now I have to get to town for back-to-back classes."

Garrett was on the move too. "I'll drive you. I need some studio time at the news station."

"Wyatt can bring me home with the kids." Brett crossed to the nearest exit and grabbed her purse from a rack that held a half dozen cowboy hats of varying sizes and a couple of lightweight jackets.

"I'll return with Tuck later on to test the lighting and sound," Garrett told Jack and Jillian. "We'll need some time, since we'll be in here for the shoot, not at the outside kitchen as usual."

He held the door for Brett, and they disappeared into the garage.

Quite shockingly, being left alone with Jack was more unnerving than all the commotion. Because he grinned and eyed Jillian like he was about to suggest a tour of the entire house that started in his bedroom. And ended there.

The flicker between her legs obliterated her previous conviction/warning.

"You sleep well, darlin'?" he asked.

His low, rich tone stole her breath. As did the twinkle in his cobalt irises.

Heat seeped through her. "I might've given a thought or two to those kisses."

Oh, my God!

Did she really just admit that?

He chuckled. "I gave 'em more than a thought or two. Actually, I'm thinking of hauling you up against me and layin' one on you that just might rock your world."

She *wanted* to be wary of that sentiment. Again, she didn't need anything related to him "rocking her world." She was only beginning to right the axis.

However . . .

She gazed up at the (not just *somewhat*) irresistible cowboy and said, "I'd tell you to have at it, but chances are damn good someone would walk in on us—"

"And be scandalized? Not in this house. We catch Wyatt and Mateo in such intense lip-locks, they don't even know we're in the same room."

"Sounds as though they're hopelessly in love."

"It's disgusting," Jack joked. "Like, get over each other already. You have children!" Jack feigned revulsion, but Jillian didn't miss the slight tightening of his jaw, revealing a hint of envy.

That brought back the twinge of emotion she was trying to keep under control.

She carefully mused, "You don't get out much, do you, cowboy?"

"Darlin', when do I have the time? And speakin' of"—he swiftly changed the subject—"we've got to prep for the show. The boys'll be here at five to help with filmin', but we've got some work ahead of us before then. And after lunch, I have several calls lined up. There's a loan I'm itchin' to close out, but it comes with a final balloon payment. So I'll be sellin' a horse or two."

His jaw clenched firmer this time. Realizing it, he relaxed. Maybe for her benefit?

Jillian's heart wrenched.

"You love those horses, don't you?"

"Can't be with them as much as I am and not admire 'em. Their strength and will. Their ruggedness and their grace."

"Hmm. Those are adjectives I'd use to describe you, Jack."

"Thought I was *sexy*, darlin'."

"That too."

He grinned again. Then his head dipped, and his mouth claimed hers.

Not with caution. With full-on passion.

Jillian's instant alarm was fleeting. She didn't even bother to deflect when Jack's powerful forearm snaked around her waist and his other hand threaded through her thick waves, his thumb hitching her chin to angle it just so as his tongue caressed hers, coaxing her into another blistering kiss. This one melting her into him, so that she clasped his biceps and slipped her other arm around to splay her palm along his shoulder blade.

Her breasts nestled below his pecs, her rib cage rubbing against his taut abs. They were sealed together, and she could feel the grooves and the flexing of his muscles.

He groaned into her mouth, and that set ablaze all those frayed nerve endings.

Was it possible to become addicted to his virility, his skilled seduction?

Why, yes. Yes, it was.

So fast. Yet again.

An insistent gnawing spread through her, making her think of ripping open the snaps of his shirt and devouring every tanned and toned inch of his wide chest. Exploring those cut abs with her tongue. Unfastening his belt buckle and unzipping his jeans.

The sensory overload had her surrendering to his demanding kiss. If this was another question, she was willing to answer it.

She wanted him.

Like nothing she could remember.

Jack released her just long enough to yank out a chair at the table and sink into it, not breaking their kiss, so that Jillian joined him, straddling his lap.

A raw intensity radiated from him that resonated within her. The gnawing sensation became a clawing one, the eruption of lust and longing eliciting near-irrational tendencies.

Jack's tongue tangled with hers, and their harsher breaths mingled. She could practically feel his heartbeats, as erratic as hers.

The hand that had been on his back now clutched at his shoulder, at the swell of his traps, further spurring her need to strip off his shirt.

She tore her mouth from his and whispered his name. Tried to catch her breath.

His remained labored.

"Christ," she mumbled.

"Yeah," he replied.

His lips grazed her neck, leaving feathery kisses. His arm around her shifted, and his hand slipped under her fitted sweater and up to the waist of her jeans. His thumb glided over her skin, the intimate contact jarring her so that a soft whimper fell from her own lips. Microtremors shot through her.

"Soft as silk," he murmured against her throat. "Just as I remember."

His fingertips grazed her side as his hand moved upward, until his thumb brushed the edge of her bra, beneath her breast. Sweeping back and forth.

Jillian's grip on him tightened. Her hips rocked in a faint, slow motion.

"Mm, like that," he said in his warm timbre.

Jillian didn't censor her movements. Not even as his mouth captured hers again with a hot kiss, keeping her entranced, lost once more in the sensual abyss that eclipsed all thought and left her with nothing but fiery sensations.

She didn't even stress over the background noise of workers on the patio. Forgot all about them and the landscaping crew. Didn't worry Avery or Chance would happen upon them either—their voices would carry from far enough away that Jack and Jillian could unravel from each other in time.

She took advantage of the moment.

When they needed air, she didn't put any space between them, just kept her head bent to his, feeling his breath on her cheek, reveling in the intimacy this time, instead of being startled by it.

"I could do this all day," he told her.

Jillian smiled. "Can't say I'd mind."

He let out a strained grunt.

She got his point. "But we have work to do."

"Should've had this reunion on a deserted island."

"We'd miss every sunrise, sunset, and ocean view."

He snickered. "If I did have you all to myself, I still wouldn't get my fill of you."

A thought that curled her toes in her ankle boots.

"We'd mostly be under the covers," he added, "existing off of room service and a well-stocked minibar."

"It's too bad we have a purpose here. Though one that's going to be fun, so . . ." She was getting her breath back. "Let's prep."

Words that came with ease, but which didn't motivate her to climb off Jack's lap.

He seemed to find that amusing. "I mean, we can just hang here for a while . . ."

Jillian could go for that. But she said, "Reality check with our responsibilities."

"Yeah, those," he grumbled.

She got to her feet. Thankful she didn't fall over.

Jack shoved out of the chair. Winced with a smile. "Damn, I'm gonna need a minute."

"Oh, come on. We were just kissing."

"Then why are *you* lookin' a little dazed and confused?" he teased.

"Because my head's spinning," she admitted. "Also, I haven't given thought to kissing or being under the covers with anyone in six years." Her teeth sank into her lower lip at that notion. It was a tricky one. Honest. Also . . . scary.

Jack picked up on this and said, "Very much like ridin' a bike."

She sighed. "You do know how to grease a squeaky wheel, cowboy."

"Mm, I like how that sounds, Jilly." He winked. "And I should get extra points for rememberin' to give your dog water." He rounded the island and grabbed a fresh bowl for Ollie, placing it alongside the table.

Ollie made a beeline for it and lapped somewhat performatively, as though to imply, "At least *someone* had the good grace to serve me."

"I wasn't remiss," Jillian told Ollie, "so much as I was distracted."

"I enjoyed it too." Jack's expression turned wicked.

Jillian's heart skipped a few beats.

So, yeah . . . she had jumped right into the frying pan.

Jack knelt next to the pup and scratched behind his ears, which was all the encouragement Ollie needed to nip at Jack's thumb. Catching on to the game, Jack offered the other, alternately, so that Ollie rushed from side to side to lick the thumbs before they disappeared in Jack's fisted hands.

"Meerkat for him, you little show-off," Jillian said.

Ollie sat on his hind legs, straightening his body, front legs outstretched.

"Would you look at that," Jack mused. "He's just beggin' for a belly rub."

"Shameless through and through." She laughed again. And damn it felt good. As did the sizzle through her, infused with that liberation she continued to experience.

Jack obliged Ollie, and the dog held his balance for a minute.

Jillian said, "Let him see your circle dance." She clapped her hands together with enthusiasm. "Circles, Ollie, circles!"

Ollie went down on all fours, ran around in a tight circle three times, collapsed to the rug on his belly, rolled over, got to his feet, and circled three more times. He repeated this. Came to a halt, sat, and stared up at Jillian expectantly as he panted.

Jack cracked up. Jillian passed him the treat bag, and Jack extracted a few paw-shaped goodies.

"Filet mignon flavored," Jillian commented. "Fine dining all the way for this mutt."

Jack gave a low whistle and said to Ollie, "You give new meanin' to singin' for your supper."

He held his palm out, and Ollie sniffed around, only needing a second to decide Jack was a reliable source. He dove in, wolfing down the treats, then meerkating again.

Jack gave him the desired rubs before standing. "Too cute, Jilly. Too damn cute."

"You can see why I snatched him up when I saw him."

Jack nodded. "You heard his story too. And it mirrored yours in some respects. Enough to form a bond."

"In a heartbeat. Even though he broke mine from the second I saw him so small and damaged. He only fit into the palm of my hands at five months. And cowered until he accepted that I'd do nothing but spoil him rotten and shower him with love."

Jack dragged a hand down his face, and then it slipped around to his neck. He massaged his nape. "Not gonna lie, that kind of trauma, inflicted by a human being, is difficult to wrap my mind around."

"You don't have to wrap your mind around it," she told him, stepping close. "It's in the past."

"Relegating something to the past doesn't always resolve the issue, doesn't always release you from it."

Were they only talking about the dog?

"I'm armchairin' it here, I know I am," Jack said. "It's just that . . . I made a mistake a decade ago that I've not let go of."

Her gaze narrowed.

"Jillian . . ." A hint of torment touched his eyes. "I adored you from the *second I met you*. Had a damn hard time of it keeping you out of my thoughts. And then that night in your dorm room . . ." His brow furrowed. "It might not have been my first time, but it was special. Because I was with *you*."

Her breath hitched.

"It was wrong of me to get involved with someone I might want a future with, knowin' what I would have to leave behind four years later. Due to what awaited me here. Worse . . . it wasn't even four years. I was gone *days* later, Jillian. Like, we had this perfect evenin' together—at least, it was perfect in my mind—"

"Don't doubt it was perfect in mine, too, Jack. Awkward on my side from time to time, but . . ." She gave him a soft smile. "You worked out all the kinks, cowboy."

Jack pulled in a long breath. Then he said, "I wanted to be locked in that room with you for a week, Jilly. Guess that's why the deserted island popped into my head for our reunion."

"That's very sweet."

"Problem is . . . I didn't tell you that. Didn't ever get the chance to tell you. We had another date, but then my life exploded, and I was . . . gone. I mean, I thought I had all this time to let us process and grow—together. To what end, I didn't know."

Tears stung her eyes because he'd agonized over this since their freshmen year. She never would have imagined.

"Damn it, Jillian. You're right. Your therapist is right. Clingin' to the past in these particular instances won't set you free to build a future. It's just not a lesson I've learned or employed."

"Jack?"

He said, "I didn't just stop thinkin' about you, darlin'. I was shocked when Garrett brought me that new line of rubs and sauces with your name as the owner of Hotter Than Haba. I was surprised when you called into my show. But I wasn't jolted by a long-lost remembrance. You were in my head before that."

She gasped.

"I didn't just forget you, honey," he said, emotion tinging his voice. "I never could. And I guess I never forgave myself for my abrupt departure. Not after what we'd shared. I just . . . couldn't do anything about it. This is my life, Jillian. From birth to death. *This* is my life."

"Jack," she whispered. "I understand that. And I never harbored any ill will toward you. I knew where your life would lead you, farther down the road, after graduation, perhaps if you ended up with a pro contract."

"A pipe dream. I'm more based in reality now."

"Makes two of us."

Jillian had severed ties with her own dreams. Being a wife, being a mother, someday a grandmother . . . she'd carved those things out of her life as she'd resurfaced.

"Jack, I'm focused on reintegrating myself into society. It's not as simple as one might think, and I haven't won many battles. But it's my next step. So. Here I am. And I'll admit, you are a fantastic safe landing."

"'Cept for the horses and the cows and the people." Now his brow crooked, challenging her to deny his statement.

"You are surrounded by a minefield, yes. And yet . . . I have a very strong feeling I can rise above while I'm here."

"Country air and cowboy kisses can do that for you?"

She leaned into him, her lips brushing his, curving upward. She murmured, "I'm willing to give it a shot, Jack."

"Me, too, Jilly." He kissed her again. "Me too."

Jillian recognized the calm seeping through her. Around the periphery, she knew her anxiety would return when the production crew was in place and there were audiences watching them . . . live.

But for these brief, stolen moments, she could allow Jack's compassionate nature to lure her into a certain security she believed he could back up.

That was a key component, while she was homing in on what qualified as an extreme reaction, rather than a faltered response—and was searching for the balance in between.

When she pulled away, she said, "Nothing to be remorseful about regarding SPU, cowboy. I have no regrets. Did I fantasize about a different outcome? Sure. But did I already know it wasn't coming? I had no delusions, Jack."

What Jillian had had was perspective—paramount in her present as much as her past.

"On to our next phase of the day," she concluded.

He chuckled. "Probably a good thing one of us can keep our wits about us."

"Don't go believing I can. It's just, you know, we have work to do." She shifted away from him.

Granted, "what could have been ten years ago" and the all-too-fleeting "what had been" intertwined with a tenuous "what could be now."

Though Jillian was wise enough to acknowledge their distinct differences, which wouldn't coalesce in the long run.

So.

She'd focus on her evolution in her current paradigm and hope she continued to grow when she returned home. Her own live-and-learn exercise *here* that might aid her forward movement *there* so that she could further progress. Shatter her glass box and surge forth.

For now, she was happy being in this kitchen with Jack.

Being with Jack, in general.

For now.

She joined him as he unloaded the produce boxes and set aside some special requests from Wyatt and their mom, while Jillian grouped what she and Jack required for their first show.

The butterflies in her stomach weren't only taking flight because of Jack. Jillian was a bit nervous about being on screen. She was only accustomed to audio.

Knowing huge audiences were going to be watching this afternoon brought on a natural anxiety that anyone would feel if they were in her shoes, whether they were used to being isolated or not.

Stage fright isn't your trigger, she told herself.

Yes, she preferred strictly audio. But she couldn't see this audience, so . . .

Just breathe.

She did.

Then Jack grinned. Jillian's next breath stuck in her throat.

His gaze was a sweltering one. Because he knew his effect on her.

"Stop being so disarming," she said as she divided out portions for each side dish they were prepping, making organized piles on the countertop.

"Darlin', I wasn't doin' anything at all," he professed.

She scoffed at him.

He laughed.

Then he grabbed two bamboo cutting boards and laid them out, along with paring and chef knives, creating their individual stations. He retrieved a tray laden with stacked glass ramekins for ingredients and spices, a nesting set of mixing bowls, and both wooden and silicone utensils. He offered Jillian a towel and slapped the other one over his shoulder.

She'd been right from the start—there was nothing sexier than a cowboy who cooked. And who kissed her the way Jack Reed did.

If he maintained this inadvertent, silent seduction, she just might be fixated enough on all the internal flickers and shudders that she completely forgot about the viewers.

And maybe that was his game.

Or . . . maybe he just couldn't help himself when it came to her.

A very appealing thought.

Only problem was, she needed some stability so that she didn't lop off a finger.

Thank God Jack had claimed the space across from her, so that he wasn't so close to her that she felt the heat on his skin, or they bumped into each other, or she smelled nothing more than his intoxicating cologne.

Concentrating on slicing and dicing helped her to focus. Along with measuring out ingredients so they were available during the show.

She covered the ramekins with cellophane and stored the ones needing refrigeration, then lined up the others on the tray.

Jack said, "Why don't we use the mini frying pans on my raclette with the rib eyes for the peppers, mushrooms, and onions? We'll reserve yours for servin' sauces."

"Perfect complement, visually. And mine won't require much heat once finished, just warming so they're not cold against the steaks."

There were numerous other details to work through. Jillian wasn't surprised when noon rolled around, and they were just wrapping up.

Neither of them wanted the show choreographed, fearing they might come across as stiff and stilted. The downside was that they'd never cooked together. Who knew how they were going to maneuver within Tuck's frame?

At least they had their food assignments nailed.

While Jillian cleaned their mess, Jack fired up the grill on the stove and whipped up carne asada street tacos on corn tortillas, topped with onions, cilantro, and one of Jillian's hybrid hot sauces. He added tortilla chips and fresh guacamole.

"Now *you're* spoiling *me*," she said with a hungry groan.

"Nothin' wrong with that."

He refrained from winking, for which Jillian was grateful. She'd finally gotten herself in check, had found a groove that didn't have her constantly pondering what Jack's next move might be.

Luckily, it was feeding her.

She returned to her saddle stool at the island, and he sat across from her again.

This time, the distance didn't provide the same reprieve from his charisma or the sparkle in his dark-blue gaze.

She managed to eat her lunch anyway. Afterward, they parted company, Jack having those calls to make and Jillian wanting to get her current wave of orders packaged for shipping.

"Meet back here at four?" Jack suggested.

She ignored the inherent twinge of panic related to filming, this being too advantageous for her to pass up.

"Four it is," she agreed.

Jillian left him before he had a chance to give her a parting kiss. Because that would just lead to another make-out session right here in the kitchen, she was sure.

His rumbling laugh chased her toward the door, telling her he was totally on to her.

"He's going to keep me on my toes this week," she told Ollie as they headed to the guesthouse.

Precisely what she needed?

Chapter Seven

Jack would have had a hell of a time concentrating in the afternoon if he didn't have such important business to conduct.

He had Mateo on the phone first.

Jack said, "I've got Jim Olsson on the hook for one of the new horses, but I haven't finished up with either of them yet. Hate to turn 'em loose while they're still riled."

"Jim has trainers," Mateo reminded him. "He wouldn't inquire if he wasn't willin' to take on the responsibility of completin' the job."

"I know." Jack sighed.

He was dragging his feet, was what he was doing. He never liked parting with the equines he broke, rehabbed, or outright purchased in excellent condition. But when the numbers told him it was the sensible thing to do, Jack couldn't put his personal feelings above the good of the ranch.

Mateo said, "I'll be overnight in Odessa for the seven a.m. auction tomorrow. Mostly cows and steers up for sale, but I'll start puttin' out feelers this evenin' for anyone interested in horses. How many you lookin' to unload?"

"Just two for now. The new ones won't make enough individually without another month or so of trainin'. Together, though, they'll yield a decent profit. But the others in the auxiliary stables are up for consideration as well, and they'll each net more on their own."

Jack wouldn't touch the horses specifically used for cowboying and wrangling. They were seasoned and proficient with herding the cattle. He couldn't afford to disrupt an effective and competent system. Not even for the sake of paying off his loan to save on the exorbitant finance charge he incurred every month.

His cell buzzed with an incoming call, identified as Luke.

"Little bro's on the other line," Jack told his brother-in-law. "Talk to me later about what you hear back when you spread the word."

"Will do."

They hung up, and Jack connected with Luke, asking, "You all set for the street festival this weekend?"

"Sure enough. Got Mom's vendor booth organized too. We're ready to rock and roll come Friday."

The annual event was one that brought people from several counties, and even though there was the tendency for the small town of Serrano to be overrun by tourists, it was beneficial for the local economy.

"You know, you ought to shoot a segment from the cantina's vendor booth," Luke said. "I'd appreciate the advertisin', sure. But it gives another perspective for your viewers."

Jack had been considering how he could capitalize on this weekend's influx, but he had too many balls in the air to begin with and couldn't drop even one.

Though Luke's recommendation held merit.

"I bet we could swing an hour on Sunday," Jack conceded.

"Let's plan on it. Anything else goin' on?"

"All's good here." Jack didn't mention his current fiscal entanglement.

Luke told him, "See you at the festival, then."

They disconnected.

Jack sat back in his big leather chair that had been refurbished three times since his grandfather had bought it.

It'd be killer if he could get Jillian to stick around a little later on Sunday before she drove to Austin.

But then Jack realized there was no way she'd agree to being in the center of that vast crowd on the main strip.

Oh, hell, no.

Jack wouldn't even present the idea to her. In his mind, he'd even rescinded the offer for her to join the BBQ bash. He'd not known about her phobia prior to blurting that invite—he'd just been so thrilled to see her, it jumped right off his tongue. Being informed now had him certain that his hundreds of on-site guests would overwhelm the heck out of her.

No, it was best if she avoided town this weekend as well as the holiday setup.

His gut coiled.

He knew she was a temporary fixture in his life. That her leaving on Sunday morning after she recorded her podcast and Jack packed her up was an agenda set in stone. That had to remain etched on his brain.

He reached for his cell again and placed more calls, signed off on urgent paperwork and payroll, then cleaned up and changed his clothes for the five p.m. filming, meeting up with Jillian at their designated time.

One look at her in a tight pink knit tank with a squared neckline and matching sweater, along with curve-hugging ankle-length jeans and low-heeled boots, and his cock twitched. His mind seized up for a few seconds as racy thoughts ran rampant, all leading to them getting naked.

Jack groaned. "Darlin', you're gonna have me twisted in knots in front of what I hope are a zillion people."

She smiled somewhat sheepishly, but more like the cat about to eat the canary. Which had Jack envisioning her crawling over rumpled sheets toward him—then crawling all over him.

He wanted her straddling his waist and rubbing herself against his abs. Rocking gently as her palms splayed over his pecs and he gripped her ass, holding her in place. He could almost feel her cream coating the grooves of his midsection and hear her rasping moans.

It took no effort at all to picture her with arms extended, breasts pressed between them. Her head on her shoulders, all those lustrous curls tumbling down her back.

He knew this fantasy would be even hotter in real life. And that now had his cock throbbing.

His blood turned to magma—and he wasn't even touching her.

Jesus, man. You have a show to do.

Fuck, he had plenty of things to focus on. Making Jillian come repeatedly should be so much lower on the list. But it sat right there at the top.

"Lost in wicked thoughts, Jack?" she teased before opening the refrigerator and retrieving the baking sheet that held the items they'd wanted to stay chilled. She put it on the island, alongside the tray containing the room temperature ingredients.

Jack's jaw clenched for a second. If he hadn't heard Garrett and Tuck in the hallway, he would have had Jillian in his arms again, kissing her senseless.

Though, admittedly, he was the one who seemed to be evading all logic.

He mumbled, "You don't know the half of it." And ducked into the pantry for the raclettes.

The twins raced into the kitchen, Ale grabbing his tripod from the storage room as Tuck collected his equipment too.

Garrett told Jack, "Miss Brett's fillin' in for another instructor this afternoon, and Wyatt's still at work, but they'll be here for supper. Kids did their homework in the sundae shop. No soccer practice for Hunt today."

"And Mateo's in Odessa," Jack mentioned. "So it's just the four of y'all helpin' out."

Jillian let out a discreet sigh of relief.

Ale got situated with his mini tablet and the extra phone stacked on top of each other and secured with the tripod, then went straight to the puppy and plopped on the floor to play with him.

Meanwhile, Hunter stood at the end of the island, awestruck.

Over Jillian.

Jack chuckled and ruffled his hair. "Yeah, I get it, boy."

He wasn't sure that *Hunter* got it—his meaning. But his nephew's jaw slackened, and Jack crooked a brow as to whether Hunt was still breathing.

Jack told Jillian, "You're a heartbreaker, darlin'."

A peculiar flash in her tawny eyes gave him pause. She looked a bit taken aback, like that wasn't something that had ever occurred to her.

Surely the woman had to know she could stop a speeding train with all she had going on.

Yet . . . she appeared doubtful.

Jack told Hunt, "Find me the double boiler, will you?"

Hunt didn't budge.

Jack mock-glowered at him. "Sooner rather than later, buddy."

"Right, right. Double boiler." Hunt went to the cabinet at the far end by the sink to find what Jack needed for the béarnaise sauce.

Jack swooped in toward Jillian and murmured, "You got him all flustered. Never seen him gawk like that before."

She nudged his ribs with an elbow. "Jack Reed."

She shook her head, then shifted away and gathered up the serving utensils and platter she wanted, setting them just out of the frame, as confirmed by Tuck, for later use.

Jack scratched his chin. And wondered what in the world would make a woman like Jillian Parks question her appeal—to anyone.

Obviously, there was more to the story of her "lost years" that he clearly knew nothing about, other than the rehabilitation she went through and the fact that she'd come through on the other side with a winning combination of a more stable existence and a successful business model.

But he did recall how being touched intimately and kissed deeply were basically foreign sensations for her. And that made him damn curious as to what, other than the physical trauma and the harrowing scare, had led her into a reclusive state.

Unfortunately, now was not the time to inquire further—or to lust after her.

Tuck was ready for lighting and sound checks. Garrett was monitoring on his computer. Ale was angling his devices just right. Hunt was organizing all the pots out of view and lining the baking sheets with foil.

And Jillian was now pacing, shaking her hands out. Inhaling slowly and exhaling in what seemed to be a cleansing manner.

He sidled up to her once again and advised, "Just forget about the cameras. Pretend you're podcastin', standing up."

"I don't do cooking demos on my podcast, Jack."

"Maybe you should. Add a visual component. You're too pretty to be hidin' behind a mic in a basement."

Her gaze locked with his.

He added, "Not discountin' what you do. Just sayin', you're fun to be around, Jillian. Attractive as hell. Savvy. A total detriment to my concentration, but I don't mind."

She sighed again, this one tinged with desire. "You being all seductive isn't going to help me get 'into character,' Jack."

His head lowered, and he whispered, "Maybe not. Then again . . . maybe."

He took just a small step backward.

She couldn't fight her smile.

"See?" he quietly asserted with a pointed look. "Just like that . . ."

She laughed. "I shouldn't concede so quickly. And yet . . ." She gave a shrug. "I will say you have a certain je ne sais quoi, cowboy."

"That's not the kind of French we speak around here, honey."

"Ha, ha." Her eyes now glowed, soft and sultry.

He tapped her nose with the tip of his finger and told her, "We're gonna be in our zone. The primary interactions need to be between us. Giving the audience some love is certainly important, but that's mostly eye contact with a camera. No one else is here but the six of us. I even sent the workers home early."

"Jack, I'm totally disrupting your schedule and—"

"Jilly, they'd make background noise. Garrett can filter some of that out, but you and I'd be hearin' it. We're not throwing any wrenches into the works with these shows, so don't go worryin' about that. This is all gonna be fine. I only want you to think of how comfortable you were with your workstation earlier and slip into that space again."

"I'm listening to what you're saying." She breathed deeply.

"I was a little freaked the first few times I did this too." He grinned. "Especially live. But thing is, darlin', when you're passionate about what you're doin' and talkin' about, the jitters fade away like that." He snapped a finger.

Jillian's expression turned appreciative. And optimistic. "I'm really looking forward to this, I promise. I just don't want to mess anything up for you."

"Not gonna happen," he said. "Now . . . let's get to it."

He refrained from kissing her in front of the small group. No easy feat.

For their new workstation, Jack had set his raclette at an angle on his outer edge and did the same with Jillian's next to her, creating a V formation, the bottom pointing toward the cameras. They were plugged into the under-the-counter outlets and firing up. Between them, the ramekins were appropriately laid out, with the warming trays stacked in fours.

Garrett gave a countdown for Jack and Jillian.

Jack delivered his standard intro before saying, "We've got two excitin' change-ups to our show today. The first bein' that we're gril-lin' inside while the outdoor kitchen's being remodeled for the big Memorial Day Weekend BBQ Bash, hosted by yours truly and my family, right here on the TRIPLE R, with a couple hundred of our closest friends and relatives."

He winked.

"Haven't purchased your tickets yet?" he continued. "What are ya waitin' for? We've got live music, dancin', and a feast for you to get your fill of barbecue. Order on my website soon, before we're sold out." He provided the link.

"Shameless self-promotion there, Jack," Jillian chimed in with a gorgeous smile that nearly knocked him out of his boots.

It took him a second or two to recover, then he told the collective audience, "Our other modification to today's show is that—obviously—I won't be grillin' alone. Folks, this is a treat for y'all, direct from Seattle, Washington, Miss Jillian Parks." He slid her a glance and a grin that he hoped gave her similar heart palpitations.

By the way the cords of her graceful throat pulled taut, he'd say, *Mission accomplished.*

"Jillian's the owner of Hotter Than Haba, if y'all remember her from our show not too long ago. She's kind enough to be on hand to offer accompaniments to the juicy rib eyes I'll be featurin'. You might wanna grab yourself a snack because she's gonna whet your appetite!"

"Thanks for that, Jack."

"She's awful strikin', isn't she?" He used his sister's words—because they were spot on.

"Don't get me blushing right off the bat, Jack. I don't have a makeup artist, and Garrett wouldn't be calling 'cut' for me anyway, to touch up."

"But I so enjoy it, darlin'."

"And so he sets the tone." She laughed. Then she said, "As I'm turning whatever shade I'm currently turning, I just want to say I'm happy to be here on the ranch with all these wonderful people. It's absolutely stunning and a fabulous place to debut my new cookbook."

She reached for the hardback just past her raclette and held it up, level with her midsection.

"Available in bookstores, at your favorite e-retailers, and on my website." She also dropped her main link. "While you're there, sign up for my free newsletter or opt in as a paid subscriber for exclusive content and a wealth of recipes for everyday dining and special occasions, plus discount codes on my hot sauces, dry rubs, and specialty hybrid chili pepper seeds."

Jack simpered comically. "Shameless self-promotion, indeed."

She gave him a feisty look and said, "They might want to know what I officially bring to the table, Jack."

"We're about to demonstrate that."

He gave a quick overview of the type of indoor grill they were using and then discussed his four different cooking methods for the steaks.

"Simple salt and pepper on one," he explained. "Steak butter on the next. Then two with spices Jillian has selected. Her ancho chili with smoked paprika, and for the other, her Carolina Reaper hybrid. Both guaranteed to wake up your taste buds and get 'em hummin'."

"So the idea is a couple traditional offerings for pairing with sauces and then two steaks that have more of a fiery flare that require no additional enhancement," she commented.

Jack walked through his prep process and then placed the four slabs of beef on his raclette.

"Don't ya just love that sizzle?" He stared into the side-by-side cameras.

When he stepped out of the frame to wash his hands, Jillian picked up the slack.

"Our main side dish will need some roasting time, then we'll finish it off on the grates." She grabbed her bowl of halved baby red and gold potatoes. "We're going to lightly coat these with olive oil, add S&P, and toss with fresh rosemary. This will give us a crispy outside, a fluffy inside, and a subtle yet distinct flavoring that's also quite fragrant."

Jack returned, but he was missing something.

"Anyone see my tongs?"

"On the counter, Uncle Jack," Hunt informed him, gesturing behind the workstation.

"Such a good kid," he said and was on the move to collect what he needed, just as Jillian was reaching for her own utensil to mix up the potatoes.

As she stretched for the silicone spoon in front of her, and he truly admired that reach, her back leg caught him right in the shin.

He hit the ground with a resounding thud—and an "Oof."

"Man down!" he quipped.

"Oh, my Go—" Jillian shrieked before catching herself as she spun around. "I can't believe I just did that!"

Jack hopped to his feet and raised his hands, saying, "Totally fine, darlin'. No harm, no foul."

He chuckled. Meanwhile, Jillian stared at him, horrified.

"Honey, I get bucked from horses. This is nothin'."

She didn't seem to think so.

Given her stricken look, he realized that the trampling had popped into her head. So he stared more intently at her.

Though his tone was light as he said, "Just takin' one for the team, honey. That's all."

She gave a slight nod, like she grasped that *he* grasped how she might perceive this little incident.

She sucked in a breath and then actually did get into character. "Might want to watch where you're going there, Jack."

He grinned. "Well, when you're crooking your leg like a starlet from back in the day, and I've just given you the ultimate Hollywood kiss . . . it's hard for a man not to get tripped up."

The splash of color on her face was the only thing he needed to see, evidence she was able to not go somewhere *too* dark in her mind.

"I gotta wash up again," he amiably commented.

"Right." She whirled around and resumed what she was doing.

But then—out of nowhere—her Julia Roberts laugh burst forth. And the crew couldn't help but crack up as well, it was so infectious.

For a moment, Jack stalled out over her unbidden response.

If ever there was a sound that made his heart almost jump from his chest . . . this was it.

Not to mention, the way her entire body shook over her boisterous laughing jag and her eyes danced as she glanced at him, she looked every bit the carefree spirit he'd once known.

His gut twisted, and his pulse hammered in his veins.

Jesus Christ.

Falling for Jillian a second time wasn't supposed to be on his bingo card.

But it just might be inescapable.

A sentiment to grind over at another time. He had a show to do.

He dried his hands and returned to his spot, saying, "Nice to see y'all get a kick out of my faux pas."

"I just didn't realize you were so clumsy, Jack," she said as she got herself under control.

He snorted.

She laughed again, more daintily this time. And added, "Just teasing. Sorry about that."

Hunt brought him the tongs to flip his steaks after they had the perfect sear on one side.

Jillian dumped her potatoes onto a baking sheet and aligned her multicolored carrots and her lengthwise-cut zucchini, sprinkling the latter with grated parmesan.

She very solemnly asked Jack, "Mind putting these in the oven for me? It's preheated. I won't move an inch. Promise."

She batted her lashes.

"Flirtin' with me will get you everywhere, darlin'."

He took her sheet to the double oven and slid it into the lower one, adjusting the heat to four hundred, per her recipe.

He returned and began slicing his sweet onions and orange, red, and yellow bell peppers.

"We'll use a little oil and some of Jillian's garlic-haba flakes on these to get a southwestern flavor." He parsed them out into four of the mini trays and added them to the grilling unit.

Jillian was moving on to the portabella mushrooms, and she held up a small glass prep bowl with butter, telling the audience, "We're going to take an extra step here to develop a silky sauce for this particular sauté. While a key ingredient is olive oil for the pan, adding butter makes this a richer topping."

Jillian snatched up a tablespoon in her other hand, as Jack went in search of the dish towel he'd misplaced. It'd been dislodged from his shoulder when he'd taken that dive, so he nabbed it from the floor.

"Hunt, will you get me a new—"

Jillian turned around to head toward the microwave.

She and Jack nearly collided.

Jillian's arm jerked upward, tilting the ramekin.

She let out a small shriek—as the lump of butter hit her chest . . . and fell lower.

Jack erupted. "Slam dunk, y'all!"

Her eyes popped.

He tried to compose himself but couldn't. Not really.

Over her shoulder, he told the audience, "That went right on down her shirt."

"Jack Reed!"

"Oh, honey, I just . . ." He fought another wave of laughter, asking the universal *everyone*, "What am I supposed to do with her hands full? Retrieve it myself?"

"Jack, it's melting!" she wailed.

"Don't hold this against me, Jilly. Y'all close your eyes. 'Specially you, Hunt." His hand plunged down her top, and he extracted the blob, tossing it into her discarded veggie bowl. "This is not how I intended to get to second base with ya, darlin'."

"Holy . . ." Her eyes rolled, and her teeth gritted.

But Jack saw the amusement stamped on her face.

"There's a smear that I need to dab at," he playfully said, not the least bit opposed to having to clean her up.

"Get it before it stains my shirt!"

He swiped at the greasy spot above her squared neckline, which the enticing swells of her breasts just barely crested. And fought a groan as lightning struck him in all the most interesting places.

"Sorry, Jilly."

"No, you're not." She shot him a humorous look.

"No, I am not." He tossed aside the towel and said, "Hunt, get Miss Jillian a half a stick of butter."

"I can't look at the camera, Jack," she murmured.

"You'll be fine, darlin'." He gently circled her around to the island.

"I don't know what to do."

"Tell the masses somethin' PG rated, honey, 'cuz I'm not sure I can."

Her lips pressed together, stifling another laugh.

Her eyes watered—in a good way.

Bumbling and bumping into each other was apparently a riot for their production crew, and Jack hoped that resonated with the audience.

For him, this was another bonding experience with Jillian. He adored how she bounced back. How resilient she was. How, even though she was swimming upstream in a sense, she was making great headway.

Proved by Garrett's thumbs-up and Ale's fist pumps as they both gauged viewers' reactions. Ale went so far as to make a heart sign with his two hands. Then he flashed ten fingers, repeatedly. Numerous times, in fact. Indicating the love emoji were exorbitant.

Jillian finally spoke, saying, "I'm going to try this again." She accepted the new portion of butter from Hunter, with thanks.

"Whatever you need, I'm just right over there." He indicated his stool at the end of the island.

Like she didn't know. Jack sniggered.

Hell, he was surprised the kid didn't keel over when Jillian smiled so sweetly at him.

Then she checked to make sure Jack was poised beside her, not behind her, before she went to the microwave.

"I'm only going to zap this for a few seconds. I don't want it melted all the way through." Her eyes still shimmered, and she glowed exuberantly.

When she had her preferred thickness, she returned to their space and said, "See how we still have this center chunk? I want to slowly turn this over with a spoon." She did just that. "Churning creates a more luxurious texture." When she was done, she set it on the counter and reached for a foil packet. "These are roasted garlic cloves. Line a muffin tin with foil, drizzle the garlic with oil, and close them up."

She unraveled a cooked pouch. Inhaled. And sighed with a hint of euphoria.

Getting Jack going again.

"Doesn't that smell amazing?" she asked.

Jack was the one at a loss for words this time.

She appeared elated—and he wanted to be the one who made that happen, not a fucking head of garlic.

Continuing on, she said, "I typically do 'bellas in a sauté pan, but these will cook up nicely in the trays, given the high heat Jack's working with for his steaks." She poured in white wine and chopped shallots and stirred. Then she combined the mushrooms to coat them before she divvied up the contents of her bowl into the trays. "I'm adding fresh parsley, which will offer an aromatic and bright element here."

She passed the pans to Jack, who loaded them up.

"We'll also keep a southwestern lobster mac and cheese bubbling on my raclette," she indicated.

Hunt collected the crockpot and then a bowl of pasta.

He grinned as Jillian thanked him yet again.

For God's sake, the kid was as smitten as Jack.

Jillian removed the lid from the ceramic pot to reveal a creamy sauce.

"I have a five-cheese recipe on my website," she informed the audience, "but for this occasion, I'm only using white cheddar, which has a velvety quality to it that pairs well with lobster." She folded in elbow macaroni and broiled seafood. Then she ladled the mixture into trays and topped them with buttery breadcrumbs and more lobster. "We're going to see a gorgeous golden layer on top that has just the slightest crunch."

While Jillian stepped away to put her baguette in the other oven, Jack took over.

"We're ready to pull these rib eyes and let them rest." He placed them on a cutting board and tented a sheet of foil that Hunt offered over them.

Jillian came back with her roasted veggies and took another long breath. "All of these melded scents are divine." She loaded up a third of her grill and then said, "Next, we're going to put romaine lettuce on this hot surface to get some marks. If you haven't grilled boats before, this is a simple way to enjoy a salad that goes with every barbecue."

She selected sturdy inner pieces and got the right effect on both sides while Jack talked about béarnaise sauce and started his demo.

As he worked with his ingredients in the double boiler on the stove, Jillian continued her dialogue.

"I'm also going to warm up a medley of sliced heirloom tomatoes, and we'll—" She halted midsentence. Sniffed the air. And said, "Um, Jack, I think something's burning."

"It's your bread, Miss Jillian!" Hunt was immediately on the case.

"Oh, good grief!"

She rushed to the oven as Jack let out a guffaw. "Darlin', you warned me you weren't a baker, but how can you burn a loaf that's already cooked?"

"Because you put my potatoes in the wrong preheated oven, Jack," she lobbed back. "So I put the bread in the free oven, which had the higher temp."

"That is one suspicious accusation, honey," he teased.

"And I'm sticking with it." She set the pan on the counter, wrapped the foil around the baguette, and discarded it, still wearing her heat-resistant gloves.

Hunt was quick to give her a replacement sheet, and she popped another baguette into the oven but switched it off, since she only wanted the bread to warm, not burst into flames.

Meanwhile, Jack whisked his sauce and admired the view of his cohost in action, racking his brain for something to say that wasn't overly flirtatious. Yet salacious comments were all that came to mind as she pinned him with a spicy expression that made his pulse hitch and his groin tighten.

Sooo not the time to be fantasizing about Jillian under the covers with him, all those soft curves of hers conforming to his hard muscles, her skin against his skin, her—

"Jack, you have to pay attention to your sauce, or it'll separate," she scolded him in her sultry voice, the subtle lilt in her tone suggesting she knew there were lascivious thoughts in his head.

He abandoned the whisk and told the audience, "There's a more efficient way to do this that yields the same result, in less time." He grabbed a cordless immersion stick from a drawer and finished up.

Jillian returned to the counter with the chimichurri, and she spooned the sauce into a tray, telling the audience, "I only want a couple minutes under the heat, since I had the bowl in the fridge so all the seasonings would blend. This is an authentic Argentinian recipe you can find on my website."

She then set out the oversize platter they were using for a display.

"Compliments of Brett Reed," she remarked, "Jack's mom and the creator of these beautiful handmade dishes, as well as pottery planters and vases."

Jack caught on to the free promo. "She'll be at the Serrano Street Festival, for those of you who are local. Check out her booth early, before she sells out. And while you're there, Luke Reed has a booth for his cantina, and he'll be whipping up the best fajitas this side of the border. Avery Reed'll be on hand, too, showin' off his cowboy cookin' skills."

"A true family affair," Jillian commented.

"I'll be filmin' from there on Sunday," he decided in that instant. "If y'all can't get enough of me."

Jillian grinned.

"Hope you'll tune in," Jack added. "Now . . . where are we, Jilly?"

"We're putting these boats on the platter, with the tomatoes on top, some shaved parmesan-romano cheese, pepper, and a drizzle of Caesar dressing, included in my cookbook, and then crumbling a bit of cheese as a final touch." She went through each task as she spoke and then scooped the veggies into the center of the plate. "Let me grab the bread."

Jack said, "I'm gonna slice two of these steaks, leavin' them bare, and arrange the others on the platter with sauces."

Jillian rejoined him. Her hands were full, so he said, "Open up," and plopped a bite of the ancho chili rib eye right on her tongue. She savored it with a stirring sigh that did nothing to cool his blazing insides.

"You cooked that to perfection," she all but moaned.

And Jack wondered if he might be hiding out behind the island until he got himself in check.

Goddamn, the things the woman did to him! Without doing much of anything at all.

She went about her business, expounding on how she prepared the baguette, hasselback-style. "I used two wooden spoons on either side of the baguette as guides when I sliced it, so I didn't cut all the way through. Then I slipped a tab of garlic butter between each one-inch slit, brushed melted butter on top, and garnished with rosemary to get this flavorful crust. Using the right temperature, of course."

Jack's expression was sardonic.

She gave him a flirty look. "So there. I successfully baked."

He chuckled. "Darlin', I'm under the impression you can achieve anything you set your mind to."

Her tawny gaze softened, and her smile was an appreciative one. "Let's hope so, Jack."

He was curious as to her meaning. And how it might involve him.

Jillian configured the baguette into two halves at the bottom of the platter. Jack retrieved the onions and mushrooms as well as the peppers, with just the right char to them. Jillian placed those trays, as well as the ones containing the mac and cheese, around the dish that Jack tilted at an angle for the camera.

"Dinner is served," she said.

"Outstanding presentation, Jilly."

"I had stellar tools to work with, Jack. A fabulous crew—special shout-out to Hunter Reed. And also a charming cohost."

"It's been my pleasure, honey."

She doled out links and info again, for both of them, and then Garrett indicated they'd wrapped and were running Jack's outro credits.

Ale went to the table that Ollie laid alongside and resumed playing with him.

Garrett took a call that came in the second he turned his phone on.

Tuck clapped his hands and declared, "Bravo! Love that this wasn't scripted."

"Well, we were a bit sloppy," Jillian confessed. "But perhaps that'll be the appeal. Other than Jack."

"Jilly, I'm guessin' you stole the show."

"Not if I'm right about your female demographic," she countered.

"I wouldn't worry too much about them." He winked. "Now, Hunt, do me a favor and get place settings for you four, plus Nana and Wyatt, who should be arrivin' soon. Y'all leave one of these steaks for them to share. And there are more fixin's in the fridge."

Which he went directly to and started gathering items for himself and Jillian. Smoked ribs, corn on the cob, and his own barbecue sauce.

Jillian took a call as well, using the speaker function as Mindy proclaimed, "That. Was. Brilliant! The two of you crashing into each other, the spicy undertones and stolen glances, the recipes, the final display . . . loved it all! And the audiences did too. I've never seen so many comments, and they're still being posted!"

"What are they saying?" Jillian excitedly asked.

"Things like, 'They make it look so fun to pull together a large meal.' Yum emoji. 'How Jillian can even concentrate with Jack flirting with her is beyond me!' Heart-eyes emoji. 'OMG, he actually reached down her shirt!!!' Triple exclamation point. Mm-hmm. A gazillion more flame emoji. On and on and on . . ."

Jillian gazed at Jack radiantly—making him think she was her *own* signature flame emoji.

She ventured, "So . . . I'm figuring . . . score?"

"Sounds like it," he concurred.

"You can count on it." This from Garrett. "Hey to you, Mindy." His first order of business.

"Hey, back," she replied.

Garrett then announced, "Just got off the line with the station manager. He said this segment was fantastic, and there was a mischievous vibe between Jack and Jillian that resonated. He's giving Jack a fifteen-minute slot on Thursday—and he wants Jillian to join in."

Chapter Eight

"He wants *what*?" Jillian choked out. Panic stricken. In an instant.

Jack was quick to tell her, "No live audience, darlin', I assure you. They built a set for me that they roll out into the parking lot—not kiddin' ya—with a backdrop advertisin' the station's call letters. And I only get a skeleton crew."

That he homed in on what would jar Jillian about this new scenario touched her. And she mouthed, *Thank you.*

He wagged a brow.

The overwhelming desire to kiss the hunky cowboy rose within her.

But Mindy kept her on point. Somewhat.

"It's a terrific idea," her producer said. "Way to maximize all these opportunities."

Mindy fell shy of mentioning the street festival Jack would be shooting at on Sunday. Because she knew that would for sure be a no-go situation for Jillian. Inconceivable.

Just the term *street festival* could make her break out in *real* hives.

And she was glad Jack hadn't brought this up either.

Of course he hadn't, knowing it'd rattle her cage.

"Anyway," Mindy continued. "Garrett and I can discuss all of this in a separate convo. Correct?"

"You have my number," he said with a grin Mindy couldn't see. But it was in his voice.

Jillian and Jack exchanged a look.

"All right, then," Jillian said. "It appears as though Jack has dinner figured out for us, and we have to plot tomorrow's theme and recipes."

"Hanging up," Mindy told her. "Congrats to all."

Garrett mirrored the sentiment.

Hunter asked, "You're not eatin' with us, Miss Jillian?" His disappointment was evident.

"Buddy, we've got a lot of plannin' to do for our next show," Jack explained. "But you were a total rock star today. And I bet Miss Jillian is grateful for your help."

"I can't thank you enough," Jillian told him. "No way could we have pulled this off without you."

Hunter perked up.

He and his brother were total gems. Already showing signs they were going to be as good-looking as the other Reed cowboys and as sharp and magnetic.

Jillian couldn't imagine stumbling upon a more dynamic family or a more compelling environment.

And when she did a hasty self-analysis, she decided the jitters over the TV show were already a distant memory.

The bouts of anxiety she'd experienced while filming this segment had abated as well. Really, the most tumultuous moment had occurred when she'd tripped Jack and he'd hit the floor. That survival instinct of hers had kicked in for her, like she ought to toss her body on top of his to protect him, which was unrealistic in this instance but ingrained after her immediate reaction at the concert.

The other option today had been to jerk Jack up by the arm, to ensure he was rapidly on his feet. But one . . . he'd done that himself. And two . . . there'd been no threat to him, other than if he sprained a wrist or smacked his jaw on the tile.

Those were improbabilities, given his agility. And, as he'd stated, he was accustomed to being bucked by horses.

So the apprehension had dissipated in a heartbeat—as hers had picked up. Because Jack was just too . . . *sensational.*

She had a multitude of other descriptors for the man, but in truth, none of them seemed to encapsulate the full depth and breadth of him.

Jillian trusted in his steady presence. So, yes. She'd do the local TV show with him—and be as chill as she could be about it.

"Let's get moving," he cut into her thoughts, and she bid everyone a good evening.

They left the main house for the guest one, Ollie nipping at her ankles because she hadn't devoted all her time to him today. He had, however, made fast friends with Jack's nephew, as Jack had predicted. And Jillian had to consider that having other sources of companionship for the dog wasn't a bad thing. By any measure.

Ollie knew how to stay out of the way, and he felt comfortable when someone came to him, rather than having to insert himself into a conglomeration. An astute dog was her conclusion. He knew his own limitations but also sensed when someone intended to be kind to him, not cruel.

They reached the deck, and Jillian opened the door to the house.

Jack deposited his stack of food on the island and then returned to the deck to uncover the gas grill and fire it up.

Jillian refreshed Ollie's water bowl and served him the mixture of raw sliders and kibble with veggies on top that he preferred.

Jack came in and eyed the ribs. Then her.

"Yes?" she queried, the corner of her mouth quirking.

"Just wondering how hungry you are."

"After what we just whipped up, I'd say I'm close to devouring your leg."

He laughed. "Gotcha."

"I mean . . . I know where your *other* thoughts are, cowboy." She couldn't deny she was on the same wavelength. But sexy times were still something to heed with caution.

Though that might be inaccurate at present. Because Jillian could envision more heated moments with the cowboy. Could almost beg for them, truth be told.

But she stayed the course as Jack grabbed the pan of ribs and put the full rack on the grill, while Jillian shucked corn husks and removed the silk. Jack came in to wrap the ears in foil with a couple of ice cubes since they hadn't been presoaked.

He then located a brush for basting the ribs in their final stage, planted a smoldering kiss on her, and said, "Try to miss me while I'm gone."

"Consider it done."

She selected pinot noir as a complement to the meat, pulled the cork, and decanted the wine. She set the table outside and lit candles so she could turn off the porch lights and minimize the dive-bombing insects. Ollie plopped into one of his plump doggie beds, content with his nightly dental "treat."

Dinner was messy, and that left Jillian lighthearted. Who could eat slathered ribs that fell off the bone and not end up with sauce all over their mouth? Who could bite into tender, yet crispy, corn on the cob, dripping butter, and not feel a dollop hit their chin? Jack had brought out the entire roll of paper towels for this feasting event.

Jillian would have rounded out the meal with a salad, but they demolished what they had, so that point was moot.

"This sauce is all kinds of wicked," she said as she licked her fingers in a very unladylike fashion. Not really caring because she knew Jack would appreciate her appetite and her palate.

"My own concoction," he told her.

"Get out."

"True fact."

She whistled. "Your talents know no bounds."

"Oh, we haven't gotten there *yet* . . ." He winked.

Her insides ignited. And it had nothing to do with the zesty sauce.

"Gettin' tingly over there, darlin'?" he asked.

"How do you *know*?" she inquired.

"I pick up on the subtle nuances."

Because he was that attuned to her.

She tried to breathe properly. As always, it was a useless undertaking.

She asked, "What are your ingredients, cowboy?"

He chuckled at her deflection, accustomed to it. But he didn't press her, just followed along.

"Main ones are serranos, bourbon, and honey. Pretty straightforward, but I add spices to elevate the flavoring."

"Well, the serranos are a twist and hotter than jalapeños, but also with an earthy texture, giving this a distinct edge."

"This is only one variety," he told her.

What?

Jillian stared at him. Blinked twice.

"You're telling me you have *many*?"

"Champion pitmasters don't use store-bought sauces, Jilly. Not that I'm aware of anyway."

"Geez, Jack . . ." She sipped her wine, then said, "Here's another gold mine your family is sitting on. You can bottle signature sauces and sell them direct to consumers, distributors, other BBQ competitors."

"Ah, Jillian . . . ," he murmured evocatively. "I do admire your entrepreneurial spirit. Only problem is, I don't have time for production, marketin', manufacturin', sales, distribution, accountin' . . ."

He heaved a sigh.

"I hear you, cowboy."

Though the thought continued to whirl in her head. He'd talked about how he had to get more and more creative with finances every year. Jillian couldn't imagine that ever changed. Like, surely from the very beginning, when the ranch was established, there'd been hardships that could have proved destructive. And while some of the variables might alter, certain ones had to remain constant. Disease running through half his herd, as he'd mentioned. That wasn't isolated to one particular generation. Nor were many other issues.

So he'd found a way to supplement cattle income with his BBQ channel. But it seemed as though there were numerous ways they, as a family, could accomplish this.

Trouble was, as he'd indicated, there were only so many hours in the day. And from what she'd gleaned thus far, everyone had more than their fair share of duties to tend to.

She bit back her own sigh.

It wasn't her place to make radical suggestions. She couldn't help it earlier with Jack's mom. But trying to convince Jack that she could also build a platform for *him* might be overly ambitious when he was stressing about current needs versus future benefits.

So she said no more. Couldn't, really, because Jack had an incoming video call that he connected.

"Mom and Wyatt," he told Jillian, then greeted both women.

"Oh, my God, we just watched the show!" Wyatt exclaimed. "Perfectly dazzling! Your analytics confirm this, Jack. You two had the audiences eatin' out of the palms of your hands!"

Jillian's stomach flipped. She knew her stats wouldn't be affected this evening but come tomorrow with her podcast and a newsletter blast . . . she'd hopefully see another notable uptick in her numbers.

She'd check her orders then, too, not wanting to know tonight if they'd skyrocketed . . . or flatlined.

She focused instead on Jack's boon. "This is great news," she said. "And, Wyatt, it's a pleasure to meet you."

"Pleasure's all mine," she replied. "Wow, what a splash the two of you made today! Sidebar," she added, "Hunt can't stop talking about you, Jillian."

"And Ale wants a dog, Jack," Brett told him.

"Knew that was comin'," he semigrumbled. "Just difficult to watch over a pet when the kids are at school and everyone's off doin' their own thing."

Jillian couldn't dispute that. And while the reasonable comment to make would be along the lines of there being breeds that did well with large animals—for example, those that herded cattle—she was too sensitive to the potential trampling scenario to chime in.

"Well, it was quite lively in the kitchen when we arrived," Brett continued. "The boys didn't even bother movin' into the dining room to eat, and I'm talking about 'em all, not just the young'uns. They were all gathered around the island like it was a prime grazin' pasture."

"Excellent rib eyes, Jack," Wyatt told him. "And all the sides were delicious. If we could get more vegetables and salads onto the table every day, that'd be—"

"All right, we're done here," Jack interrupted. "Jillian and I've got to decide on tomorrow's menu."

"'Night to you both," Wyatt said with a smile.

Brett blew a kiss.

Jack hung up. And laughed.

"Swear, my sister'll have us hitched up in a heartbeat if we're not careful."

Jillian considered this for all of a second and reminded him, "We really haven't been careful."

He pinned her with a look she felt all the way to her toes. "Believe me when I say this, Jilly, I've employed every ounce of restraint I can muster."

She thought of his sexy kisses and got his meaning. He'd pretty much hit his threshold.

She let that simmer in her brain, discovering she wasn't terrified of the notion of him coming close to reaching his breaking point.

Was enticed by it, in fact.

Because if ever Jillian was going to "get back in the saddle," this was the man she'd *want to do it with*. Literally more so than figuratively.

"There's plenty to be said for your slow burn, cowboy." She smiled.

Jack sat back and drummed his fingers on the table. "Honey, I'm not an impulsive man."

"Duly noted, from the time I met you," she told him.

"But I do go after what I want, when I'm ready." His penetrating stare spoke volumes.

And sent a wild shudder through her.

Though she regulated her response by saying, "Repercussions have become a huge part of my life, Jack." She paused to give this further consideration and added, "But overthinking sexual tension when it's genuine . . ." She shook her head. Didn't say more. Didn't have to.

"Yeah," he agreed.

They left the conversation at that. Gathered their dishes and cleaned up.

Then Jack snatched Jillian's cookbook from the counter and took it into the living room. He switched on the fireplace and picked a comfy spot in the crook of the L-shaped sofa.

Jillian poured more wine, gauging where her anxiety sat on a scale of one to five, if Mindy were to ask, and was delighted she could contend it was a solid two, with nothing to kick it upward at present, not even being alone with Jack.

She *wanted* to be alone with Jack. More important, she wanted to be open to whatever might happen *while* she was alone with Jack.

So.

She delivered a glass to him. Slipped out of her boots and assisted Ollie onto the very end of the couch, where he burrowed into the folds of a chenille throw.

She sipped her wine and asked, "What's our next protein?"

"Pork shoulder."

"Oh!" Jillian shifted into cooking mode with that golden nugget. "We can do *so* much with a ten-pound shoulder."

"Pulled pork sliders, cubano sandwiches—"

"Carnitas," they said in unison.

"Damned if I'm not hungry again," he joked.

"Not even possible."

"Well, darlin', I do tend to work up an appetite with my daily activities. And you stir up cravin's too."

"Yet somehow I sense the food is more tempting than me."

He chuckled. "Don't go making any assumptions, honey."

Jack crossed a leg over the other, resting his ankle near his knee. "Why don't you scooch on over here, and we'll select all the right accompaniments."

"I do have a wonderful pineapple-and-teriyaki jam that goes with *everything* pork," she informed him. And inched toward him.

He scoffed. "Closer, darlin'."

Her stomach fluttered.

She sat alongside him, curling her feet underneath her.

"I pretty much meant *snuggle up to me*," he told her. And draped his arm along the top of the sofa as he leaned against a mound of pillows.

Jillian eyed the cozy spot he indicated.

And couldn't stop herself from narrowing the gap between them.

"Closer," he murmured.

Suddenly, she was nestled against him, her head on his shoulder.

His leg that was crossed had the book propped up, and she flipped through pages. Mindlessly. Because her thoughts were elsewhere.

"Obviously, we'll need a slaw," Jack said in a low voice that made lust ooze down her spine like warm molasses.

"My broccoli slaw has slivered red cabbage and carrots as accents," she said, breathy again. "With a light champagne dressing. Crisp and peppery."

Jack recommended, "How about sweet potato wedges for the sandwiches?"

"With a habanero dip. And cilantro-lime rice to complement the carnitas."

"Now you're talkin', darlin'."

"We should simmer the pulled pork for the sliders in your barbecue sauce, Jack, and you should do—"

"Honey." He tossed aside the book. "You should do *me*."

"Jack!" Her head popped up.

"We're discussin' one of my favorite topics—food—and I'm inhaling that arousing scent of yours and practically feelin' your lips on my neck, and I just . . ." He gave a primal grunt and said, "Darlin', a man can only take so much."

She nipped at his earlobe. And whispered, "Your move, Jack."

He didn't hesitate to toe off his boots and stretch his legs along the couch.

"Just a wee bit closer, Jilly." He maneuvered her—with no resistance from Jillian—so that she was on his side of the sofa, sprawled on top of him.

"There we go," he said. "Just like that."

Their legs tangled, and her fingers coiled in the opening of his shirt.

He splayed a palm at her lower back while whisking waves of hair from her face with his other hand.

Their lips brushed as they stared into each other's eyes.

"Shorter fuse than you let on, Jack Reed," she teased.

"Honey, you can't even begin to fathom my range of desire for you."

That sparked burning sensations as much as being sealed to his muscular body did. Her breasts were pressed to his pecs. Her belly trembled against his rib cage. One hand clutched his shoulder.

His chest rose and fell in time with hers. A titillating combination of excitement and anticipation arced between them.

Jillian could sense he tempered his more aggressive nature, but she also knew that thread had pulled taut. Would snap any second now.

He was giving her the chance to process, to acclimate to what was about to transpire.

She had some insecurities to wade through. All the obvious ones related to her isolation, of course. Also . . . she had scars from her surgeries, which no one outside a clinical setting had seen or touched.

Though it couldn't surprise Jack that she'd have residual damage. She suspected he had his own wounds from training horses.

She didn't want these things holding her back. Not tonight. She remembered how sensitive Jack had been as a lover, when he'd known it was her first time, when he'd understood her hesitation.

Causing her to reassure him now.

"I'm not saying no, Jack."

His eyes filled with lust *and* acceptance.

Then his mouth was on hers.

But Jillian was the one to take charge, her tongue glancing over his and then twirling in a flirty way. That didn't last long, though, because a darker, needier sensation flooded her veins, and they were both caught up in a deep kiss that went on and on.

A hot-and-heavy make-out session with Jack not only amped her exhilaration, it also brought to light so many possibilities. The potential to connect with someone intimately, yes. And the opportunity to sate a yearning she'd had for this man since college, a longing she'd had to suppress, even before the trampling. She'd had to let him go, in every way, when he'd left school.

Yet burying feelings didn't always mean they disappeared entirely. They were just hidden, shoved into shadowy corners, forgotten until unexpectedly tapped into.

Every time Jack kissed her, those feelings emerged and strengthened.

She recalled all the daydreams that mirrored this moment, convincing Jillian even more that this was not a mistake. Regardless of how fleeting this ranch adventure was, she could reconcile in her mind and in her heart that a week with someone who evoked feelings she hadn't felt in years and resuscitated physical needs she'd doubted would ever spring to life again was the next phase of therapy she required.

That was *her* acceptance.

When she writhed in his loose embrace, Jack murmured between kisses, "Lemme get rid of this buckle so it doesn't scrape you."

Jillian rose slightly off him so he could wedge a hand between them and work the buckle, then yank the belt from its loops and toss it onto the floor.

"While we're at it," she said, "these snaps are a huge nuisance."

She clutched the material with both hands and ripped his shirt open. Right down to his waist. She pulled the tails from his jeans and then laid her palms over his abs as she took in every inch of exposed flesh.

"Jesus, Jack," she said on a sharp breath. "Do you bench-press your cattle?"

"Ha, ha." His voice was strained. "And while we're on the subject of things that are in the way . . ." He stripped off her cardigan and let it fall to the side. His gaze slid over her, and he said, "This has to go too."

He fisted the hem of her sweater-tank.

Panic slammed into her.

"Wait, Jack," she was quick to say, a specific thought returning to her.

He halted. Stared at her. One brow crooked.

"I . . ." Her gaze drifted upward to the ceiling as she searched for the proper words.

"Jilly?"

"I just . . ." She blew out a puff of air. Glanced at him and said, "I have scars, Jack. They've become a part of me. I don't know how they look to someone else."

Their eyes remained locked. She gave him a moment to think this one through.

His jaw worked, as she'd expected.

When he spoke, it was in the quiet, rich timbre that never failed to induce emotion.

"Darlin', I won't deny that knowing or seein' the evidence of what happened to you doesn't or won't affect me, but like you said. They're a part of you. And I don't take exception to anything about you, Jillian Parks."

Her eyes glistened. She brushed aside his hands.

"I might not have said that right." Now his brow furrowed.

She sniffled. And told him, "Pretty much nailed it, cowboy."

Jillian took over, ridding herself of the top, adding it to the mounting pile.

She paused again, allowing Jack's gaze to sweep over the front of her.

Then she said, "I used scar cream to help minimize the damage from the surgeries, but you can still see them if you look close."

"I'm lookin', honey. And I'm mesmerized."

Her heart constricted.

"They're worse on my back, around my spine."

"Nothing about you is short of sensational, Jilly."

That made her nose twitch in the way that led to tears. She held them at bay, though. And smiled with a sense of peace she hadn't experienced in a long time.

Her hands skated up his chest and to his traps as she resumed her position of covering him like a blanket.

She kissed him again and that sent heat vibrating through her.

She squirmed a bit, her pelvis lightly grinding.

Jack tore his mouth from hers. "That's not gonna keep this train on the rails, Jilly."

"I want you, Jack."

The brightest green light of them all.

He maneuvered them so she was straddling him, the oversize sofa accommodating them, despite Jack's wide frame.

He held her hips still while he seemed to work on some semblance of composure. But then threw caution to the wind. He sat up, one arm around her, the other lifting so he could thread his fingers through her hair again, something he clearly enjoyed doing. It was helpful, too, getting the mass off her temple and away from her face.

He kissed her ardently.

Jillian had to grip his upper arms to steady herself from the rush of adrenaline and the restlessness clawing at her.

When he broke the kiss so they could breathe, his lips skimmed along her neck. Her head fell back on her shoulders as he nibbled her flesh, then soothed the skin with his tongue.

A moan escaped her parted lips.

Jack's hand in her hair now followed the trail his mouth had blazed, then drifted lower, over her collarbone and to her chest. He cupped her breast and massaged with just the right amount of pressure to hitch her pulse.

"Jack," she whispered, her eyelids still closed from his previous kiss.

His head bent, and his tongue flitted over the inner swell of her breast, then the top. Teasing her with the suggestion of wicked things to come—that being divesting her of her bra, only needing the one hand at her back to release the clasp. Then he slid the straps down, and it went the way of her other clothes.

He tightened his embrace so that her breasts pressed to his chest again, bare this time.

"Fuck, Jillian . . . ," he mumbled.

She couldn't even speak. Scintillating zings ricocheted through her, all culminating at the heart of her. A tantalizingly uncomfortable prickle along her clit had her in desperate need of scratching that particular itch.

But Jack was kissing her again, and she couldn't bring herself to pull her mouth from his to beg him to do something about the fires he sparked. Though she did rock her hips, creating a degree of denim-on-denim friction that helped to quell the ache. At first. But stroking his erection through their jeans taunted her.

Jack as well.

He took action.

With a firm hold on her, he rotated them and transferred her to the other sofa. He wasted no time peeling away her pants. But he held her in suspense as his fingers twisted in the strands of her thong at her hips, while he seemed to absorb the vision of her, almost naked and breathless.

"The sight of you does more than get a man hard, Jillian."

He dragged her lacy lingerie down her thighs.

Then he whipped off his shirt that had been hanging open.

Jillian bit her lower lip, forcing back a greedy whimper.

Ollie hopped off the couch and went to his bed in front of the fireplace, likely so that he wasn't dislodged by them.

Jillian reached for a plump pillow just beyond her head and used it to prop herself up. She gazed at Jack, cataloging all the reactions he had to her. The pull of the cords of his neck. The setting of his jaw. The burning need in his eyes.

All those flexed muscles.

Jesus, the man was magnificent. Carved in stone.

But then he broke from his trancelike state and angled her just so, one of her legs dangling over the side to form a wide V he could fit between as he knelt on the floor. His hands skimmed along her calves, over her knees, his thumbs grazing her inner thighs as he approached his intended target.

Jillian wanted to close her eyes again so that she didn't give *herself* away. But she was riveted as Jack watched her, in turn.

His thumbs caressed sensitive flesh that quivered.

Every inch of her was hypersensitized.

And all she could think of was Jack's mouth on her, pushing her higher and higher.

The tip of his tongue traced the delicate skin at her apex, still toying with her inner thighs, leaving her teeming with anticipation. Especially considering how close he was to the part of her crying out the most for his attention.

She wanted him to speed up. But, no . . . she really didn't. This was a seductive torture she relished.

He knew by the way her fingers curved around his powerful forearms, with the ability to urge his hands that final millimeter upward to glide over her slick folds, that she was the one employing the most restraint now. And it'd disintegrate soon.

"Jack," she whispered.

His hands pushed her legs wider. His searing breaths against her sex had her writhing—and fighting to voice the demand to *please, please put your mouth on me!*

As though her plea echoed in his own head, his tongue swiped along her labia, jolting her straight to the core.

"Jack! Oh, God . . ."

She needed a second to catch her breath.

But the genie couldn't be returned to his bottle.

Jack's tongue licked. His lips tugged. His mouth suckled.

He took his time. Holy Christ, did he ever.

His thumbs opened her to him, and his tongue fluttered against that pearl of nerves that had somehow become the center of her universe.

He had a maddening technique of butterfly strokes, then assertive suckling, then more of the light flitting, all of which drew Jillian in as every thought fled her mind. She was lost in sensation and heat, both consuming her until there was nothing she needed more than a climactic release.

And she knew he was on a mission to deliver it.

He eased a finger inside her. Jillian gasped as her body tensed.

He caressed her inner walls as his tongue continued to tease and titillate, until Jillian was moaning and wriggling on the cushion, reaching for something that had been elusive for so long but was now within her grasp. Because she permitted it.

And because Jack was damn persuasive even when he wasn't saying anything at all.

The tip of his finger swirled—something new and sinful.

He drew her clit against his teeth—and *that* was pure magic.

"Yes, Jack," she murmured. "More of that."

The fluttering was the foreplay. The suckling and swirling were the main act.

Jillian's breaths came in razory slivers as all the sensations collided.

And burst wide open.

She cried his name, still clutching his forearms, her lids squeezing tight as tiny golden orbs exploded behind them.

"Oh, my God, Jack," she said on a wisp of air. "Oh, my God!"

The only words she could muster as bliss overcame her. Delirium spread through her because she'd hit a pinnacle she'd secretly worried she might not be able to achieve ever again.

Yet somehow, she'd known that if anyone was going to jump-start her, it would be Jack Reed.

His chuckle was good-natured and triumphant at once.

Jillian cracked open an eye. Quirked a brow.

He smirked, all victorious and quite pleased with himself. Clearly, understanding the significance of this particular breakthrough.

He was entitled.

She would have said as much, but she was still blissed out and breathless.

He kissed his way up her body, nipping here, leaving feathery sweeps of his lips there, in no particular hurry. With no true destination in mind. When he reached her breasts, his tongue curled around a beaded nipple, then flickered over it. He devoted ample attention to the other one. Keeping Jillian's body thrumming and her head spinning.

There were myriad things to unpack here, related to this being her first orgasm in forever. And by way of how masterfully Jack had lured her in while leaving her all the power. So that she was driven by her own wants and desires, and he was there to oblige them with every page they turned, together.

Their first time ten years ago had been poignant not only because Jillian had offered him something she'd never offered anyone else but also because Jack had recognized the significance. Had taken great care with her, while also delivering a heat level she'd never fathomed.

And here he was tonight, reawakening every sexy emotion and sensation within her.

That resonated so deeply, she opened her mind—and her heart—to other possibilities.

When his soft lips grazed her throat, and he kissed a delicate spot below her ear, Jillian whispered, "Make love to me, Jack."

Chapter Nine

A carnal sound escaped him.

Jack told her, "Darlin', for all my suggestive comments, I came here neither prepared nor presumptuous. Granted, I was lookin' forward to foolin' around. But I had no intention of guidin' you down a path you might not want to—"

"I know you weren't being presumptuous, Jack. And you know I can't be swayed against my will."

"No denyin' that."

She was silent, contemplative. Because this was tricky territory for them both.

She asked, "How long has it been for you, Jack?"

"A while," he confessed with a grim look that implied a drawn-out *looong* in between those two words.

She didn't have to mention her six years. They'd covered that, obviously.

She said, "I take the pill to normalize my periods." It was a bit more complex than that, but Jillian knew she couldn't get pregnant, so she added, "I think we're safe."

His thumb swept along her temple. "You sure about this?"

"I'm sure about *you*."

One corner of Jack's mouth lifted in a bad-boy grin. "Hasn't this just been my lucky month?"

"If you like roller coasters with corkscrews in them." She held his hand against her cheek for a moment.

"Maybe I do. Or maybe," he said as he reached for the button on his jeans, "I know which rides are worth takin'."

"Oh, with the charm . . ." She sighed.

"You're my undoin', darlin'." He slid the zipper down its track.

Excitement rippled through Jillian, along with a renewed sense of urgency to have Jack inside her, filling her.

He stripped down, and she admired the view.

Her breath caught in her throat, and her nipples tightened further.

His powerful legs were the perfect complement to all his sculpted hotness. Even the man's feet were sexy.

But, of course, her gaze had to drift upward to his thick cock, throbbing and tempting.

Jillian hadn't exactly been driven by her libido, ever. That changed instantly.

"Jesus, Jack," she murmured. She couldn't even think of a joke to save her from salivating. She just . . . stared.

Jack peered down at her with a dubious look on his face.

"No lie," she said. "I'm impressed."

"Good to know, darlin'. Good to know."

She whispered, "All that and a bag of chips?"

He chuckled again. "If that's all you've got, I'll take it."

"I might be having a brain aneurysm." At the very least, she was suffering the wildest eruptions of those damned flame emoji—within her.

Jack moved in close, settling on the sofa in a manner that allowed him to prop himself up on the pillows she laid back against so that he wasn't crushing her.

Naturally, he'd think of that. He thought of everything.

Downside was . . . he was correct in her need to not feel anyone bearing down on her. Yet she *wanted* his weight on her. She wanted to feel every inch of him, from head to toe.

But she was smart enough to recognize that could incite a triggering moment, and Jillian was doing her absolute best to ensure that didn't happen. Jack was too.

Though he was also doing his best to be certain that *other* things happened. Like keeping her pulse racing and her insides sizzling.

His fingertips caressed her skin, from the valley of her breasts, down the vertical line between her ribs, circling her navel, then continuing south. Goose bumps popped, and her breaths ratcheted.

"We're gonna take this slow and easy," he told her.

The tip of his erection nudged her opening.

"Don't move," he muttered.

Jillian wasn't confident she could follow that lead.

He said, "Just take me in a little at a time, Jilly."

"There's nothing little about you, Jack," she retorted. "And there's something to be said about the heat of the moment."

"I don't want to hurt you." The primary point he was trying to get across.

"You should be more worried about me shaking the rafters."

"Now that's how you compliment a man, darlin'."

He eased into her. Just the tiniest bit.

"Oh, God." The words fell from her mouth. And her eyes nearly rolled into the back of her head.

He was only getting started.

Still, there was a distinct anticipation that came with him entering her for the first time, years after the fact. Particularly given their circumstances.

This was pivotal for him too.

"Jack . . ." Just the slightest taste of him had Jillian's inner muscles clenching and releasing, seeking and demanding all of him.

"Breathe, honey," he whispered in her ear. "Relax. I already know you're damn tight. No need to—"

"Jack, *more*," she said on a throaty moan. "I want more. Of you."

Their gazes locked. He was fighting his restraint. But began to cave to her dire request.

He pushed deeper into her, wrenching a small cry from her.

"Yes, Jack. Oh, God, yes . . ."

He slipped a hand around to cup her ass, tilting her pelvis just so. He pumped farther into her, and Jillian felt the friction, the sting, the slippery sliding, the measured thrusting . . . the absolute pleasure of him stretching her, of him awakening that mystical spot within her as his cock massaged with just the right cadence, just the right pressure.

Jillian's eyelids closed. Her head fell back. Her breaths came in soft whimpers that mingled with the crackling in the hearth.

Jack was cautious with her, even as the insistency seemed to mount within him and radiate outward to her.

Jillian draped a leg over his waist, pinioning him to her as their hips moved together, finding the same rhythm.

Her spine arched to get her closer to him, so that his skin brushed hers.

Liquid fire replaced her blood.

"Jack," she repeated, not having anything else to say other than screaming, *Please don't ever stop!*

Which she refrained from doing.

She didn't need to traumatize the man with the way her body so vehemently responded to his, how she wanted to claw at him, how impossible it was not to drag her nails down his back or raise her hips higher to take him in deeper.

She wasn't an animal, for Christ's sake.

And yet his commanding strokes lent a feral edge to her desire.

"You feel so damn good," he told her, following her pace as she picked it up. "Careful, Jilly."

"This time, we *are* being careful, Jack." Their bodies weren't smashed together. He wasn't pressing her into the cushions. That was fine because he seemed to have the right leverage with this position.

And the wetter he made her, the more that tether within her threatened to break free.

Jillian wanted to hold on as long as she could—knowing it was impossible. Jack's hips rolled, and he pumped a bit faster, and that was all she could stand.

The sensations converged once more—*so fast*—shattering her.

"Jack!"

She squeezed him firmly.

"Oh, fuck, Jillian," he said on a strained groan. "Like that, honey. Just like that."

Her inner muscles milked his cock, working him involuntarily because Jillian's climax went on and on.

Jack lost it, pushing deep. Grinding out her name. Filling her with his hot seed.

The fiery river and the sheer knowledge of it caused another shuddering release within her.

The tremors didn't subside.

Neither one had their breath for endless minutes.

Eventually, Jack brushed away strands of hair from her cheek.

"Well, that tells me my stamina's shot to shit," he said. "Or that I flat-out can't resist you."

Her lids flitted open. She smiled. Knew she had a dreamy look on her face.

"Funny thing about riding that bike, Jack. You *can* get right back on it."

He chuckled. Then asked, "Are you all right?"

"Never better. Like I stuck a bobby pin in a light socket for kicks, and it totally worked."

"You crack me up, Jilly," he warmly said. "You really do."

"In all seriousness," she told him in a softer voice, "that was beautiful, Jack. All of it."

And similar to those sunny days that followed a bout of rain and clouds in Seattle, when the whole world seemed refreshed and renewed, alive and vibrant, so that Jillian basked in their symbolism, she now basked in her personal afterglow . . . with Jack.

◆　◆　◆

He couldn't remember a woman ever saying anything like that to him.

Then again, Jack had never been with a woman like Jillian Parks before. Well, except that one time—with her. And back then, she'd seemed so overwhelmed by having given up her virginity that she hadn't had much to say for a half hour or so. Had just sort of appeared dazed and drained. Like what *he* was experiencing now. He couldn't bring himself to move even the tiniest centimeter away from her.

Though he was cognizant of not bearing down on her. He remained braced on one forearm, their bodies only grazing, not melding together.

That this registered in his mind was somewhat of a miracle, given he was all sorts of twisted up. In the feel of her, the smell of her, the taste of her. In the sheer exquisiteness of her.

Another out-of-the-blue thought for him.

Exquisiteness wasn't in his everyday vocabulary. But it popped into his brain as he gazed down at Jillian, who wore a delirious expression and still tried to draw in breaths that weren't thin streams of air.

Meanwhile, the throbbing between his legs, even low in his gut, kept his own breathing on the labored side.

Man, what the woman did to him. And lying partially alongside her, her leg twined around one of his to keep him close, had Jack curious as to how to play his cards.

One hand seemed to be stacked with aces that could lead him to the bedroom—where he wanted to spend the night. The other warned he might be pressing his luck if he didn't get dressed and head home.

This was a delicate situation. Also an arousing one. Jillian naked, with her breasts brushing his chest, kept the testosterone pumping through his veins and the fantasies forming in his mind.

But he thought of what she'd said about his "slow burn," and realized Jillian likely needed these new experiences in measured doses. He didn't want to overwhelm her.

So he folded the aces and unraveled from her (reluctantly). He draped the throw from the end of the sofa over her, not just to ward off a chill but also because if he gazed at her creamy skin and her feminine curves much longer, he'd forget chivalry altogether.

He headed toward the bathroom.

"You realize you strut, cowboy?" Her voice was wispy. Sultry. Heat continued to roar through him.

"Nice of you to notice, darlin'."

He tidied himself and slung a towel low on his hips. Then he went back to scoop her up and carry her to the master suite. With one arm around his neck, she reached down to pull back the bedding. He set her on the mattress.

He kissed her—not at all chastely—and then said, "You get some rest. Another big day tomorrow. And somethin' tells me you're gonna be inundated with orders, making it even more hectic."

"Such a gallant retreat," she murmured.

"Not one I'm interested in makin', really."

Jillian stared at him. The soft rays of moonlight filtering in around the edges of the drapes caught the mist covering her eyes.

He kissed her forehead. "Believe every word I tell you."

She gave a slow nod. And whispered, "Then stay."

His teeth ground for a moment. He asked, "You sure?"

"Never surer," she promised.

"Let me get your dog."

He coaxed Ollie outside and watched him like a hawk until he was ready to come in. Jack had the fencing secured with a tight metal mesh trim to keep the snakes out, but it wasn't always a foolproof system.

He returned to the bedroom, Ollie right behind him. The pup ran up the three steps that Jillian had brought with her and placed alongside the bed. He snuggled on one side of her, so Jack took the other.

Jillian rolled toward Jack, and he put an arm around her.

"He's not gonna bite me in the middle of the night 'cuz I'm poachin' on his territory, is he?"

Jillian's laugh was faint yet arousing. "I really can't say. No one's invaded his turf before."

"Right, gotcha. So this'll be a crapshoot."

"Indeed."

"Well, he seems to like me, so . . ." Jack eyed the dog and said to Ollie, "I'll feed you a leftover rib if you'll spare mine."

"You will not!" Jillian scoffed. "This dog has a fabulous digestive system. Don't you dare disrupt it."

"You did hear her say that, correct?" he asked the pup, who just burrowed in deeper. Jack gave a half snort. "Can't even rile him with threats of not bein' fed."

"Told you he can barely be bothered to bark."

They fell into a comfortable silence. Jack's fingertips drew lazy circles on her shoulder and glided up to her neck, then back down.

Her breaths on his skin intensified a yearning that even sex couldn't fulfill. It was this quiet intimacy that felt substantial.

The emotional connection when he was inside her and staring into her eyes was significant, of course. Amazingly so.

But knowing that connection transcended their physical need for each other was most poignant for him. Perhaps because he'd experienced the reassuring glances and touches his parents had shared when they thought no one was looking. Similar to Wyatt and Mateo getting so wrapped up in each other they could almost shut out the entire world. If one of their kids wouldn't come along and interrupt them.

Jack couldn't deny he paid attention to these types of relationships. Longed for his own. But he'd resigned himself to the inevitable. His love affair was with the ranch. Not a woman.

Making it complex to have Jillian Parks in his arms.

He wondered if she was mulling over something similar, particularly as a tear dampened his skin. Then another.

"Darlin'," he murmured. "Don't go breakin' my heart."

"Not regretting anything," she said. "At all."

"Then what?"

"Just thinking . . ."

He let out a breath. "Yeah, me too. This feels right, doesn't it?"

"Yes." Her voice quavered. She added, "It's just . . . I feel like we're setting ourselves up for failure."

"Epically," he said on a laugh that held no humor.

She sighed. Paused for a moment. Then told him, "I was engaged, Jack."

Okay, yeah. That blindsided him.

His brows knitted. "When?"

"From about the time I graduated SPU until I was put into a medically induced coma after the fire."

Jack was stunned.

And envious. Hell, yes, he was.

Except . . . now she *wasn't* engaged.

"What happened, Jillian?"

Her breaths quavered. More drops fell.

His gut wrenched. But Jack wanted to hear her story.

She said, "We met when I needed to try out an indoor hydroponics growing system for my apartment, since I didn't have a yard, no soil. He owned a nursery, specializing in cherry blossoms."

Jack groaned. Wasn't that a match made in heaven?

Though . . . he could think of a better one, fueled by chili peppers.

Jillian told him, "We dated, fell in love, agreed to spend the rest of our lives together, with a small family and tons of pets. The entire white-picket-fence dream. All lovely and perfect."

"Until it wasn't . . ."

"Yeah."

"Jesus, Jillian, please don't tell me he died at that concert."

"No, Jack, he didn't die." She sucked in a breath. And said, "He left me."

"What?" Jack shifted slightly so that he could glance down at her.

"After that whole ordeal," she went on, "he was just . . . distraught. And drowning in guilt because he couldn't get to me in the auditorium. I only heard pieces of his story as I was drifting in and out of consciousness in the ambulance. And before the coma, he mumbled a lot about how this was all too much for him. When I was lucid a couple weeks later, an ICU nurse read me a letter. From Scott."

Jack's spirits took a deeper dive south than when he'd thought her fiancé had been killed.

Jillian said, "He'd been at a concession stand, getting us beers, when people came barreling through the doors on the mezzanine, screaming about the fire. He'd tried to get back in, pushing and shoving his way through the crowd to reach me. But he was working against the tide of mass hysteria, and they carried him right out the main exits."

Jack felt a shiver run through her.

But she continued.

"He just couldn't deal with it all. He left me. In that hospital room. All alone."

"Jillian." Jack's arms tightened around her as she trembled from sobs she attempted to contain.

"He knew I had no relatives in the area—my mother's in Nova Scotia. He didn't take the time to tell anyone we were jointly friendly with where I was. I guess people just assumed I went with him to California. My name was never in the paper or on TV. I didn't want the publicity, and I was in critical condition, so not available to any reporter who might have learned this private hospital was harboring a victim."

A peculiar rage tore through Jack. Riding a wave of empathy. And his own guilt.

How anyone could just walk away from a situation like that was completely beyond him, and he burned to put a fist in her fiancé's face.

He also felt sympathetic toward Jillian and all she'd suffered.

In addition, Jack wanted to tell her that if *he* was engaged to her, he would *never* leave her.

But he had left her.

So. He bit his tongue.

Jillian said, "I spent months and months in the hospital, rehab facilities, back in the hospital for more surgeries, back to rehab. It was almost a year before I was released. I lived in a hotel at first because I had no place to go. Tried to get my bearings. Then I bought a house with money I had from my dad's life insurance policy. Had the greenhouse built and . . . started all over. Literally from scratch."

"I wish I'd known." Jack winced. "That's a dumb thing for me to say. What could I have done for you?"

"That's an interesting question. Had you posed it five years ago or even five months ago, I would have said, 'Absolutely nothing.'"

Her hand rested on his abs as though she were gauging how twisted up his insides were over all she'd revealed.

"And now?" he prompted.

"Now that I know you better in this lifetime, I believe we could have helped each other. Geographical differences notwithstanding, we share some remarkable similarities, don't you think?"

She wasn't just talking about the chilies.

He said, "We could have commiserated, long distance."

"In a sense, yes." Her head lifted, and she gazed at him. "You're lonely, aren't you, Jack?"

It was a painful query that speared him straight to his soul.

Jillian nestled against him once more.

"I didn't quite grasp the concept at first," she confessed. "Because I couldn't be around people. And because I was still slain from the inside out over Scott abandoning me—when I needed him the most. Maybe I was bitter. For sure terrified. And convinced that people were evil and I didn't need them in my life. I mean, other than to buy my products." She gave a half laugh. "And listen to my podcast and subscribe to my newsletter."

Her attempt at levity didn't quell the roiling within him.

She said, "I came around, though. Mindy's wonderful. As are my courier and my postal carrier. The twins down the street. The restaurant managers and the third-party vendors I deliver sauces to. I like people, Jack. I'm just . . . horrified to be around most of them."

"My life of irony ensues," he murmured. "I like them too, darlin'. I just don't have the time to be around them."

"And you can live with that, for the most part."

"I'm too busy to notice?" he ventured.

"Exactly. But here we are, and I'm consumed with thoughts of how I can't remember the last time someone's fingertips brushed my skin. Or the last time my cheek was pressed to someone's chest and I could hear their heart beating."

"How's mine doin'?" he asked.

"Little erratic."

"That's all you, darlin'."

They let the silence envelop them again.

Jack comprehended everything she said. Oddly, two extroverts had reached a point of self-preservation, where they existed—and even thrived—within the confines of a near-isolated shelter. Jack had all the activity on the ranch, yes. But he didn't spend time in town, unless for business purposes. Didn't go to local dances or the county fair. Didn't really associate with anyone not in his immediate sphere of influence. Hell, he didn't even engage with his audience beyond his show. Wyatt answered those particular emails, and Ale responded to social media comments with canned responses drafted by Wyatt.

"Guess we're two peas in a pod," he concluded.

"Not necessarily. You have tremendous potential for more, Jack. But I chose what I've created for myself. I'm not someone who gets a happily ever after."

Another admission that shook him.

Though she added, "I am content, however, with a happy for now."

Jack wasn't pleased that was her resolution.

Then again, he couldn't deny it was also his.

◆ ◆ ◆

The next morning, Jack was on a video call with Mateo at five thirty. Chance had joined him in his office, and Mateo was conferencing in from Odessa.

Jack was doing his damnedest not to be sidetracked by thoughts of Jillian—the sexy ones as much as the disconcerting ones.

He found it nearly inconceivable to count back in time when he'd woken up with a woman in his arms. It'd been years. Because Jack didn't stay the night. Brief encounters had satiated some of his needs. But then he'd sort of lost track of the notches on his belt and couldn't even really assign a date or a month to his last two-hour stand.

As usual, similar to Jillian, he could now recall what he'd been missing out on.

Making it more complicated in his heart and in his mind to determine how he was going to close the door Jillian had opened.

A different problem for a different day, absolutely. This morning, he had serious business to conduct.

"Any nibbles on our horses?" Jack asked his brother-in-law.

Mateo rubbed the back of his neck and said, "You know these ol' boys out here are well versed with your cattle horses, Jack. They're familiar with your setup and your trainin' process, not to mention the way those bunkhouse cowboys have them skilled at herdin'. There's money to be had if you're willing to part with any of 'em. Other than that, Olsson's the only one bitin' on the newbies."

"Then those are the ones we'll sell," Jack decisively told him.

He slid a glance toward Chance.

"Jack, I'm not the one attached," his cousin admitted. "I do get that breakin' a horse makes him a part of your soul and vice versa, but my job is to handle operations. Yours is to figure out the finances."

Jack always had appreciated Chance's candor. And his wise observations. Chance had learned as a kid what this ranch meant and how complex it could be to run. Regardless, he and his brother, Avery, had expressed their respect for the TRIPLE R and had also dedicated themselves to it, to being an integral part of its legacy. They'd easily found their niches while growing up, and everything they contributed layered on to what others had to offer, and that was why they were all still in business.

He told Chance, "You find me some more horses to train, to replace these two. The lost causes that are given up on are the ones I work with the best. They come cheaper, too, so that we net a decent profit." To Mateo, he said, "Do me a favor and call Olsson. We'll sell. But make it a good sale," he added.

Mateo grinned. "Don't I always?"

"True fact."

They disconnected.

Chance went to work while Jack headed to the kitchen to start breakfast. The production was the polar opposite of his and Jillian's haphazardness, but as Ale and Garrett both confirmed, he and Jillian were a hit.

The trouble therein, of course, was fear of the sophomore slump.

They could be too obsessed over not being in perfect sync with each other and overcompensate in an effort to correct that.

They could continue with their innate reactions to one another—and the audience could quickly tire of that.

Or they could lose track of what they were doing with all that damned pork he'd be cooking.

Jack raked a hand through his hair.

He'd not thought this all through when he'd come up with the grand plan to bring Jillian out to the ranch to cohost with him. He didn't want to mess with her subscriber numbers any more than he wanted to flub his own.

He'd seen a great opportunity, yes. He'd also latched on to the notion of spending time with her. Getting to know her again.

To what end, he wasn't sure.

But while that weighed on his mind, so, too, did their online "careers." Social media could be a fickle beast, and tables could be so easily turned against them.

This was a perilous thought as Jack's holiday event drew closer. Though he didn't give that more precedence over Jillian being in the midst of a new product launch.

She had as much to lose as he did.

A stressor he recognized. And took responsibility for. Though, in his heart, he had to give credence to how well they fit together—and how his family, the station manager, and both their producers were fanatical about their partnership.

When Hunt said, "Uncle Jack, I wanna skip this afternoon's practice so I can be here for the show, when I'm done with my homework," Jack regained a sense of faith in what he was building with Jillian.

He told his nephew, "Boy, soccer has been the light of your life since you came out of the womb. My show'll still be here for you to help with when you're available. And FYI, Miss Jillian's here for the week. I have a feelin' she might even join us all for dinner tonight."

The kid grinned so damn wide, Jack couldn't help but laugh.

"Okay, okay!" Hunt said. "We'll be back by then!" He went off to gather his backpack and gear.

Wyatt sidled up to Jack. "My son's first crush." She sighed and placed a hand over her heart.

Jack raised a brow. "He's eleven, Wyatt. He's gonna have a dozen more before he's even in college."

"You didn't bother with crushes *until* you were in college, Jack."

He rolled his eyes.

She continued. "All those cheerleaders who batted their lashes at the star quarterback when you were in high school . . . you just couldn't be bothered with them."

"Well, I did have grades to maintain and practice and ranch chores, so . . ."

"I hear ya, I hear ya. Still." She wound an arm around his and rested her head on his shoulder, mocking him. "Excuses are one thing, and they're acceptable. But the way you're all tangled up with Jillian . . . that says sooo much."

She kissed him on the cheek. Unraveled from him. And ushered her kids toward the door to take them to school.

Jack stared after them.

In his mind, his eldest sister had the perfect life. She understood the peaks and valleys associated with the ranch. She and her husband pitched in whenever, wherever, however they could. So did their small brood.

At the end of the day, Wyatt had a familial infrastructure that was centered around everything she and Jack had been raised to embrace. Only difference was, Jack being the firstborn son had left him in the position of taking over the ranch in his dad's absence.

He was okay with that.

There were no resentments when it came to his situation or his kin. Aside from his uncle, Caleb Reed. That man had caused one hell of a ruckus around this ranch—and had nearly destroyed Avery's stellar BBQ reputation.

One bad apple, however, hadn't toppled the legacy cart.

And through it all, Jack had learned to just keep ranchin'. The best he could.

As he did now.

His mom had the water running in the sink, and everyone else had stacked breakfast plates and linen on the island.

"Chance and I are inspecting the new fencin' up north," Jack told her. "You're home today?"

"No classes," she confirmed. "I can make the farmers' market run this morning with Garrett. Later on, I want to assess the picnic area and talk to George about more seatin' for the holiday event."

"Luke's lendin' us vendor tents that he sponsors for the street festival. That'll provide ample shade for the food stations. So far, we're only lookin' at mid-eighties for the temps. I'm not expecting a heat wave to cause people any discomfort."

"Fingers crossed," Brett said and went to work on the dishes.

Jack left the house and was crossing to the stables as Chance emerged on his horse—and had Jack's saddled and ready to head out.

Jillian and Ollie were just coming up the drive, and they veered over toward Jack, though she kept a reasonable distance.

"Bit early to be riding off into the sunset, cowboy." She scooped Ollie into her arms.

He grinned and said, "A cowboy's day starts before sunrise, honey. And lasts as long as it has to."

"Anything I can help with?"

"All's under control at present." He spied her tote bag and asked, "Whatcha got there?"

"Just thought I'd show your mom my processing and shipping routine. She'll be surprised at how seamless this is."

"Am I next on your to-do list, darlin'?"

She batted her lashes and asked, "We talking about websites or something else, Jack?" Never mind that Chance was listening in.

Jack felt the innuendo in his groin.

Maybe for some cowboys it was too early in the day to get a rise from a woman. But Jack wasn't an ordinary cowboy.

He said, "I'm still thinkin' about last night, honey."

She blushed.

Tick mark in his favor.

He chuckled. "I'd like to say I'm teasin' ya, Jilly. But I'm not." He gave her a searing look. "I do have to ride off now."

"I'll just watch you go," she said with a sigh.

Jack hooked his foot in a stirrup and swung his leg over, then settled into his saddle with the comfortable sound of leather adjusting to him. He touched the brim of his hat. Chance did too—as he fought what was sure to be a zinger Jack would get an earful of later. They loped off before breaking into a gallop, then cresting the drive and hitting the dirt road, kicking up a plume of dust in their wake.

"Well, if that just isn't the sexiest . . . ," Jillian muttered as she stared after them. Then she glanced down at Ollie, who had no clue as to what she referred.

Didn't matter.

"Let's see if I can concentrate on anything other than that man's hands on my body."

They entered the main house, and Jillian went to work helping Brett with the breakfast cleanup.

Afterward, she set her laptop on the kitchen table and retrieved her slim wireless printer from her bag. Brett joined her, offering a cup of coffee as she took a seat with her own mug in hand.

"So, the coolest thing about this online store software," Jillian said, "is that I can manage start-to-finish sales on this one site or their mobile app." She pulled up the program on her screen. "I just log in, go to my orders page, confirm the payment has been processed, and then I select the mailing options. I automatically have the flat shipping rate calculated based on the items purchased. A step or two later, and this happens . . ."

Her printer quietly spit out a narrow label.

Jillian ripped it from the device and said, "This top portion is the mailing label. The bottom half is the inventory list. I put the latter in the box before I seal it and slap the label on the front. Then I schedule a pickup and voilà. There you have it." She smiled. "Piece of cake."

"I wouldn't have to open up different tabs and toggle between them?"

"Not at all." Jillian showed her the screen, where every function was clearly denoted. "I have everything packaged and physically protected, but this is an entire tracking system from the time the order comes in until it's delivered to the customer. Anyone who's missing a shipment or doesn't have a complete or correct order can be pulled up and researched. Not complicated at all."

"Does sound simple," Brett agreed. "Unless I push the wrong buttons."

"You get used to what's what," Jillian assured her. "Anyway, that's just a demo to consider."

She was about to close the lid on her laptop when the urge to check her sales numbers struck her.

She clicked on her new orders.

And gasped.

"What is it?" Brett asked, instantly alarmed by Jillian's sharp intake of air. And her bulging eyes.

"I—These numbers are—Oh—Holy—*Oh!*"

She stared. Now gaping. In shock.

"Jillian?"

"It's just . . . I can't even believe what I'm seeing." Her heart nearly burst from her chest.

She'd hoped for a surge in sales due to her joint venture with Jack. But *through-the-roof, astronomical* sales were beyond her greatest expectations.

"I can't believe it," she repeated. And slumped back in her chair.

Never mind the logistics of how she was going to get these orders out. She'd expedite the hell out of them, and when she ran out of stock, she'd send a follow-up email to say the shipments would go out when she returned to Seattle. She'd already mentioned the potential for a delay—and customers had purchased anyway.

Brett couldn't take the suspense a second longer and peeked over Jillian's shoulder.

"Those are new sales?!" she exclaimed. Then covered her mouth with her hand. Then dropped her arm. "From *yesterday*?"

"And today." Jillian was astounded. Mind blown. "Wow," she murmured. "Just . . . wow."

Brett sank back into her chair as well. And said, "Tell you what. I'll help you fill as many orders as you have stock for. If you'll show me how to create my own online store."

"I'm getting the better end of the deal, you realize."

"This afternoon, sure. But in two years? Who knows what *my* numbers are going to look like."

"Hopefully, even more stunning than mine," Jillian said. And tapped the rim of her cup to Brett's.

"Well," Brett said after a sip. "I'll leave you to the processing so I can get my tasks done. Then after your prep with Jack, we'll meet at the guesthouse to package?"

"That's a wonderful offer," Jillian replied.

Brett stood again and smiled. "We don't require tit for tat around here. But when someone can lend a hand, they always do."

"And I'm grateful for that. Also happy I can reciprocate."

"Wait'll Wyatt finds out I'm gonna be open for business."

"Sooner than you can probably imagine," Jillian told her. "I have a fabulous manufacturing company that can customize all your shipping boxes and materials for fragile items."

"Don't tell Jack, but I have a storage room at Luke's that is full of pots." She made an "Eehhh" face that had Jillian laughing.

"Something tells me he knows, Brett."

She shrugged. "Chances are good, Jillian."

Brett departed. Jillian stared—for at least five minutes—at the figures she'd not ever seen in a twenty-four-hour period.

Then she got a grip. And went to work.

Chapter Ten

The prep for the show went smoothly—because Jillian and Jack were on opposite sides of the kitchen island, with their hands preoccupied.

The only real issue was . . .

"Honey, you stealin' those not-so-secretive glances at me is distractin' as all get-out."

"Can't help it, Jack. Unless you can somehow be less appealing?"

"Hmm. I'll suffer through the distraction."

She laughed. "Keep working on those vegetables."

"Tell me that's not really what you're thinkin'."

"No, it is not. But we have work to focus on, cowboy."

He eyed her a moment longer.

"Don't slice off your finger because of me, Jack."

He harrumphed. Then said, "Little bit of a ballbuster, Jillian. Little bit."

They continued on. Then Jack made lunch again. Though, while the country-style meat loaf cooked in the oven, he couldn't keep his hands off Jillian.

"I'm trying to get the lumps out of these mashed potatoes," she reprimanded him as he stole behind her and kissed her bare nape, because her hair was pulled up.

"Chance and I like the lumps, darlin'. Garrett and Tuck too."

"Nobody likes the lumps, Jack."

He chuckled. "You added all the right flavorin's with the garlic-herb cheese. Trust me when I say, a lump or two here or there won't cause any hiccups."

"Fine." She set aside her masher and turned to him. "But if you mess with my timing on the biscuits, cowboy, you're in big trouble."

He grimaced. "Oh, honey. You know if word reaches Avery that you smacked a canister against the edge of the counter and laid out premade rounds of dough on a bakin' sheet . . . there'll be hell to pay."

"Guess I ought to spend some time with him, learning his flaky southwestern earth-oven biscuits."

"You do like to tease me, don't you?"

Jillian laughed. "As if you have competition, cowboy."

"You step in front of a reflective surface every mornin', right?"

She kissed him. "Eye of the beholder, Jack."

"You gonna use that adage on Hunt? 'Cuz he won't get it."

"Not my target audience. He'll be over me tomorrow. Some cute soccer goalie on an opposing team will deflect his shot, and they'll gaze at each other with stars in their eyes. He'll forget my name on the spot."

"So you think."

"Universal reality for the demographic, Jack." She kissed him again. Then said, "If you'll kindly let me finish the potatoes."

He grunted. "I can actually pass up food for you, darlin'."

"Well, I can't. I'm starving. Oatmeal only powers you through so many hours."

"Then you should be havin' breakfast with us. And now that I've mentioned dining with the family, you should definitely partake in the cubano sandwiches and the sweet potato wedges this evening. I've got a recipe to knock your socks off, honey."

Jillian didn't doubt it.

Nor did she feel anxiety over *dinner with the family*.

She gave Jack a lingering gaze as she considered how meeting everyone in separate stages had helped her to piece them all together in a big-picture sense. The entire group embraced her—and she wanted to embrace them.

So she told Jack, "Yes to dinner tonight. Under the condition that I don't spectacularly blow up our show today."

He gave a low chortle. "That's not gonna happen. Now . . . let's eat."

Jillian set out the buffet just as Chance entered. Followed by Garrett and Tuck.

Jack ensured they all settled at the island, rather than the table. He sat next to Jillian, opposite the others, providing ample space for her.

She did another "if Mindy were to ask my scale of anxiety" assessment. And felt quite strongly she'd dipped below two.

She slid a glance Jack's way, only to find him gazing suggestively at her. So much so, she laughed. Her really big one.

Jack appeared taken aback. Looked around the group and said, "No idea what gets the woman goin'." And chuckled along with her.

Jillian smiled as Jack hacked off a chunk of meat loaf and savored it. She gave the loaded loaf a roll, too, liking the velvety ketchup glaze and the perfectly seasoned ground beef, carrots, bell peppers, and onions.

The men had ranch business to discuss. Jillian listened in, though it was hard to concentrate when Jack was dazzling her with fiscal terms and private grins.

She cleaned up as they finished their meals. Folks continued on their way, including Jack, who gave her a breath-stealing kiss before heading out. Jillian returned to the guesthouse, soon to be visited by Brett.

"This is organization at its finest," Jack's mom said as she took in the layout on the long dining table and the stacks of supplies and inventory in a semicircle on the floor.

"The wooden holders are precut and easy to assemble. Saves money and space to put them together myself." Jillian demonstrated.

She had another process so successfully in place that she only had to make mention of this and that to Brett and the two of them fell into sync with the packaging and labeling. They filled the storage bins with shipments as quickly as they drained them of products.

In one afternoon, Jillian was bone dry.

"I can't believe it," she reiterated. "I was certain I'd brought enough of everything to last me a week. I haven't been here three whole days."

"Anything we can do to keep you in production?"

"No, unfortunately. I've called in an exorbitant amount of supplies to be sent to my home in Seattle for when I return and can dive in. There's nothing I can do about lack of sauces and rubs at this point."

"All right, then. Good to know you have a booming business awaiting you."

"That is a nice feeling," Jillian said.

"Well, let me help you tidy up."

They had discarded tape that'd gotten tangled up, label backings, and scraps of foam to put in the trash.

Brett said, "Wyatt's willing to deliver your crates to the mail service in town, but with this many . . . you and Jack should probably load up his truck, since you're drivin' in for the TV show. The bed has a cover, so everything'll be safe."

"Excellent idea."

Brett said, "You know, you're really on to something with your cookbook. It'd be great if you could convince Jack that more vegetables in his diet would be a benefit to his longevity." She said this lightly, though Jillian understood it was a grave concern.

"You worry he's following too closely in his father's footsteps."

"He stays in shape," Brett said. "But so did his daddy. You don't see many overweight cowboys."

"All that red meat and financial burden and stressors. The endless responsibilities. That can certainly affect someone's health."

"Just somethin' to think about," Brett told her. And headed to the door. "I'm guessin' you're gonna change clothes before the segment. I'll leave you to it."

Jillian watched her go, knowing Jack's mom planted a seed for her to cultivate. Problem was, the man did like his barbecue.

But they were augmenting with her dishes, and he'd not shunned them. So perhaps there was hope. A favor she could return to Brett in addition to it benefiting Jack. The entire family, really, in more ways than one.

She got around and returned to the main house, Ollie scampering into the kitchen in search of Ale.

"Traitor," Jillian joked.

Jack joined her at the island while Ale rolled a small ball on the tile for the dog to chase.

Jack was all spiffed up in a white shirt that, as always, accentuated every inch of sinew the man possessed. He had on button-fly jeans that were worn and comfortable looking, and tan boots. His dark hair was the typical strategically mussed style that Jillian longed to run her fingers through. And his cobalt eyes glimmered mischievously.

So the station manager had been right. That was exactly the vibe that arced between them.

Jillian had donned khaki capris and a sage-colored tank and sweater set, the sleeves pushed up to her forearms. During her quick online shopping spree before she'd made the trek here—since athleisure wear was her norm—she'd basically selected essentials in every shade offered. She chastised herself for not being more creative, but the soothing hues looked good on camera, so she wasn't too self-conscious about not being a fashion influencer.

She told Jack, "You in a white shirt and faded jeans does not make you any less devilish."

He grinned. Bent his head and whispered, "And you in clothes doesn't make me *not* see you naked."

"Jack!" She swatted at him. "I'm not even sure that was a proper sentence."

"But you get my point."

"Duly noted."

"That's all that matters, darlin'." He gazed at her. And added, "Don't blame me that the visual sticks. All I could think of this mornin' was that deserted island and a California king with rumpled sheets."

"The regular king was a little cramped for you last night. Long legs you've got there, cowboy."

"I just curled around you, honey. Prayed to high heaven that Ollie wasn't going to take exception. And enjoyed the feel of your body next to mine."

"Which you took advantage of this morning."

He groaned sexily. "Don't think for a second I wanted breakfast more than I wanted you."

"Now you're pulling one of *my* long legs."

He feigned innocence with a hand over his heart. "How can you possibly believe that?"

Jillian laughed.

Garrett stepped in to set up his laptop and asked, "What's so hysterical?"

"Jack passing up food for . . . *anything*," Jillian sputtered.

"I'd agree. But . . ." Garrett grinned. And left that sentiment as it stood. So that Jillian's face flushed, and she had to busy herself elsewhere, while Jack gave one of his rumbling chuckles that chased after her.

At five o'clock, they got the show on the road.

Jillian demonstrated the prep for the pork shoulder as Jack pulled the one they'd had roasting in the oven for the past several hours and let it rest.

She whisked together the ingredients for another batch of the Asian marinade they'd used, which acted more as an outer-shell glaze when properly encrusted. She couldn't wait for Jack to slice into the pork and reveal the juicy inside.

"If you'll pass the ginger, Jack, I'll mix it in, along with the lime juice." Which she reached for at the exact moment he was stretching toward the ramekin of ginger.

They collided. Again.

The sauce in the bowl Jillian held in her other hand went flying—all over Jack's chest.

Like . . . Right. Off. The. Bat.

It was too comical and fated for the two of them—along with Garrett, Tuck, Ale, and Brett—not to erupt.

"Well, darlin', that's one way to get me out of my shirt," Jack quipped. "Do I just strip it off right here and now?"

Jillian's stomach nearly launched into her throat at the thought—and at the image of his wide, hulking chest that flashed in her mind.

"Jack, I wouldn't be able to get another word out of my mouth," she confessed.

He shot a look toward the camera. "I'm convinced she did this on purpose."

"You know I did not!"

He snickered. "I'm gonna need a towel to mop this up with, Mom. And please don't harangue me for not wearin' an apron."

"The audience would not go for that," Jillian contended.

Ale made bizarre hand signals behind his cameras, and Garrett circled his index finger in a *keep rolling with this* motion.

"No need to cover up all this hunkiness," she flirted.

Garrett gave a double thumbs-up. Ale nodded with enthusiasm. So all manner of emoji must be floating over his screens.

"Think my PG rating's about to be tossed out the window," Jack remarked.

"I'm certain it was never that solidified," she said. And winked.

"Aw, darlin', you're turnin' the tables on me."

She flirted some more, making his gaze smolder.

He dropped a slice of ham for the cubanos on the floor.

They spilled a bottle of toasted sesame oil when their hands touched.

And joked their way through the whole episode.

Wyatt and Hunter were just coming in when they wrapped.

"I watched on the drive home!" Hunter exclaimed. "You were hilarious!"

"And sexy," Garrett commented.

"Jillian puts the 'hot' in hot mess," Jack teased.

Wyatt went straight to the breakfast table and whipped out her laptop. Garrett and Tuck gathered behind her as she rattled off staggering analytics.

Jillian's cell rang, and she connected a video call with Mindy as she moved out of earshot.

"If you'd just take the man's shirt off," her producer said, "I'm certain you'd land a prime-time network spot."

"Get out!"

"Just sayin'. I had to put more ice in my iced tea. All I could imagine was you shredding the buttons on his shirt and just . . . melting at his feet. Proverbially speaking, of course."

"Sort of already did that," Jillian mumbled.

"You did not!"

"I did so!"

"Dirty girl."

"You betcha. Now . . . ," Jillian said. "What's happening with my numbers on the podcast and newsletter?"

"Increasing by leaps and bounds. But it's your cookbook rankings I want you to check out."

"Oh, Mindy . . . I can't." Now Jillian's stomach bottomed out. "I mean . . . what if I'm still tanking? I'm not sure I can handle the—"

"Just look. I'll wait."

Jillian secured the phone in a slot on Ale's tripod. She took a deep breath. Then she retrieved her laptop from her bag to quickly access the bookmarked page.

And almost dropped her computer.

"Whoa, honey," Jack was quick to steady the device—and her. "You okay?"

"No," she choked out. She set her laptop on the counter and pointed to the screen.

"Holy hell," Jack mumbled.

"Jack Royce Reed," his mother scolded. "You know the rule in this house."

"Which is repeatedly broken, Mom," Wyatt reminded her. "Jack, what is it?"

"Editor's Pick and Number One Bestseller banners for Jilly's cookbook," he announced.

Jillian covered her mouth with her hand to hide her quivering lips. But she couldn't disguise the tears that misted her eyes.

"Told you," Mindy said.

Jillian swallowed a lump of emotion. But the shocking reality staring her in the face kept her supercharged.

She bounced on the balls of her feet, wanting to shout from the rooftops that her cookbook had finally gotten the attention she'd dreamed of. But she didn't want to startle anyone.

Brett was the first to break through that cage. She jumped from her seat and threw her arms around Jillian.

Who didn't hesitate to hug her back.

"Congratulations!" Brett cried as though she truly understood the significance of this feat.

Wyatt was next. "It's beautiful from cover to cover. Of course it's a bestseller!"

Garrett and Tuck offered handshakes.

Ale and Hunter didn't quite get the importance of the moment, but they were both all smiles and applause.

Jack swooped in and wrapped an arm around Jillian's waist. "You have a winner on your hands, honey."

"This cookbook would have faded into oblivion without you, Jack," she averred.

"I don't believe that's true, but I'm happy to provide a little limelight. Fact is, Jilly, I think it's your own charisma that's drivin' sales."

"Oh, Jack," she said on a dramatic sigh. "If only you were a woman. You'd see the appeal you present and that *you* fuel sales."

"We'll agree to disagree. Point bein' . . . that's an online page worthy of a screenshot, so get on it. We're gonna move this party into the dinin' room. Join us when you're ready."

The group fell into formation.

Jillian released her phone and took it to the table everyone had vacated. She told Mindy, "This is surreal."

Her producer tsk-tsked and said, "You've worked hard for this, Jillian. And you took a gigantic leap of faith by going to Texas."

Her brows scrunched. "Thought you labeled this 'easy-peasy promo'?"

"That's because I'm your representative, and I have to convin— never mind. Bottom line is that it was the right decision, yes?"

"A million times over," she admitted. "It's almost like I've rediscovered civilization. And I like it, Mindy. I really, really like it."

Now the tears came. She reached for a napkin she'd laid out earlier for tomorrow's breakfast service.

She dabbed at her eyes as Mindy said, "You've come a long way, Jillian. The past few weeks, and this one . . . these milestones are substantial and life-altering."

"Yes."

"I won't pretend to know what it's like to walk a mile—or even a few feet—in your shoes. But I can say this." Mindy's expression softened. Her eyes glistened. "You are incredibly brave for enduring all that you have—and continuing to progress. Some people . . . they might've given up. They might just stay in that shell they created and never consider leaving it, never push themselves to step outside. You've done so much recovery, Jillian. And you keep plowing through obstacles. I admire that so much."

Tears tumbled along Jillian's cheeks. "That's a very kind and encouraging thing to say."

"Consider me a lifelong fan. And a friend."

Jillian was taken aback.

Mindy was just so . . . Mindy. Never one to exhibit this sort of emotion. It gripped Jillian in a way that had her fighting back more fat drops she didn't want to have to sop up.

She took a moment to regroup as Mindy said, "If you need someone to talk to, Jillian, I'm always just a phone call away."

"We don't really do that . . . ," she breathlessly said.

"We do now."

Jillian clung to some levity like a life preserver, saying, "Look at me making a BFF."

"I was in need of one myself. All work and no play . . ."

"Guess I'll hit up Garrett for his take on you."

"Do that," Mindy said, helping to lighten the mood.

Jillian sniffled. Tossed aside the napkin. And told Mindy, "I have to give a family dinner a chance now. Sixteen chairs that I'm sure will mostly be filled."

This was confirmed as Chance and Mateo came through the patio doors, tipped their hats at her, and gathered up the rest of the platters on the island, taking them to the dining room.

"I'm thinking you might want to come spend a couple days with me," Jillian said as she watched the good-looking cowboys exit. "All this Texas breeding stimulates the . . . mind."

Mindy laughed. "Yeah, I'm sure that's what's stimulated."

"Fine. Consider it a holistic environment. Definitely something in the water."

"Now that sounds intriguing."

"Speaking of . . . ," Jillian surprised herself by adding, "I have to go so that I don't appear as though I'm hesitant to be a part of the festivities. I'm actually quite curious as to how they all interact."

"Call me tomorrow after the TV show."

"Will do." She paused a moment.

Mindy's brow raised.

Jillian said, "I appreciate you sticking it out with me all these years."

"You're not a hardship, Jillian." Mindy gave her a pointed look.

"I'm not a walk in the park either," she acknowledged.

"Says you." She smiled. "Go. I have huge plans of my own. Microwavable chicken piccata with shriveled asparagus and a glass of pinot grigio."

Jillian winced. "Perhaps you ought to buy my cookbook."

"I was the first one to do so. But joke's on me because I can't cook."

"Everyone can cook, Mindy."

"Yeah, I said that to you about baking."

"All righty, then. I'm out."

Jillian tucked her computer and her phone into her tote and trailed after the others, waiting for them all to settle into what she assumed were their traditional seats.

When Brett touched Jack's elbow and gently jutted her chin toward the chair at the head of the table, Jillian's heart clenched.

Jack gave a slight shake of his head.

Brett gave a decisive nod. Then took the seat to the right.

As Jack conceded, Wyatt said, "Hunt, honey, pull back a chair for Miss Jillian."

The most obvious one was to Jack's left.

Jillian bit back more emotion and joined Hunt. "Thanks for being such a gentleman."

He beamed. "This is my chair." He indicated the one next to her and sat, with Ale on his other side.

"Perfect arrangement," Jillian told him. Then she spared a glance at Jack.

He seemed to still be struggling with his new reign. Jillian deduced this was his dad's position at the head of the table. And Brett now wanted her eldest son to deem himself worthy of the honor of sitting there.

Jillian was overcome with feelings—and she wasn't the only one. The other adults found this critical occasion moving. If she wasn't mistaken, they took their own moments of silence in memoriam of Royce

Reed. And then raised a glass to Jack. Like he'd become the godfather of the ranch.

Jillian suspected that was an accurate assessment.

Jack said, "Y'all know family members come and go. What never changes is the bond we share. Whether we're here on the TRIPLE R or explorin' other passions, we have this commonality. And that commitment is what keeps us goin'."

They all tapped rims, even the kids with their glasses of milk.

Brett blinked away tears. She sipped her wine as Jack told everyone to dig in. There was an elevated serving platform in the middle of the table where the entrées were placed. The additional dishes were arranged underneath.

Jack said, "Boys, start passin' the sides."

The orchestration was commendable. Jillian let Jack load up her plate, primarily because he was in charge of how this all played out.

The meal was terrific and topped off when Avery came in with huckleberry pie, lemon cake, and blueberry campfire cobbler, along with a pot of campout s'mores for the kids.

Later, Jack walked Jillian and Ollie to the guesthouse. Jack swung the gate open and supervised Ollie while Jillian took the steps to the deck and then opened the door.

She turned back to him. "You are coming in, right?"

He propped a hip against the railing. "Well, we're not in need of plottin' out tomorrow morning's menu for the TV segment. I have to decide a week in advance and provide the list of ingredients to a production assistant. So that's all taken care of."

"You are coming in, right?" she repeated.

Heat flared in Jack's eyes. "Wild horses, Jillian. Wild horses . . ."

An apropos adage, even if he didn't complete it.

He joined her, Ollie following them.

Jack went into the kitchen and poured a glass of the pinot noir they hadn't finished the night before while Jillian and her pup situated themselves on the sectional.

"So what are we making for the segment?" she asked.

"Breakfast."

Jack handed her the wine. She sipped as he took the corner spot again and eased her back to lean against him. He draped his arm over her shoulder. They shared the glass.

"The meal I assign the lowest priority to," she commented.

"That's because you're not eatin' mine."

"I have no doubt it's beyond fabulous."

"I like to think so." He chuckled. "And they all keep comin' back for more, so."

"Modesty is not your strongest suit, Jack."

"No, it is not."

She sipped again and asked, "What are we whipping up? Breakfast burritos? Tex-Mex skillets? Huevos rancheros?"

"All favorites of mine. But I've been doin' this show weekly for over a year, and I've nearly run the gamut with southwestern recipes, so I toss in a variety to supplement. Tomorrow, it's strawberry-cream-cheese-filled crepes with berry toppings and my own bourbon syrup drizzle."

"Did not see that one coming."

"Keeps the menu fresh, and they continue to give me the slot. Though . . . with this extra bit of time, we don't have to premake anything. We can do it all on the fly."

"And you have a bourbon syrup too?"

"An award winner, darlin'."

"Jesus, Mary, and Joseph."

"Beg pardon?"

"Nothing," she said. "Just one thousand percent swimming in *ways to help Jack make money*. But I understand your time constraints. It's a conundrum."

"So shelve that and get naked with me."

Jillian laughed.

But her mind churned with more thoughts than sex. *Surprise, surprise.*

Tonight's "crowning" still held her spellbound.

"You're awful quiet, honey," Jack murmured.

Jillian's eyes squeezed shut for a few seconds. She was once again curious as to what she'd see.

What she'd expected was exactly what she got.

Visions of Jack—with his own kid. A son.

Perhaps the imagery was more prominent now that the passing-of-the-torch-type symbolism had occurred. Sure, it'd been subtle. But it'd been substantial. And Jillian had not missed how it had affected Jack, even if the recognition, the silent sentimentality, the acceptance—and the appreciation for what had been left to him—were fleeting so that he didn't get mired in the deep emotional aspect of the coronation.

He'd held this prestigious position since he was nineteen. But, clearly, out of love and respect for his father—his mother too—he'd not occupied that chair.

Until tonight.

That brought to light a future Jack might not have dreamed of for himself, focused as he was on making ends meet and providing for a family that extended well beyond those living under the roof of the main house.

Jillian placed the wineglass on the coffee table and turned to him.

She said, "You could have so much more, Jack."

His gaze narrowed. "Look around, darlin'. What does this ranch lack? We've got green pastures and fat cows. A bunkhouse full of cowboys who love to cowboy. My relatives use every tool in their toolboxes to maintain this lifestyle, to see us all through, season after season. Only drought or famine can take us down, Jilly. And at that . . . I'm bankin' on us because of our dedication and resourcefulness."

She nodded. "I'm not discounting any of that—or anyone's contributions. I'm referring to you."

"I don't know what you're sayin', honey. I've got everything intended for me."

Culminating with him taking that particular seat at the table tonight.

Except . . .

"Jack . . ." She groaned. She could seriously be stepping on his toes, but she had to tell him, "You're not the sum of this ranch. That's a huge part of you, yes. Absolutely. But you're destined for even greater achievements. I can feel it. In my soul."

The backs of her eyes prickled.

He let out a harsh breath. "Jilly, maybe I'm not meant for a happily ever after either."

"I think you are," she insisted. "And, Jack, you deserve it. You deserve the complete package. I'm not just talking about acres and acres of bluebonnets and rolling hills, relatives to help you keep it all in your collective possession. I'm talking about a wife. Kids. Dogs and cats. Whatever. Fish."

Tears popped on the rims of her eyes. Because she wanted the entire kit and caboodle for Jack Reed.

He brushed away the first drop that fell, even before it hit her cheek.

"Jilly . . ." His grave expression lightened as he sought to mellow the tense mood. He teased, "Are you proposin' to me, darlin'?"

She let out a strangled laugh. "I'm not your match made in heaven, Jack. I'm what will eventually become a distant memory. Again." *That* was their fate. "Hopefully a fond one."

"Don't forget," he said, returning to his solemn cadence. "You never were a distant memory. I thought about you more than might be deemed socially appropriate. The fantasies did get pretty steamy."

Heat tinged her cheeks. But she didn't falter.

"That's not really what I'm getting at, Jack."

"Then why don't you tell me point blank what it is you're attemptin' to convey. So that I don't get mixed signals or make assumptions."

She stared into his beautiful blue eyes.

Then glanced away.

She shook her head and said, "I can't have children, Jack. No pill necessary. After all the surgeries, it's just . . . not possible."

"And you think havin' kids would define me? Make my life richer?" he challenged.

Her tears spilled.

She slipped from his loose embrace and stood.

"Jack, you ensure your family has everything it needs. That *you* have everything you want and desire—for the moment. But legacies are built on generational succession. And when you're the king of the mountain, you want to pass the dynasty on to the son or daughter who bears your name in any capacity. First name or middle. Like yours."

"Jillian—"

"More than that, Jack," she continued, "I see how you interact with your nephews, how great you are with them, how they look up to you. And I hear the longing in your voice when you talk about the magical love affair Wyatt and Mateo share. I just think—"

"Enough, Jillian." He got to his feet, reached for the wine, and drained the glass. "It could very well be that I'm still single because I *choose* to be," he said. "Because I won't settle for less than what fills my heart with joy."

"There's your *point blank*, Jack," she replied. "And you *shouldn't* settle. Ever."

He raked a hand through his hair. Gave her an intent look. And told her, "Maybe you should let me determine what's best for *me*, Jillian."

"That's what I want, Jack!"

His jaw set. Then he asked, "And what about you?"

"Obviously, this was more than I was intending," she said, forthright. "I like your family."

"They like you, too, darlin'."

"I enjoy being with you as well."

"Ditto." He rubbed his jaw now, as though to loosen it. And asked, "What happens when you leave?"

She knew what he was insinuating.

She told him, "We've already covered that, for the most part. I go back to my life and business and try to incorporate more social activities into my routine. What I'd take solace in is if I could eventually get back on a ferry to Puget Sound. Be on a boat with dozens of people and not be terrified, not be panicked."

"That's your big goal?"

"Yeah, Jack. It is."

He placed his hands on his waist. Continued to hold her gaze. "I understand that's a lofty objective. That it comes with all sorts of emotional thorns and perceived physical threats. But beyond that, Jilly . . . what's the ultimate evolution for you?"

Chapter Eleven

Jack knew he was pushing her boundaries.

Hell, maybe he was pushing a boulder uphill. Especially since she didn't answer his question.

But, no . . . Jillian wasn't rooted within her personal limitations anymore. He knew that because she'd come to Texas. She'd remained on the ranch when every fiber of her being had likely screamed for her to retreat to her safe haven in Seattle once she'd gotten a good look at this place. Once she'd met his family. Once she'd found herself integrated within their circle—and had had dinner with nearly a dozen people. In the same room.

She'd trusted in him from the beginning.

And just as she was pressing him to see his bigger picture, if that even existed, he was doing the same with her.

Every time the woman's laugh bounced around in his head, and every time she gave him a seductive smile, and every time she kissed him, Jack got lost in what-ifs.

What if she stayed?

What if she truly was the one?

What if she recognized that too?

Never mind what she'd said about not being able to have children. That was a painful revelation that sliced through him on levels he couldn't even begin to process, yet they had less to do with his legacy than the ache in his heart over her inability to potentially fulfill that white-picket-fence dream she'd once had.

That dream that had been ripped from her fingers. Through no fault of her own—other than she'd tried to save a life at a concert. (And had succeeded.)

Jack knew how a blindside could cut to the core.

He'd grown up on dreams and grand plans. From learning how to tend cattle and assess the market, to finding all the sweet spots with BBQ to win competitions, to playing football, to achieving good grades, to wanting to be a provider even when he was just a kid. That inspiration had been born from watching his dad manage every aspect of this place—and being damn proud to do so.

Jack had thought he'd had the prime solution to anything that had, at the time, or could possibly in the future, ail this enterprise and devastate his family—pro ball.

His rug had been yanked from beneath him too.

He heaved a harsh puff of air. He wouldn't simplify his current situation with Jillian with an "it is what it is" resignation.

For one thing, he still clung to the what-ifs.

Second, as much as she was rallying hope for more for him . . . he had the same inclination where she was concerned.

For the time being, however . . .

"We agree we're at an impasse?" he asked.

She sighed. Hauntingly.

"Jillian," he murmured. And closed the gap between them. "We have a good sense of each other's lives but not the deeper entanglements. I want to know more. But whatever you share has to be based on how we acknowledge and accept our different nuances. One day at a time."

She gazed up at him, notably confused.

He added, "I like that you're here. I think you like it too."

She nodded.

"That's what matters most. *Today.*" He kissed her.

Jillian didn't miss a beat.

She wound her arms around his neck, her body melding to his.

There was agony and relief in that first kiss.

Then . . . nothing but a soul-deep sensuality that consumed Jack.

He swept her into his arms and took her to the bedroom, setting her on her feet along the edge of the bed.

They gave up on words.

He rid her of her tank and sweater. She divested him of his marinade-stained shirt.

Her hands skimmed over his biceps as his palms rested in the curve of her waist.

Their next kiss was even more evocative, stirring, fervent.

Jack's erection strained against his fly, and he had the desperate need to discard the rest of their clothes. Fast. But savoring every second with Jillian became his new norm.

He kissed her until she needed oxygen.

Even at that, her lips didn't stray far from his. They tangled in sensuous kisses as they both got their breaths back.

She whispered, "Remind me to never argue with you. I'll lose every time."

"That wasn't an argument, honey. That was a difference of opinion that has more connotations than either of us have delved into."

"Goddamn, you're smart, cowboy."

He chuckled, albeit tightly. "I can call 'em like I see 'em. But I can also read between the lines . . . and piece together a puzzle."

"Unless those pieces are incongruent." She stared into his eyes.

He got her meaning. And said, "Sometimes you just have to find a work-around." He basically dropped the mic. *Boom.*

Jillian smiled. "Kissing me as though there's no tomorrow is one guaranteed work-around."

"Honey, Sunday's a million miles away."

And with that statement, he guided her down onto the bed, removed their clothing, and crawled under the covers beside her.

He pulled her to him, on top of him.

The moonlight streaming in through the cracks in the blinds created a silhouette around her thick caramel waves. She flattened one palm alongside him on the mattress as she poised herself against him, midthigh. Her other hand stroked his cock from base to tip.

"Just so you know, darlin', I'm a sure thing."

She laughed. And that alleviated the pressure in his chest.

"I'm taking in the view, Jack. And just so *you* know . . . it's mind blowing."

"There you go again, strokin' my ego."

"If that's what I'm doing . . ."

He let out a primal grunt. "What you're doin' is driving me wild."

"Me too."

She shifted and drew him into her body. Slowly. Tortuously slow.

The initial penetration into her tight, wet depths stole his breath. Jack was certain he'd never get over the lure of her. The beautiful body. The impish smile and all that hair. Not to mention the way she lowered herself provocatively so that his cock glided along her inner walls, with a hint of friction that was titillating, while also eliciting in him a thrill of knowing how wet he made her.

She slid her hands up to his pecs. Stretched her body and arched her back so that their skin almost touched. The ultimate in temptation.

He gripped her ass and led her into a grinding rhythm as she rode him with panting breaths and heavy-lidded eyes.

"Jack," she whispered.

"Don't say anything, Jillian. Not right now, honey. Not when we're like this . . ."

Her head bent to his, and she kissed him. As though she comprehended that this moment wasn't conducive to a dissection of them. It was better suited to uniting them.

He sat up. Her arms circled his neck again. He swelled inside her, felt her adjusting to him, accommodating him. Quite welcomingly, if the gentle contracting and releasing of her pussy was any indication.

Jillian checked the conversation at the door for him, remaining focused on the intimacy they shared, rather than all the conflict surrounding them.

Jack's hands slid up her sides. He felt the lines of raised skin—and honestly accepted that her scars weren't flaws; they were their own story, a composition of her.

His palms pressed to her shoulder blades. They moved with each other, rocking in time, gradually picking up the pace, finding that perfect, stimulating cadence, and . . . giving themselves over to it.

So that all that registered, all that was left between them, was a searing eroticism that turned all the doubts, the anxiety, the agony to ash.

◆ ◆ ◆

He hated leaving her in the morning.

Like, full-on loathed it.

But Jack slipped from the bed anyway and returned to the main house to shower and dress. Breakfast was its usual organized chaos, and then Wyatt took the kids to school, Mateo herding them out the door before getting his own day underway.

Jack checked his emails in his office and then went back to the kitchen for another cup of coffee. His mom finished loading the dishwasher and then cleaned herself up. She rounded the island and took a stool, folding her hands on the countertop.

"Where's Jillian?" she asked. "I'd hoped she'd join us for breakfast."

"Likely primpin' for the TV show." He gave a half snort. "Not that she needs it. The woman wakes up gorgeous."

His mom grinned. "You know this personally."

He smirked.

She would have baited him more under different circumstances, he was sure, but she caught his melancholy and asked, "What's on your mind, Jack?"

He shook his head. Let out a long breath.

"Go on, now," his mom encouraged. "I'll just prod you till you cave, so spare me the indignity of my cajoling."

He rubbed the knot at his nape. Dropped his hand. And said, "I could spend the rest of my life with that woman and die a happier man because of it."

Brett's eyes glistened in an instant.

She nodded and said, "A mother can tell when her son's in love. And see that the feelings are reciprocal."

"The latter doesn't matter, even if it's true," he told her, his stomach coiling. "The situation is essentially moot."

"If it's about geography, Jack—"

"It's a hell of a lot more than that, Mom."

He raised his mug to sip, but the rim didn't touch his lips. He returned it to the counter.

"Jack?" Concern etched Brett's face and laced her tone.

He told her, "Jillian's broken inside, Mom. Deep in her heart." He blew out another stream of air. "And I can't fix her."

This had a peculiar rage ripping through him that he couldn't quell. He was angry Jillian had suffered so much. And he was agitated there was nothing he could do to help with her predicament.

He took his cup to the sink and poured out the rest of his coffee because his gut burned from the admission he'd just made.

"I don't understand," Brett quietly said.

He glanced over his shoulder. "She was in a really bad accident. Laid up for almost a year. And that changed her."

"We all know she's been isolated. We're just not aware of the reason. But she's clearly made strides, Jack, since comin' here. Huge strides."

"And yet her greatest aspiration beyond growing her business is to get on a boat with a bunch of strangers and not be horrified to be among them." His heart twisted. "When it should be somethin' like . . . gettin' married and adoptin' five kids."

"Adoptin'?" Brett's brow arched.

"Jillian's life is different, Mom." That was all he said in that vein.

He washed out his cup and set it in the dish rack.

He turned around, propped his backside against the apron of the sink, and shoved his hands into his front pockets.

"I'm a man who prides himself on solvin' problems," he said in a grim voice. "This one's so far out of my wheelhouse, I can't even wrap my mind around it."

"Jack."

"Mom . . ." He gave another shake of his head. He wouldn't betray Jillian's confidences. Nor would he pretend he had any answers.

He started to walk off.

"Jack," Brett called after him.

He halted.

Coming up behind him, she gripped his arm and said, "Take it from someone who knows—love *can* heal wounds."

A notion he'd pushed aside long ago.

"And you have so much of it to give, son."

"This isn't a carrot I can chase, Mom," he ground out.

"I'm a survivor because I'm surrounded by my family and my friends," she persisted. "Because they fill my heart with joy. And I know you and Wyatt worry too much about what I might be missin' out on, but the truth is, I have plenty of wonderful memories of your father—and of current good times—to keep me warm at night."

Emotion rose within Jack, almost choking him.

"I'm grateful for that," he managed to say.

"I am too."

"Things are just . . . not ideal for me and Jillian."

"How so?"

"Mom, I've always been on your side when it comes to happiness being derived in various forms, not always the traditional ones. But Jillian insists I should have my own family. Issue bein', she's the only one I want to have it with. And goddamn it, I don't care if we have to adopt."

Fuck!

He was divulging too much.

190

"I have to go," he said. "We've gotta get to town."

"Jack—"

"It's complicated, Mom."

"But she's only here for a short time!"

He felt the knife twist. "I'm well aware of that fact."

They stared at each other.

Eventually, his mother said, "Don't waste any of it, Jack."

"Always one step ahead of me."

"That's how moms are."

"And I love you for it." He kissed the top of her head.

"I love you, too, Jack."

She released him.

Jack continued on his way, grabbing his hat as he strode toward the door.

◆ ◆ ◆

His teeth ground pretty much all the way into town. The only time his jaw slackened was when he pointed out a landmark or other feature of interest. Primarily, though, it was a quiet ride for him and Jillian.

He turned on the radio, and that seemed to cut some of the tension. But Jillian mostly stared out her side window, watching the meadows and streams pass by.

Once in Serrano, she took note of the brick buildings and the awnings above the large storefront windows. The tree-lined walkways and the flowerpots.

He said, "The city council pulled together a beautification committee a few years back and spruced up the town proper with funds collected from the annual street festival vendors."

"It's lovely," she commented.

He pulled into the news station parking lot and told her, "Don't go losin' your faith in our sophistication when you see my set rolled out onto this very lot."

She said, "Jack, you have your own TV spot. That's something."

"Two minutes, darlin'," he reminded her.

"Not today."

"That's likely because the station manager has a crush on you."

She laughed. Sweetly enough to ribbon through him, twine around his heart, and pull tight. So that he could barely breathe. Seemed to be the bane of his morning.

Damn, but he needed to shake off the consternation because he had a segment to do.

"Not a chance," she commented. "He knows a good thing when he sees it with ratings potential. I bet he'll keep you at fifteen minutes. Then he'll give you a full hour."

"Well, I wouldn't say no to that. It is a payin' gig. Now why don't you collect your dog, and I'll come 'round to get you."

"Thanks for not saying you'll 'fetch' me."

He chuckled, and it helped to ease the strain of emotion he'd been battling since last night. Maybe since she'd arrived on the ranch.

They entered the studio, Ollie in his soft carrier. Garrett greeted them and escorted them past reception, through the double doors, and to the inner sanctum. Only to have them follow to the set outside.

"Almost made you feel like a celebrity, didn't it?" Jack quipped.

She smiled up at him. "I'm duly impressed, regardless."

The backdrop looked like a backyard with a real grill to provide a barbecue setting. Though, as he'd previously mentioned, the call letters were stamped across the blue sky. So that killed the illusion right there.

Still, it was elaborate enough to get the job done.

There was a long counter with a sink, a minifridge, and a stove top and oven. All the equipment he needed, including mixers, bowls, utensils, and dishes. And the multitude of electrical cords that gave him juice, which were being taped down so no one tripped over them.

Garrett grabbed a director's chair for Ollie, and Jillian placed his carrier on the seat so he could see her.

She said, "That was very considerate of you."

"Dogs get star treatment around here too. Can I get either of you water—or do you want coffee?"

"We'll share a bottle, thanks."

When Garrett passed a cold one to her, she poured a small amount into the collapsible bowl that fit in the carrier and gave the pup a few treats.

Then Jack offered his hand to assist her up to the platform of the set. He gave her the "five-cent tour," since everything was laid out in a simple format, mostly hidden under the counter on shelves.

They started their prep, but as Jack had said, there was no need to make anything in advance. It could all be managed within their allotted time, with the two of them working together.

When the cameras rolled, Jillian walked the audience through the slicing-and-dicing portion, also combining the softened cream cheese with the strawberries—using a silicone paddle, rather than a blender. Jack put sausage and his signature steak hash browns on the grill, then crafted his batter and warmed the crepe pan on the stove.

The production was as smooth as silk, though the set was small enough that they were shoulder to shoulder, and that provided its own comedic scenario.

"This is my cooking space, Jack." She indicated a small square with her index fingers. "That's your cooking space. Kindly refrain from edging me out of the frame."

"Honey, you've stepped on my toes three times already."

"Your big feet are not my problem, cowboy."

Tuck gave thumbs-up signs to let them know all was well with the shooting—and probably to indicate that Ale would be making his love emoji signals if he were here.

That, of course, presented its own peril. Even the audiences were falling for him and Jillian.

But Jack couldn't fixate on that right now. They had a different clock ticking down. So they filled the crepes, plated them, added sliced strawberries and whole blueberries, drizzled his syrup on top, and dusted the display with powdered sugar for a dazzling presentation. He set out his sausage and hash browns and spritzed them up with a bit of syrup.

"There you have it, folks," he announced.

They each took a bite.

"Mmm . . ." Jillian sighed. "Sublime. That bourbon mix is superb."

"Pop open a bottle of bubbly for mimosas or mix up a pitcher of spicy Bloody Marys, and this is a brunch that won't break the bank or take up your mornin' making."

Jillian chimed in again with all the links—and then they were out.

Garrett clapped his hands together once before spreading his arms wide. "You two just get better and better."

Jack felt the same. Didn't matter about internal turmoil. They harmonized perfectly, even when they were stumbling into each other. Hell, he suspected that was what humanized them and made them personable, not like arrogant chefs yelling out insults for ratings.

As Mindy synopsized the comments on speakerphone while Jack and Jillian left the station and drove to the post office, she contended they were absolutely relatable.

Jillian was still listening to her producer's take on their shows as Jack and one of the mail clerks cleared out the bed of his truck, which he and Chance had loaded up earlier.

Jack returned the folded tonneau cover to its place when they were done. Jillian disconnected her call with Mindy and thanked the worker for his help, pulling a twenty from her front pocket and offering a tip.

As they were leaving the shop, Jack said, "That was mighty kind of you."

"It's a big shipment, Jack."

"Yeah, I'm impressed by your sales."

She wound an arm around his and gazed up at him. "Bet we could net *you* sales like that."

"Let's not travel that path at present."

He didn't take their route to the truck either. Instead, he led Jillian down the walkway, Ollie alongside her on his leash.

"Where are we off to?" she asked.

He noted there was only the tiniest hint of hesitation in her voice. Because she trusted him. Because she knew he wouldn't lead her into a massive crowd.

Also because . . . there was no massive crowd. People were working, not milling about at ten o'clock on a Thursday morning. And the tourists who would normally window-shop were deterred from that currently, as streets were blocked off to allow the festival staff to bring in the tents, staging, and equipment for the event that started tomorrow.

Jack said, "Thought we'd swing by Luke's. His cantina's not open yet, but he'll be there—and more than willin' to feed us."

She laughed. "Didn't you just eat at the ranch?"

"Darlin', you know me. I could eat all day. Especially after smellin' those steak hash browns. Took all the willpower I possessed to leave 'em be for the crew."

"Yeah, I noticed you didn't offer me a bite," she teased.

"I'll make 'em for breakfast tomorrow." He gave her a pointed look.

She pulled in a deep breath. Exhaled. And said, "I shall endeavor to be there."

"Good girl. Now . . . Luke's gonna knock your socks off, so be prepared."

"I expect nothing less from a Reed."

They rounded a corner and walked another block.

Jack retrieved his phone from his back pocket and texted Luke, alerting him of their approach.

Luke swung the door open for them.

"Well, color me surprised," Jack's younger brother said with a wide grin.

He was Jack's height but with slightly lighter-colored hair and eyes. Similar build because he'd played ball too. Just sans the goal of it landing him a college scholarship. Luke had gone to a two-year culinary school instead and had worked as a chef at a hotel in Austin until he'd hit it big with his poker winnings.

They shook hands, and then Jack introduced him to Jillian.

"Don't go fallin' for those sky-blue eyes, darlin'," Jack chided.

"Your gene pool should be studied and replicated, cowboy."

"I'm gonna take that as she approves of my stunning good looks," Luke said and stepped aside to allow them in. To Jack, he whistled under his breath and murmured, "Nice catch, bro."

"She's not mine to keep," Jack replied. And felt an anvil to his chest over that sentiment.

Luke appeared taken aback as well but let the comment slide. He led them past the hostess stand and into the restaurant.

"This place is fantastic," Jillian said as she took in the authentic Tex-Mex décor, with tiled tables and Saltillo floors. The vibrant patterns mixed with darker undertones and the neon lights behind the bar.

"Do you mind if I take photos and a video or two?" Jillian asked Luke. "For my blog and newsletter."

"I'd be honored, darlin'," he said with a hand over his heart.

"Okay, dial down the charm," Jack snapped.

"So . . . Avery was right," Luke taunted. "You've got it bad for this woman."

Ignoring him, Jack said, "Honey, take your time. Luke'll make you a margarita."

"And fajitas. Girl, you haven't lived until you've had my fajitas."

Jack sighed with resignation. "That's a fact."

Luke popped the top on two Mexican beers and tapped the neck of his to Jack's. To Jillian, he asked, "You prefer frozen or on the rocks?"

"On the rocks, please."

"This is my own concoction, and it's guaranteed to go down smooth, so be careful," Luke warned. And yet he set out the standard glass that was akin to a double serving. He salted the blue rim and went to work.

Jillian continued her inspection of the place.

When her cocktail was ready, they all cheersed, and then Luke directed them into the kitchen, where his lunch staff was prepping. The fragrant bell peppers and onions hit them first, laced with the scent of crispy homemade tortilla chips, followed by the sound of sizzling garlic-guajillo steak and jala-poblano chicken.

Jack crooked a brow at Jillian. "I'm gonna have to work extra hard to win you back, aren't I?"

She said, "Jack, you're holding my dog's leash so I can double-fist a fishbowl of a margarita. There's just no way a woman recovers from that." She was being feisty. And yet . . . obviously serious.

"Well, to be fair to Luke, he hasn't gotten started yet."

"And, oh, God," she said, "we shouldn't even have Ollie in here."

"He's fine in the dinin' room," Luke told her. "I allow service animals, so we'll pretend he qualifies."

"That's where we'll be." Jillian made a slow about-face so as to not spill her drink.

Jack went with her, and they selected a table in the corner. Jillian set out water for Ollie and then sucked down more of her margarita.

Luke joined them minutes later carrying a tray laden with plates and a tortilla container. He snapped open a tray jack and then transferred everything to the table. Chips, fresh salsa and guacamole, and all the fixings to go with the fajitas.

"I could move in here," Jillian jested.

"Tastes even better than it smells," Luke assured her.

There was no standing on ceremony with a feast such as this. They all dove in.

"This is too sensational for words," Jillian said. In between bites, she asked Jack, "Did you mention to Luke our thoughts on getting vid of his booth at the festival for tomorrow's show?"

"Hadn't had a chance, but . . ." He glanced at Luke. "Ale will be shootin', and Wyatt'll be with him."

"You dare to have my handsome mug on your show?" Luke playfully taunted. "I'll steal all your female viewers, Jack."

"That is a definite possibility," he agreed. "Avery too. But it'd make for a more diverse agenda. Highlight the local flavor and sights. That sort of thing."

"Happy to do what I can," Luke told them. "Though if you wanna come in person, I'll set out another grill, and you two can—"

"Ehh, we'll stick with our setup at the house," Jack said.

"The street fair's a great venue, Jack," Luke contended.

Jillian sipped. Then said, "I'm not a fan of crowds, Luke. Jack's keeping me in my comfort zone."

"Ah, gotcha. Okay, well." He held his hands in the air, in immediate surrender. "I certainly do understand that. Y'all heard of Whit Tatum?"

"No," Jack said, eyeing his brother with curiosity, not knowing what his query was about.

"He's a country-western singer. Amazingly talented," Luke said. "But he has stage fright. Can't sing in front of a crowd. Literally freezes up."

Jillian's brow furrowed. "But he's a singer?"

"Amazingly talented," Luke reiterated. "Riley's written a few songs for him. Anyway, he's indie-produced two albums and shoots his own videos for his YouTube channel. Even built himself a stage in his back-yard so he can film his band performin' on it—without a live audience."

Luke wiped his hands on a linen napkin and reached for his phone. He tapped the screen to pull up the app and then set the cell on the table, leaning it against the tortilla warmer. He hit play.

They listened to a song as Luke said, "That's one of Riley's."

"Wow," Jillian murmured.

"That's stellar stuff there," Jack agreed.

Jillian slid a glance Jack's way and smiled prettily.

"Uh-oh. I spy trouble."

"Stop," she joked. "How awesome would it be if Whit Tatum closed out our show on Saturday? Singing one of Riley's songs, of course."

"Darlin' . . ."

"Come on, it's a fabulous idea," she goaded.

He conceded with a nod. "Right up there with all of mine."

"Well, yes," she agreed, "your side did start it."

"I owe Garrett for contactin' Mindy, no doubt."

"Might want to let him know she thinks he's the bee's knees."

Jack chuckled. "Honey, are you drunk?"

"Just a slight buzz." She held up her hand and pinched her thumb and index finger almost together. Then she laughed. "Get it? Buzz . . . bees?"

"She is too much, Jack!" Luke roared and slapped his palm to his thigh.

Jack could swear he fell even more in love with her.

He wanted to say that was a straight shot to eternal misery, but . . . he couldn't deny he got a kick out of her.

They finished up, and Jillian excused herself to use the ladies' room.

Luke more seriously said, "She's a beauty queen for sure, bro. And she's got you wrapped around her finger."

"How do you figure?" he countered. Though he knew it to be fact.

"You're feedin' my chips to her dog, refilling his water bowl, and keepin' a weather eye on him to make sure he's all settled in."

"She likes her dog," Jack scoffed.

"*You* like her dog. And *her*." Luke took his last swig of beer and added, "And the three of you are about as perfect as Wyatt, Mateo, and their brood."

Jack winced.

At the exact same time his heart was finally released from that ribbon she'd twisted it up in earlier, allowing him a full breath.

He grinned. Shook his head. And said, "If ever there was a woman to put me in that frame of mind . . ."

He bit his lip. Tried not to *thoroughly* unravel in front of his younger brother.

But Jack already knew it was too late.

Luke gazed at him as though Jack had been the one to win that poker tournament.

He said, "Jack, I've always admired your commitment to the ranch." His expression turned sincere. "To see you awestruck over a woman . . . that's the sort of reward you should earn for all that you do, bro."

"I don't do all that I do for a reward, Luke."

"Yeah . . . about that." He sat back in his chair and gave Jack a laser-sharp look. "I heard about the sale of the horses."

"Needed to be done."

"And you didn't think to mention that to me when we were on the phone?"

They stared each other down.

Till Luke sat forward, extracted his wallet from his back pocket, flipped it open, and pulled out a slim folded piece of paper. He tossed it onto the table.

Jack snatched up the slip, opened it, folded it back up, and returned it to the decorative tile. He pushed it toward Luke.

"I don't want your money," Jack said.

"It's not really for you to say, Jack. If I wanna give you some of my dividends from my investments, I'm allowed to do so. And no one but you will argue, so you might as well not."

Jack crossed his arms over his chest. "I sold those horses to pay off a loan because it was the sensible, economical thing to do. The finance charges I'm savin' the ranch are enough to give us a better margin than we've seen in years. And I can always get two more horses to train. Though we don't need 'em right now, so I'm savin' there too."

"You do realize the TRIPLE R is my legacy as well?" Luke's jaw worked rigorously.

Jack took a long pull from his beer, draining it. Then he said, "You and Riley both have a forever home there. No fiscal obligation required. You take care of Mom when she's in town, Luke. You make sure her craft booths are set up and her inventory is displayed. You bring food to her so she doesn't have to leave her booth. You pack her up, and you repeat the whole thing the next day or two. You store the pottery she makes in her classes—yes, I know about that. Luke . . . you contribute."

Jack splayed his palms on the table and pushed himself up, leaning toward his brother, for emphasis.

"When Mom's in town," he said, "I don't worry about her. Because of you. Do you know what a huge relief that is? So that I can concentrate on things goin' on at the ranch?"

Luke combed a hand through his hair. Gave a slight nod that wasn't convincing. And told him, "Let's not argue in front of your girlfriend."

Jillian arrived with a new coat of lip gloss and fluffed hair. Her eyes danced from the food and the margarita—maybe even from the company.

Jack attached the leash to Ollie's vest harness and told Luke, "You do you. That's acceptable to all. Don't second-guess that." He reached for his own wallet.

Luke said, "If you even think you're payin' for lunch—"

"Don't be daft. I know you'd never take my money. This is for your staff."

Luke glowered, with humor. "You're too much to live up to, big brother."

"Well, you keep on tryin'." They shook hands again.

Luke guided them back to the entrance minutes before customers would start filing in when he flipped the **OPEN** sign.

To Jillian, Luke said, "You come back anytime. With or without him."

"I do sort of enjoy his camaraderie."

"Seems mutual. Just promise to stop by on your way out of town."

"If you'll fix me a to-go box."

"Consider it done," he avowed.

Jack and Jillian departed. On the stroll back to the truck, she asked Jack, "What offends you when he attempts to help out?"

"You overheard that, huh?"

"Some. Mostly, there's tension between the two of you. It's palpable."

Jack groaned. "Honey, that's family. You get along, you admire and respect, you butt heads."

She gave this some thought, then said, "At the end of the day, you shake and make up?"

"Why wouldn't we?"

Chapter Twelve

Jillian had to take Jack's question to heart.

With her mom, there'd been no shaking hands or hugging it out.

With her dad, there really hadn't been conflicts to rectify.

But Jack lived in that alternate universe she'd distinguished from the beginning. He had numerous relatives. Higher stakes. Differing opinions from time to time.

Yet he had an affinity for taking the highs and the lows in stride.

As they reached the truck and drove back to the ranch, she thought of how crucial it was for him to be an arbitrator as much as he was a leader.

She glanced his way and said, "My tipsiness aside—because that was hands down the best margarita I've ever had—I think you should know that being a soup-to-nuts person is incredibly commendable." She paused. Did a mental rewind. And asked, "Is 'soup to nuts' right? I mean . . . what do the nuts have to do with the soup?"

Jack chuckled. "Soup can be your main course. Sometimes nuts are your last."

"Holy cow! How did I not know that?"

He choked out his next laugh, evidently attempting to stifle it.

"You 'buzzed,' Jilly, is highly entertaining."

"Thank God we don't have a show this afternoon."

"No, but we do have to come up with tomorrow's menu and figure out with Garrett and Tuck how we're gonna factor in the street festival footage."

"Oh, and Jack!" she exclaimed. "Wouldn't it also be fantastic if you joined me on my podcast tomorrow? And Saturday—if you can swing it."

"Jillian, I am all about maximizing our PR ops."

She breathed a sigh of relief. "So am I. Mindy is blowing my mind with analytics I can't process, but seeing that Number One Bestseller banner on my cookbook?" She closed her eyes, trying to keep her composure.

"Pretty fucking amazing?" he asked.

"To the nth degree."

"Look at you quantifyin' with mathematical terms."

Her lids fluttered open. "You can rib me all you want, cowboy. I'm having the best week of my life."

That sentiment lingered between them.

Jillian acknowledged its significance.

So did Jack. No mistaking it.

The silence ensued again.

In her slightly impaired state, Jillian could embrace this entire new existence. Where everything was wonderful, the scenery was glorious, the people were extraordinary.

But she was currently wearing rose-colored glasses that blinded her from her shortcomings—and all those things she'd said to Jack the night before.

Another reality blasted her when they pulled up to the guesthouse and had to stop there because a large truck with a trailer attached was blocking the drive.

Jack parked next to her SUV.

He said, "That's Jim Olsson's team about to load up the horses I sold him. Those wild ones aren't gonna be amenable to the transfer." He gave her a daunting look.

"I understand." She gathered up Ollie and went inside the house.

She paced for a few moments, pondering what this excursion might entail. Then she heard the aggravated neighs and snorts of the horses and the clamoring within the trailer.

She took Ollie into the second bedroom where he lay in his bed while she put on her noise-canceling earphones.

Her clipboards were spread out, and she perused the topics to discern the viable options where she could insert Jack into the narrative. With the endless pepper content she had, she realized it wouldn't be the least bit difficult to include him.

She selected two perfect outlines she could modify to fit in Jack's "grillin', 'cuein', and smokin'," techniques and made ample notes.

Later on, she took Ollie up to the main house and found Jack out on the patio, admiring the manicured event lawns and all the repairs to the pergolas and the furniture. There were some new additions that Jack had mentioned, and they seemed to be progressing nicely.

She came up behind him and wound her arms around his waist, pressing her cheek to his shoulder blade.

"This really is a sensational setting," she said. "The perfect backdrop for your event."

"It's a big enough space too."

"You could host lots of other festivities here," she noted. "For an exorbitant fee, no less."

"Too disruptive, honey. I don't want weddin', birthday, or anniversary parties ruinin' the landscape. Or guests roamin' about."

"Right. This is a working ranch."

"Practical for one big hurrah each year, if this upcoming holiday bash pans out." His hands covered hers that were laced against his abs. "You're still welcome to come back and cohost with me."

"You know my answer to that," she softly replied.

He sighed. "Yeah, I do, darlin'."

He unclenched her hands and turned to her.

Jillian was remorseful as she said, "A couple hundred people, Jack . . . that's much too ambitious for me to tackle this early in my reclamation phase."

"I get it." He kissed her. "Promise I do."

"I'll be watching, though."

He swept strands from her temple and grinned. "That's good enough for me, Jilly."

Her heart melted. Emotion rose in her throat. She spoke around it. "Jack, I'd do more if I could, but—"

"Jillian." He kissed her once more. And murmured against her lips, "You're doin' just fine, in my book."

She held his gaze.

He shot for levity, as usual, whispering, "You didn't even fall for Luke's charm and swagger."

"I'm more a fan of the Jack Reed strut. And I bet you kick the crap out of his fajitas too."

He chuckled. "Honey, that's his pride and joy. I don't even attempt to compete against that. When you devote your life to a specialty, you master it in a way others can't."

"Mm . . . yes. Your brisket."

"Had some of that, did you?"

"Your mom insisted. But more than that . . ." She briefly rolled her eyes skyward. "Everything you pull off a grill or out of an oven is divine."

"The pork was spectacular because of your glaze."

"You cooked it flawlessly."

"You know I'm gettin' hungry, right?"

"Early lunch, early dinner?"

He grinned. "You read my mind."

"Hmm. Not quite so difficult in this instance." She stepped away from him and asked, "What's the plan, cowboy?"

"I have the perfect one."

"You always do." And Jillian adored that about him.

Hell, the entire day was just one more example of how incredible Jack was in every capacity, right down to squaring up with his younger brother so they didn't leave each other with a bad taste in their mouths.

Even when they weren't on the same page, they were still tightly bound. Jillian thought that was exceptional.

She let Jack take her hand and return her to the kitchen where she sat on a stool as he went about his business, assembling whatever he wanted, foodwise.

He packed up a cooler and crooked his finger at her. She and Ollie went through the garage doors with him, and Jack secured the cooler to the rack of an ATV.

She was a little perplexed but didn't say a word.

She trusted Jack.

He retrieved from a shelf a medium-size backpack that was likely one of his nephews'. Rigged it slightly and set Ollie inside, his head popping out of the hole. Jack slung the straps over his broad shoulders so that Ollie nestled against his chest, gazing forward so he could see where they were going.

To Jillian, he said, "Hop on, darlin'."

She couldn't move for a moment.

He had this down pat—how to nudge her just so, not upsetting her emotional balance too much. Also, how to accommodate Ollie and always include him.

There just couldn't be a more considerate cowboy. Man. Friend. Lover.

She shook her head at all the labels.

She didn't have to define him. She didn't have to confine them.

She just had to go along with him and be grateful for every moment.

So she climbed onto the back of the ATV and twined her arms around Jack's midsection, one palm pressed to Ollie to keep him from being jostled.

Jack puttered down the graveled drive and then veered off toward the multitude of outbuildings, skirting them to head into a vast meadow that was breathtaking and led to the river. They approached a huge deck with a tall ramada housing picnic tables. A pier jutted out into the water. More tables were arranged in the grass, along with grills and storage bins.

He halted at the deck and cut the engine. Jillian slipped from her seat and took Ollie. Jack gathered the cooler and directed her up the steps. Then he collected some cushions and other necessities from one of the bins and put a playlist on the sound system.

He told her, "This is our summer escape. The river's widest here, and gentle. Kids can swim. We can fish, stick our toes in the water, whatever. There's a nice breeze through those trees on the opposite shoreline. We can whip up a feast for fifty."

"Fifty?"

"We've got relatives in other states, darlin'. Mateo's and Mom's, primarily. Garrett's too. They come in every year for a July Fourth reunion."

This was a revelation that made her think of all she'd said about him having a wife and kids, the complete package.

This time, however, she didn't say a word. Just let him get one of the grills going. She didn't even know what he'd be putting on the grates, and that was okay.

She could do spontaneity with Jack.

She set a small portion of the main table on the deck and unpacked the rest of the cooler, finding a container of wet dog food someone had apparently picked up on one of their market runs. Jillian's heart swelled.

Jack said, "The potato and pasta salads are compliments of Wyatt—and straight from your cookbook. She was home this afternoon."

There were also condiments.

Jillian ventured, "We're having hamburgers?"

"Oh, darlin' . . . hamburgers." He snickered.

"What new devilry is this, Jack?"

"A little somethin' I worked on after you agreed to come out to Texas. Featuring your own scorpion hybrid."

"Jack, that borders on deliciously dangerous."

"You don't know the half of it."

She squirmed in her seat. "I'm going to be *re*-reworking tomorrow's podcast based on this experience."

"Chances are good, honey. I spent ample time on figurin' out harmonious spices."

She could already smell them smoking up, and that made her stomach growl.

She laughed and said, "Much as I enjoyed those fajitas earlier, I've got drool pooling over the scents wafting our way."

"Sure it's not because of me, darlin'?"

She gave a shrug. "Think what you want, cowboy."

His mouth scrunched with a sardonic expression.

That was pretty much enough to wither her.

He flipped the burgers and added pepper jack slices.

Jillian spared a glance at Ollie. "I'm going to be as melty as that cheese."

Ollie was more interested in his treats.

Jillian told the pup, "If you only understood the level of 'sear' I'm dealing with here."

"Talkin' about me again?" Jack asked as he set the tray of burgers on the table.

"I'm certain you know where I'm going with these thoughts."

His grin was a cocky one. "Indeed, I do."

He sat across from her and Ollie. Jillian plopped a generous spoonful of each salad onto Jack's plate and passed it to him as he handed her a plate with a fully loaded burger. Oozing her hot sauce along the sides.

"Holy hell . . . ," she murmured. "Diablo burger all the way."

The aroma was as evocative as the man sitting opposite her.

She eyed him. Eyed the burger. Eyed him once more.

Jack chuckled.

"This is going to be crazy-wicked," she surmised.

"Too crazy-wicked."

"I don't believe I need that extreme, and yet . . . I'll be disappointed if you don't deliver, cowboy."

"Oh, I'll deliver, honey. Don't you doubt that for a second."

"No doubting. At. All."

She bit into the huge sandwich. Moaned. Savored. Then bit in again. Despite the scorching sensation burning through her.

"I'll assume you won't be uttering another word for the next half hour."

"At least," she confirmed with a full mouth.

She sampled the salads and sipped the wine Jack poured, quelling some of the heat but leaving behind the fiery flavor that lit her from head to toe.

When they'd demolished their meal and cleaned up, Jack took her hand and led her to the wooden swing at the river's edge, cozying himself into the corner with her leaning against him. Ollie found a space on the far end.

They stared out at the glittering colors on the placid water and the blazing sunset as it dipped below the horizon.

"It's so peaceful here," she mused.

"Sometimes, it's all you need."

"You're right about that."

They paused again, with myriad thoughts on their minds.

Until the sky darkened, and the stars twinkled.

"As usual, you've set one hell of a scene, Jack."

"Just wanted you to see the sights, darlin'."

"As beautiful as all the others on your sliver of paradise."

"We capitalize on what we've been given," he told her.

"Clever to do so."

After they packed back up, Jack returned them to the house. They unloaded in the kitchen. Then he wound an arm around her waist and guided her to the stairs. He glanced down at her. She nodded her acquiescence.

Jack picked up the dog, and they crested the second floor and continued on to the third.

He said, "I have this whole level to myself."

She didn't miss the doors they passed as they rounded to the far corner. It wasn't a stretch to assume these rooms were meant for his kids.

She let that thought dissipate, for both their sakes.

Though it seeped into her psyche once more as they entered Jack's spacious suite. His large bed faced a wall of tall windows that looked out on the vast property. There were seating areas and a desk with his laptop resting on it. At the far end of the room, a massive fireplace filled the corner. It was trimmed in river rock and featured a thick mantel, with a flat-screen mounted above. More windows decorated the wall and led beyond the sleeping area to a hallway.

Jillian poked her head around that bend and found opened doors to a cavernous bathroom and a dressing room.

She glanced back at Jack. "You've got the penthouse here."

"Wyatt's is bigger than mine. Mom's is even bigger."

Her brows raised. "I'm thinking my living room and kitchen would fit in here."

"Well, the suites are meant for privacy—and family time."

"Or for you . . ." She eyed the desk. "Work."

"Sometimes it's nice to not be interrupted."

"I get it."

She helped Ollie onto one of the sofas while Jack flipped the switch for the hearth.

He even had a wet bar, and he set the dog up with water and popped the cork on a split of champagne for him and Jillian.

"We haven't properly celebrated our successes," he said as he handed her a glass and tapped his rim to hers.

"Really, Jack . . ." Her gaze swept the room. "This is like a five-star experience."

"My ancestors have added on just about every generation. Knocked down some walls when necessary, so they could all spread out."

"Your own village." She'd considered that when she'd seen the formal dining room for the first time.

"Well, we're way out of town, and the majority of our time is spent tendin' to the ranch, so it helps to have all the bells and whistles we can afford, all the conveniences at our disposal."

"At the end of a long, hard day, you don't want to be skimping on comfort."

"Definitely not."

They clinked rims again and sipped their drinks in front of the fire. Interestingly, the sight of flames hadn't been a monumental issue for Jillian to overcome during her therapy. She'd only witnessed the initial eruption of them around the stage, and then she'd been facedown until the rugby guys had rescued her. It was the screaming and tromping crowd, the physical pain, and the "every man for himself" mentality that had manifested itself within her. Followed by the emotional gutting when Scott abandoned her. She'd lost more than him, though.

A shudder ran through her. Jillian shook it off. Took a deeper drink and tried to relax.

Jack retrieved his tablet from his desk, then rejoined her on the sofa. He opened her cookbook.

She laughed, chasing away her previous melancholy. "You downloaded this?"

"Of course. I've gone through every page. Impressive offerin's, Jilly."

"Speaking of . . . more leafy greens and veggies in your diet, and a little less red meat, would be very healthy, Jack. And alleviate some of your mother's worry."

"Teamin' up on me, darlin'?"

"Just sayin'."

"I hear ya. Don't go expectin' me to swap breakfast for green smoothies, though. I'd wither away before I even made it to lunch."

"I do understand you're burning plenty of calories in your everyday life. Just suggesting some modifications. Like more fish and chicken."

"Then why don't we maintain the Mexican theme that'll be featured at the festival tomorrow and make shredded chicken tamales with tomatillo verde salsa, chicken empanadas with jalapeño poppers as the fillin', and grilled fish tacos."

"Baja sauce and a spicy avocado salsa for the latter."

He moved through a few pages on screen and added, "Black beans, rice, and Mexican street corn salad for sides."

"Plus fresh pico de gallo."

Jack flipped the cover closed on his tablet and set it aside. He gazed at Jillian and said, "You realize we're instigatin' a cook-off with Luke and Avery."

She beamed. "Mission accepted."

"And you know Avery'll make his chopped salad, right? Since you'd brought it up."

"Have faith in my street corn salad, Jack. Fully loaded with a swift kick in the behind."

He grinned, his blue eyes sparkling. So that she had to fan her face.

He said, "I do like a challenge."

"All right, then. Game on."

"Cheers to that." They polished off their flutes.

Jillian yawned, and Jack said, "How fortunate it is that I have a comfortable California king just yonder." He hitched his thumb over his shoulder.

"Is that why you brought me up here?" she teased.

His tone turned serious as he said, "I want you in my bed, Jilly."

Words that made her stomach and her heart flutter.

She slid her hand into his, and he tugged gently, helping her to her feet.

Ollie was fast asleep and didn't even stir as Jillian walked away. Demonstrating he trusted in Jack as well.

He peeled back the lightweight bronze-colored duvet. The sheets were a sateen cream. A masculine palette to go with the dark-brown leather furniture and the framed Western paintings, mostly of wild horses.

Jack was out of his shirt and belt in a flash, laying them on the bench at the foot of the bed.

Jillian's gaze flitted over him, the corners of her mouth curving upward.

He said, "It's okay to just take it in, honey. I'll wait."

"If you're going to put on a show, cowboy," she sassily told him, "then let's see *all* the goods."

"You should be ashamed of yourself, darlin', eyeing me as though I'm a juicy rack of lamb."

"Oh, Jack! What a fabulous suggestion for Saturday's segment!"

He grimaced. "Honey, I get that our daily focus is on food, but at night . . . I'd prefer to be the only thing occupyin' your mind. I mean, other than the dog."

"Who had a very yummy meal, thanks to someone in your household."

"I believe that was Ale's request to Mom, to make sure the pup doesn't go hungry when he's here with us—with the hopes that he'll be here with us a lot while you're visitin'."

"I have to say, the Reed-Martinez hybrids possess the best of both genes. He and Hunt are wonderful."

"They're a handful in a manageable way. Not even capable of bein' troublemakers. But . . . why are we discussing them when I could be takin' your clothes off right this very second?"

"Rabbit holes," she said by way of an apology. Then gasped. "Jack! Rabbit as an appetizer! With a chili-cumin rub!"

"Darlin', you make my head spin."

"Okay, I'll stop. But don't forget about the rack of lamb."

He moved in close and pushed the sweater over her shoulders and down her arms. "Honey, I'm about to forget my own name."

He added her clothes to his current pile. Then finished the job he'd started on himself, toeing off his boots and discarding everything else.

He turned Jillian around so he stood behind her. She twisted her hair into a loose knot, high up and out of the way, for whatever he had in mind. His warm breaths caressed her skin while his fingers glided along her outer thighs to her hips. His hands settled at her waist as he left soft kisses on her nape. Exhilaration cascaded down her spine.

"That's a sweet spot, Jack," she whispered on a quavering breath.

"Happy to have discovered it, Jilly."

"I'm quite pleased as well."

He laughed, and that blew another faint stream that made her tingle.

"Jesus," she mumbled. "I'm about to become a live wire."

"That is the intent."

His hands skimmed upward and cupped her breasts, kneading as his mouth continued to wreak havoc on that new erogenous zone, alternating between tender kisses and the flickering of the tip of his tongue.

The restlessness he incited returned full force. She gripped his hips behind her and wiggled her ass against him, eliciting a low growl.

"You grindin' on me leads to all kinds of dirty thoughts," he muttered in a strained tone.

"The dirtier the better," she prompted.

"How you provoke me, woman."

"I know you're capable of following through."

One of his hands skated down the front of her, and the pads of his fingers brushed over her slick folds, making her pulse jump.

His strokes were slow and tantalizing.

"Mm, already wet for me," he said.

"Hard not to be."

"Speaking of things that are hard . . ."

She wedged a hand between them and fisted his cock, pumping in taunting measures.

"Yeah, that's gonna get you laid, honey."

"Joint goal, right?"

"It's all I can think of."

Two of his fingers slipped inside her and massaged with a hint of insistency.

"You do enjoy getting me off," she said.

"Over and over."

The heel of his hand rubbed her clit, and Jillian was damn certain he'd achieve his objective in record time.

Especially when he changed up their positioning, withdrawing from her and easing her toward the bed so she placed a knee on the edge. He directed her to do the same with the other knee, and then he grabbed a large pillow and placed it before her, quirking a brow.

She went down on all fours, excitement shimmying through her.

Jack knelt behind her and spread her cheeks. His tongue whisked over her folds, and her breaths quickened. She needed the pillow to keep her angled just right but also for support as tremors shot through her.

Jack took a more aggressive approach than the last time he went down on her, bypassing the initial teasing and getting right to business, his tongue licking, his mouth suckling.

Jillian's eyelids drifted closed. She gave herself over to the sensations he sparked and anticipated the mounting tension he evoked.

"Jack," she said on a fractured breath. "More."

He drew the pearl of nerves against his teeth, and she let out a small cry. He soothed the electrical jolt with his tongue. Then his lips swept over hers, and Jillian felt herself creeping closer to that sinful precipice, so ready to fall over.

Jack didn't relent. He kept her open to him as his tongue swirled around her opening and then dipped inside.

He licked her folds again.

Suckled her clit. Deep. So very deep.

"Jack!" she called out.

And shattered.

Chapter Thirteen

"Goddamn, woman," Jack said on a sharp groan. "I could do that to you mornin', noon, and night."

She let out a wispy laugh. "I'd be glowing brighter than the Texas sun, cowboy."

"Your compliments are really comin' along, Jilly."

"Not the only thing coming, Jack."

"Yeah, about that . . ."

He stood with a slight grunt.

She mustered the strength to glance over her shoulder at him. No easy feat, given the way her body vibrated.

Jack's muscles were rigid, his erection, thick and full.

"Now there's a mouthwatering feast," she mused.

"For another time," he told her. "'Cuz I know exactly what I want to do to you, Jillian. I don't need to be sidetracked."

His fingers curled around his cock, his hand stroking.

"Don't think you need more wrangling to get the job done, cowboy."

"Just enjoyin' the visual of you with your ass in the air."

She bowed her spine and raised her hips farther, providing ample access.

He palmed her cheeks again, giving them a scintillating squeeze. Then his tip nudged her opening, and Jillian braced herself for the wild ride he was about to take her on.

He pressed into her, an inch at a time, letting her assimilate to his girth.

Her breaths turned to shallow pants. Her nipples tightened.

"Jack," she urged. "Don't take too much time. The suspense is plain cruel."

"We've established you're my undoin', right? I don't want to be that guy who loses it two seconds in."

She ignored the comment and pushed back with her pelvis, effectively driving him into her.

She cried out once more, as the rush of adrenaline rode a fiery wave of excitement.

Jack practically roared in response to the immediate sheathing of his cock.

Then he pumped with a steady tempo.

"Like that, Jack. Oh, my God, just like that."

He placed his knee alongside hers for leverage. Twined an arm around her waist to keep her stable. Increased the pace.

"Yes, Jack," she whimpered. "Fuck me."

Jillian wanted all of him. She wanted him hammering into her, making her crazed with lust, pushing her to that edge again.

He caved to her whim.

Jillian gripped the pillow. Buried her face in it to keep from doing what she'd suggested at the guesthouse—shaking the rafters. Still, her stifled moans filled the suite.

Jack's free hand shifted around to her front, and he rubbed that knot of nerves with the pads of two fingers, sending her barreling toward climax.

"Jesus, Jillian," he said as her inner walls clenched him.

Jillian had no control over the involuntary reflexes.

And as Jack hit that sensitive spot within her, and his thrusts were deeper and deeper, she didn't hold on to her composure. She let him push her over that taunting precipice.

Her head snapped up. "Jack!"

The explosive release was intensified when his body stiffened, then convulsed.

He surged inside her, filling her with liquid heat and keeping the tremors moving through her.

"Jillian," he said on a harsh breath. "Fuck . . ."

She wasn't the only one trembling.

His torso almost curled around her, like he needed *her* to steady *him*.

Jillian's pussy contracted, holding him in a vise grip—and Jack's body jolted.

"You're killin' me, darlin'," he panted.

"Just don't move for a minute," she pleaded, loving his hot skin on hers, absorbing the shock waves emitting from him and echoing within her. Not to mention how he clung to her while also keeping her from collapsing.

His mouth was next to her ear, and he whispered, "Thank God I recover quickly."

An enticing thrill rippled through her. "I do look forward to that."

Eventually, he unraveled from her, seeming reluctant to do so.

He flopped onto his back on the mattress. His eyes shut briefly. Then he gazed at her, as she snuggled into the oversize pillow, staring at him.

He grinned. Ran his knuckles along her upper arm. And said, "You just keep the juices flowin', darlin'. I swear there's magma runnin' through my veins."

"So round two will commence soon."

"Think we'll make it to the seventh-inning stretch tonight."

She laughed. "You do realize I'm limp and boneless—and my inner thighs feel as though I've done a marathon workout this week."

"Little sore?"

"A lot sore. But . . . well worth it."

He rolled toward her. "Serious question. You're not afraid of me bein' pressed up next to you?"

"At first, I thought I might be. But it's not the same with you, Jack. It's not like being on those steps in the auditorium and feeling immobilized. Not to mention . . ."

"Yes?" His gaze turned more expectant.

"I'm well aware you're only trying to get closer to me. And I want that too."

He kissed the tip of her nose. And murmured, "I'd never hurt you. Not purposely, Jilly."

She waited for the consternation to swell within her. It didn't—because she knew Jack spoke the truth.

"Cowboy, you don't have to convince me of a damn thing. Your heart is as pure as they come."

He nodded.

She added, "If ever there was a truer Prince Charming, I'd be shocked."

"Don't go knightin' me, Jilly. Not when my still-dirty thoughts are focused on our next go-round."

She smiled and said, "You can be all-encompassing, even in bed, Jack. Soup to nuts."

"Don't make me hungry again."

She pushed him onto his back and straddled his lap. "No time for food. I'm ready for you."

◆　◆　◆

Jack was the first to wake the next morning. He texted Wyatt, asking her to bring a change of clothes for Jillian and a new toothbrush to his suite.

She replied with a wink emoji.

He didn't bother explaining the circumstances. No point to that, right?

As Jillian showered, Jack collected the tote Wyatt had assembled, leaning against his doorframe, taking her ribbing for a minute or two.

Then he said, "I'll be down shortly. Once everyone's in the kitchen, I'll text Jillian that the coast is clear, and she can stroll in like she just came from the guesthouse."

"Got this all figured out, do ya?"

"Thinkin' she's not interested in the walk of shame."

"Not much shame to it when everyone can see how into each other you are. Even Hunt's sulkin', he's so on to you guys."

"He'll get over it."

Wyatt pinned Jack with a solemn look and asked, "Will you?"

He groaned. Rubbed his nape. And said, "No tellin'. But here's the thing." He drew in a long breath. Let it out slowly.

His sister's gaze narrowed with curiosity—and concern.

"I get one week with her. Out of the blue. That's somethin', Wyatt. That's . . . so much."

"One week is enough, Jack?" she asked, incredulous.

"It's more than I'd ever expected after I left SPU. It's more time than I've wanted to spend with any other woman in this capacity."

"Thanks for sparin' my feelings. And Mom's."

He gave her an exasperated look.

"I get it, okay. I was just jokin'." She placed a hand on his arm. "Jack, it's fantastic that you've reunited with your deep infatuation. But . . . can't this be more than the cryptic one-week affair you're making it out to be?"

"Wyatt." He stared intently at her. "Not every 'affair' is meant to be everlastin'. And don't go spoilin' my next few days."

She threw her arms around him. Hugged him tight. Then stepped back.

"Totally not spoilin' anything, Jack. We'll see you both downstairs."

She turned away. Though not before Jack caught the watery glint in her eyes.

Christ.

This reunion with Jillian was turning his family inside out.

How was that even possible?

He was the one suffering the consequences of bringing her here.

But just like him, his family was gelling with her and vice versa. She melded with the dynamic. And everyone had caught on to how he and Jillian meshed in a more romantic vein.

Jack grimaced. Then took the tote into the bathroom as Jillian was emerging from the shower.

Naked. Naturally.

Everything within him seized up. In a heartbeat.

She stood on the bath mat and asked, "Maybe a towel would be helpful here?"

He shook his head. "Nope. Not at all."

"I'm just supposed to drip dry?"

"I could lick the drops from your body. If you'd like."

"Well, that's one option . . ." She gave him a saucy look. "Do we have time for that?"

He debated this for a moment or two.

"I know the answer to that, cowboy."

"Interestingly . . . I don't. I mean . . . there's cereal and fruit. Oatmeal. Do I really have to feed everyone every single mornin'?"

She held his gaze. "How would you feel if you didn't?"

His jaw worked as he considered this. Then he said, "Like I wasn't fulfillin' all my obligations."

"And how would *they* feel . . . ?"

He got her point. "That I took a break and proved they could fend for themselves."

"That's a poignant revelation." She crossed to the rack of towels and wrapped up in one. "However, knowing how important it is that you start your day in this way, I'll get dressed and wait for your signal before I show myself."

She went to the long vanity and rifled through the bag Wyatt had provided.

Jack folded his arms over his chest. "You can concede, just like that?"

"Jack." She gave him an earnest look over her shoulder. "It's not only about how your family might depend on you to offer specific things; it's about you *wanting* to offer these specific things. Could your family survive without you for a meal or two? Absolutely. They're more than capable. But . . . do they know how much you love being the provider?"

She faced him and stared deeper into his eyes.

"Yes, they do, Jack. This is who you are. And this is why . . . this is part of why . . . this is . . ." Tears suddenly tumbled down her cheeks.

"Say it, Jilly," he urged. Not pressing in on her, just . . . giving her the space, the opportunity, to confess what he thought she felt. What he was convinced of, in his soul.

She didn't retreat from this. Merely faltered.

She sucked in a breath. Leveled her gaze again. And said, "All of this—everything about you—is one thousand percent why I'm in love with you, Jack Reed."

"And that's exactly why you should stay, Jillian," he asserted.

"No, Jack. It's not." She reached for tissues. Dabbed her eyes. Blew her nose. Turned away. Though she captured his gaze in the reflection of the mirror. "Being in love doesn't solve the world's problems, cowboy."

"I don't give a shit about the world's problems, Jillian," he said. Then he scowled. And amended, "I mean, I fuckin' do. But in this particular silo, I only care about what's happenin' between us. Knowin' full well that my family can figure out life without me for one breakfast . . . or more. Of course for more. It's just that—"

"Jack." She whirled around and moved toward him, splaying her palms against his pecs. "Listen to yourself, chasing your tail. There's no denying your family can fill in the gaps. But it's your desire and your *need* to do what's right by your good conscience, by your inherited place in this family, by your own passion, to check all the boxes. To be this man everyone can count on."

It'd been his dad's way. His grandfather's way. And so on.

More than that, Jack really did embrace this lifestyle.

The crux of his problem with Jillian, he now realized.

He couldn't abandon his world to join hers.

Not ever.

It was simply impossible. Jillian knew that too. He believed that wholeheartedly.

Which presented the other heavy dread—not abandoning his world meant he was abandoning *her*.

And for fuck's sake. Hadn't she had enough of that?

Yet . . . in Jillian's fashion that had emerged in such a valiant manner, she kissed Jack and said, "Right now, we can have breakfast. We have a show to produce. And Jack . . . we have more days together."

It wasn't the solution he sought.

But it was a temporary salve to the sting.

He said, "Dry your hair, honey. I'll check my emails. Then I'll go downstairs and text you when everyone's in the kitchen."

He turned to walk away.

"Cowboy?"

The splinter in her voice nearly shredded him.

But he bucked up. Glanced over his shoulder. And grinned. "Yeah, darlin'?"

"We might not have stars perfectly aligned for the long run. But I can accept how we feel about each other today."

His gaze held hers.

He asked, "What if I said I feel the same. All the way around?"

"Still doesn't change our situation. But . . . for now . . ."

"We're livin' in the moment?"

She pulled in a breath. Nodded. And said, "Living in the moment."

Jillian got ready and awaited Jack's signal so that she came through the living room and into the kitchen without it being overly evident she'd taken the stairs from the third floor.

The cleanup was nearly done. Wyatt corralled her boys and ushered them toward the door, though not before Hunter commented, "Hey, my mom has a shirt just like that."

Jillian cringed on the inside but didn't miss a beat. "She has very good taste."

Wyatt winked. Jillian stifled a laugh.

Brett went into town with Wyatt and the kids to set up her booth. The men had places to be. As Jillian finished the few leftover chores, Jack made omelets.

They settled at the table, and she said, "I'm fine with going to the farmers' market. Everyone's super busy, and with the festival starting today, the market shouldn't be overrun, right?"

"Most of the vendors maintain their regular booths to accommodate customers who don't want the hassle of navigating a street fair to get to them."

"Cool. After that, we have the podcast. Then we'll figure out our winning strategy against Luke and Avery."

Jack said, "Almost feels like old times with my dad. Avery and his father hit the circuit with us in the beginning, and it was always a head-to-head battle."

"Where's your uncle now?" Jillian asked before biting into her tasty omelet.

Jack also chewed, swallowed. Took his time replying.

"Jack?"

His sudden tension was notable.

"Well, darlin'. Avery and Chance's father is . . . to be blunt . . . an absolute asshole." He blew out a breath. "No other way to say it."

"How, exactly?" she asked.

"My uncle put this ranch in jeopardy when he and my dad butted heads on some financial issues."

She glanced up from her plate. "That sounds a little too Jack and Luke—"

"No, honey, Jack and Luke are nothin' compared to Caleb and Royce. And, primarily, this was an issue of the embezzlement of funds. By Uncle Caleb, to be clear."

"Oh, holy fuck."

"Yeah. Anyway, more than that, my uncle has a bad temper. Violently so. And a drinkin' problem. That caused Avery plenty of trouble on the circuit. Till he had to flat-out quit so that he didn't get pulled into the shitshow his dad created for himself. Avery could have lost his reputation altogether . . . if he didn't sever the ties."

"That sounds ominous."

"It's actually worse than that."

Jack didn't say anything more, though.

Jillian didn't prod.

Yet she certainly felt a stab of pain over Avery's misfortune. She took solace, however, in the way he'd protected and preserved something that meant so much to him—his excellent standing in the BBQ community. He was a huge asset to the ranch as well, and Jillian was glad Jack could rely on him.

They finished their breakfast, washed their dishes, and then went to the guesthouse to record their impromptu podcast. Then Jillian stuck with her commitment to accompany him to the farmers' market.

Jack had the process down to a science. And while there were vendors who gushed over him—and even wanted autographs from him and Jillian—it wasn't overbearing. She breathed almost normally for the hour they were there.

They returned to the ranch and prepped. Jack got Luke and Avery on a video call to loop them in on the menu he and Jillian were working on.

The first thing Luke said when he connected the call was, "You're lookin' mighty pretty today, Miss Jillian."

"Thank you, Luke."

"Ditto," Avery said. "Think Wyatt's got a shirt like that."

She hadn't changed yet.

"Guess we shop at the same store." A lame excuse. She hadn't seen a chain boutique when she'd been downtown with Jack the day before.

Jack bulldozed right through that awkward moment, saying, "Jillian and I are gonna be cooking up a feast over here to complement your booth fixin's. Thought we'd let y'all know that Ale's gonna put up a poll for what looks most appetizin'."

Luke erupted with laughter.

Avery pointed out, "You do realize that everyone here will be smellin' these fajitas and everything else we're grillin' up—also tastin' 'em?"

"Yeah, but Jillian's got the advantage on presentation."

Luke finally came around. "Oh, this is just easy pickin's. No offense, Miss Jillian."

"None taken. It's a little something extra for the viewers, and it might drive more sales for your cantina."

"You bet it will," Luke agreed. "Consider the gauntlet dropped."

He gave a wicked grin, and Jillian could absolutely see how this augmentation would garner more subscribers for Jack—and likely more orders for her.

They disconnected and continued their work, Jillian feeling a spike in excitement with this competition and knowing Jack was getting into it too. He was more than just a showman—he delivered on the perfect execution and exhibition of food, as much as on the flavorings.

She only wished she had some of her hybrid peppers on hand, to replace the jalapeño popper addition to the empanada. She used jalapeños frequently, but they weren't nearly as edgy as one of her specialty chilies.

And while her thoughts ran in that direction, she whipped out her phone to check on her greenhouse.

"Whatcha got there, honey?" Jack asked as he glanced at her.

"All my gardens, in quadrants, monitored by cameras and an app that helps me to maintain growing conditions remotely." She showed him. Then she said, "I can adjust the lighting and the irrigation. See this section here?" She tapped the screen to maximize that neatly arranged square. "These peppers require less moisture and more sunlight. My numbers indicate we're off balance—as does the texture of the leaves."

Jillian made adjustments that were in real time.

Jack whistled. "Fancy."

"I tend to the plants throughout the day, but they can go up to a couple weeks without gardening, as long as my app's working properly. Difficulty is, I've cultivated them at different intervals so . . . these here," she said as she pulled up another quadrant, "are close to needing harvesting. Really close."

They shared a look.

He nodded. "I hear ya, darlin'."

The sand was running out of their hourglass. Jillian couldn't let her crops go to waste. Especially when she was in desperate need of batching more sauces and rubs to complete orders that were paid for, due to this venture.

A trace of anxiety made her fingers tremble. She put the cell back in her pocket.

"Anyway," she continued, striving for a calm voice, "it's advantageous to have the ability to immediately correct any variances so none of my levels remain off long enough to cause mass destruction."

"That would be a damn shame," Jack said, deep in thought. Because he grasped the criticality of safeguarding her infrastructure—and how important her labor of love was, in general.

While he left to get the smoker ready for the chicken, Jillian made the Baja sauce and the spicy avocado salsa. She also scrolled through her mental database of recipes for a solution to elevating the heat of the empanadas.

The moment Jack came through the opened patio doors, lightning struck.

In multiple ways.

First . . . geez, the man was so broad and tall and gorgeous. And this challenge with his brother and cousin seemed to have him supercharged, because his eyes were flaming with mischief and anticipation.

Jillian lost her train of thought.

One corner of Jack's mouth quirked. "You never fail to peg me with a look that suggests we forget cookin' and go get naked."

"'That's not exactly *not* on my mind," she admitted. "But I just came up with a surefire way to stack the odds in our favor this afternoon. Granted, it's going to take a bit of time to pull off, and I'll have to raid your spice rack and pantry—also ascertain what I've got tucked away in the kit I brought from home."

"I am all ears," he said as he turned a stool lengthwise and straddled it.

"What you are is all kinds of tempting, Jack Reed." She let out a sigh.

His expression turned expectant. "Much as I enjoy knowing I turn you on, honey, you're leaving me in suspense over your latest idea."

"My latest . . . oh, right!"

Christ, she was fixated on that wide chest of his and those powerful thighs.

But they had so much to do.

She said, "I want the empanada filling to be chicken mole. A velvety, decadent mole that melts on your tongue, oozes down your throat, warms your belly. Then gives you a burst of peppery fireworks."

"I'm all for that—an awesome twist. However . . . Jilly, an authentic mole has like thirty ingredients."

"Yes, that's true." Though she was undeterred. "The majority need to be spot on, not substitutes. But I have a few tricks up my sleeve. A fabulous recipe my dad taught me. Authentic, with the right umph to it. And I'm guessing with your gourmet palate, Jack, you're going to have precisely the enhancements we need."

"You're welcome to anythin' and everythin'," he told her. "You know that includes me, right?" He winked.

"Save that delicious notion for later. The mole requires my full concentration."

"Then I'll get rollin' with the pico de gallo. I like it to chill awhile so the diced tomatoes, onions, and cilantro blend with the lime juice."

She clapped her hands together. "Let's do this!"

Jillian was revved. And relieved she had her spice kit with her. She also attacked the pantry, having the very distinct feeling she was going to find the one key ingredient she wanted the most.

Lo and behold, there it was in a bin of treats—Mexican chocolate.

"Holy hell," she murmured, a thrill cascading down her spine. "Now we're talking."

She gathered up what she could, then went back for more, also searching the veggie crisper in the fridge.

Jack eyed her with that devilish combination in his glowing irises that he'd had when he'd walked in on her epiphany.

Jillian couldn't ignore the spark in her core—or the way it spread outward, upward, downward. So that her stomach fluttered, her heart-beats picked up, and her clit tingled.

Such an inopportune time to get all lit up!

"I must resist the allure of Jack Reed," she said. "Crucial recipe to concoct here. Can't miss a step."

Jack chuckled. "I do like how you don't bother denyin' I get you goin', darlin'."

"It is truly a wonder I've gotten anything done since arriving on this ranch."

"Long as you're doin' me, I've got no complaints."

She shook her head. "I'll never accomplish this sauce if you keep saying things like that, Jack."

"Something tells me you can do this in your sleep."

"It is one of my favorites."

Knowing her way around this kitchen now, she quickly located all the accessories she needed and dedicated herself to sweating onions and hydrating dried spices.

Jack prepped two chickens with rubs that were going to smell divine as the poultry smoked for several hours. The meat would fall off the bone and be a breeze to shred with BBQ claws.

Jillian was tempted to add chicken tortilla/enchilada soup to the menu, but the mole was pretty ambitious—and time was of the essence. They also had tamales and fish tacos to make. Not to mention the tomatillo verde salsa.

Her pulse raced.

She asked Jack, "Is Luke going to step up his game with shrimp for the fajitas?"

"You know it. Barbacoa too. And, shoot . . . I gave Avery your Hotter Than Haba's smoky chipotle meco chili powder after I featured it on my show."

She made a face. "Damn it."

"No worries." He tried to smooth that over. "It's just fajitas."

Now she groaned. "I've tasted those fajitas, cowboy. They are not for the faint of heart. Truly a masterpiece."

"Against a thirty-ingredient mole?"

"Well, we do have a secret weapon." She held up the bar of chocolate.

"Oh, boy. Hunt hears you snagged his chocolate, and I swear the crush'll be over before you can even tell him you'll buy him a new one. That's akin to gold in the kid's mind."

"It's a sacrifice I'm willing to make. We'll distract him with ice cream or something."

"You don't quite comprehend his personal love affair with that particular treat."

"I'll get him a lifetime supply."

She continued on while Jack snickered.

Considering they'd be sharing this extensive meal with the family, they made extra. Jillian barely had a chance to get back to the guesthouse to change and primp for the show.

Mateo brought home Hunt, and they joined in the kitchen. Neither Jillian nor Jack made note of how Hunt had unwittingly taken one for the team. He was too busy helping Jillian gather everything from the fridge. Jack came in from the patio with a baking sheet holding the chickens. He tented foil over them and followed Jillian's directions on what would be served on which plate or in which bowl so that he didn't mess up her presentation.

When they were live, Jack announced the impromptu cook-off, and then Garrett provided a split screen for Ale's feed from the festival. Jack and Jillian saw this on the second laptop, turned toward them so they could view the monitor.

Jillian winced. Luke and Avery had a grated grill loaded with meat and the right height of flames beneath it. They also had a flat grill for the onions and peppers. All of which smoked and sizzled and snapped. She could almost smell the fragrant veggies and her meco rub.

Son. Of. A. Bitch.

"Y'all look as though you're about to burn the booth to the ground," Jack joked, in a vain attempt to detract from the operation the two men had mastered.

"Not a chance, Jack," Luke lobbed back. "We are nothin' but pure precision—and damn temptin'. I'm not just talkin' about the fajitas." He winked.

Score one for the festival cooks.

"You're gonna have to put extra effort into flirtin' with my audience," Jack told him. "They're loyal—and I have a special treat for everyone."

Jack revealed the chickens that not only had the perfect crisp to the skins but also gave off a smoky aroma that filled the kitchen and made Jillian's stomach rumble.

"Those are beautiful, Jack," she commended him. Then she turned to the camera. "I believe we have a war of the spices happening here, folks."

Jack shared his process, then carved a chicken to get to the juicy inside. He sampled a sliver and nodded. "This is perfect on its own, but we're gonna use this bird for other dishes."

Jillian explained the menu. Then the feed returned to the festival.

Avery said, "I'll admit that anything Jack puts in an offset will come out tasty. But just look at this barbacoa."

Ale zoomed in.

The beef had a beautiful char and a tender pink inside.

"Yeah, that's the jam," Jack agreed. "But Jillian's gonna do you one better. She made mole."

"Ah, come on!" Luke feigned pain in his heart with a hand over his chest. "No one mentioned that this mornin'!"

"Just popped into my head," she casually said. Though that was a serious understatement. "And you've never seen nor tasted a richer mole, guaranteed."

She dipped a spoon into the sauce, held it up in the air, tilted the utensil, and let the chocolaty goodness flow back into the bowl.

"We didn't assign any sort of stakes, did we?" Avery asked. "'Cuz even I'm eatin' the heck out whatever's left over when I get back to the ranch."

"You wound me, you do," Luke told his cousin. "Defectin' already? I haven't even put the prawns on yet. Yes, y'all heard correctly—jumbo ones at that, seasoned to perfection."

The competition heated up from there, with Luke and Avery pulling some rabbits from their collective hat to combat every offering by Jack and Jillian.

Mindy was on Jillian's phone, attached to the tripod, and she was all but dancing in her chair and giving air-kisses like nothing Jillian had ever seen before.

Jillian's laughter seemed to spawn more love emoji that Mindy indicated.

And when Jillian and Jack smashed together over a bowl of the Baja sauce that splattered on both their shirts, she was certain they'd win Ale's poll, hands down. Regardless of Luke and Avery blowing up the screen with their magnetism.

The show wrapped on high notes and the promise of secret variations to Jillian's recipes in her exclusive newsletter, not the free one. Fingers crossed those subscriber numbers would soar.

Jack finished shredding chicken and piled the meat onto a separate plate for soft tacos with Jillian's hot sauces available. They all dove in at the island, once again not bothering to move to the dining room—or even the breakfast table.

"Y'all don't forget to save some for Wyatt and Ale. Mom'll eat Luke's food before Avery brings her home."

Chance and Mateo strolled in.

"Ah, just in time." Chance rubbed his hands together.

Jillian was delighted over all the compliments, and Mindy stayed on the line for a while, previewing Ale's social media snippets and giving status updates on his poll.

"Honestly, I figured the female contingent would skew the results toward the two guys," Mindy said, "but you're neck and neck."

"Maybe we're making an assumption on the demographic as a whole," Jillian pondered. "Beyond that, variety truly might be the spice of life, given the array of dishes Jack and I presented."

"Excellent points, Jillian," Wyatt said as she and Ale joined in. They commanded the commentary with Mindy, centered on the survey.

Suddenly, Ale declared, "You're pullin' ahead, Uncle Jack!" He bounced in his seat and flashed his screen to everyone nearby.

Jillian was on her own springs while she cleaned up, delighted by the positive vibes.

Wyatt joined her.

"I owe Hunt his special chocolate," Jillian said. "If you can tell me where to pick it up, I'll have a stash returned to the pantry before he notices the last bar is gone."

"Don't even worry about it. I have an entire box hidden behind a bag of dehydrated prunes, knowing he'd never in the history of ever reach for that bag and discover the loot."

Jillian laughed. "Clever of you. Also . . . I washed your clothes. They're in my tote. Thanks for the loaners."

"Anytime," Wyatt said with a twinkle in her eyes. "No one minds Jack's lady friend sneaking around the house the mornin' after. 'Cept Hunt. But he wouldn't get it, so. Moot."

Jillian waited for her cheeks to flush.

Didn't happen.

Interesting.

She told Wyatt, "I appreciate the discretion, anyway. Now how's your mom doing with her pottery?"

"Luke had to bust open the storage unit to get a dozen more pots and vases. Some dishes as well. Last I saw when we checked on her before leavin', she was runnin' low on that inventory too. And taking fistfuls of cash with a big smile on her face."

"That's incredible. I'm happy for her."

"She told me about your online store idea. After this weekend, I'm convinced she'll be all in."

Jillian said, "Doesn't make sense for her to have all those beautiful pieces locked up where no one sees them."

"Agreed. So I'll create a website, and we'll get her in business."

They shook hands.

Wyatt more seriously added, "You do know you're a breath of fresh air through this house, right? We don't lack for laughter, that's certain. Just seems more vibrant this week."

Emotion churned in her stomach and stung the backs of her eyes. Because Jillian felt more vibrant herself. "That's a kind thing to say, Wyatt."

"I have a younger sister who radiates positive energy. Yours can be a little . . . haunting . . . at times. But when you and Jack are in the same room, the vibe is infectious, Jillian."

"He's got charisma to spare."

"It's not just him," Wyatt pointedly said. Then she gave Jillian a hug. A quick one, presumably to not throw her out of whack.

But that wasn't really an issue anymore with this family. Jillian had been accepted from the beginning with open arms—hell, from the moment she'd driven through those tall wrought iron gates. She'd learned to open hers, in turn.

An inspiring reality. One she'd not been expecting, but then again, upon setting foot in this house, she'd been surrounded by people who demonstrated resiliency, commitment, love. And, yes, laughter.

"You doin' okay?" Jack asked as he sidled up next to her.

Wyatt made an excuse to dispatch herself elsewhere.

Jillian said, "I'm really happy about how the show went today."

"All right. I'll let you slide on that one."

She nudged him with her elbow. "Just girl talk, Jack. Wyatt's terrific. Everyone is. And whatever comes of Ale's poll . . . well, the entire event was just plain good fun, and I think it established more of the camaraderie that the audience likes to see—and was great advertising for Luke."

"I'm gonna have Wyatt add 'single' to his bio," Jack jested. "Take some of the pressure off me."

"You seem to remain elusive. Your bachelorhood is still intact."

"Shame about that," he murmured. Then took her hand and led her back to the island where dessert was being served—cinnamon churros and tres leches cakes.

After more cleanup, Jillian and Jack each took a glass of wine into the main living room where Ale and Hunt were spreading out a board game on the coffee table, the dog curling alongside Ale.

Jillian and Jack settled on the sofa adjacent to where Wyatt and Mateo sat. They chatted about the festival and some ranch business. The kids told them about their day in school.

Brett and Avery eventually came in. Jack's mom didn't stay for long, though.

"I'm exhausted, and Chance is takin' me back tomorrow mornin'," she said. "He needs to hit up the tack and feed store for supplies, so if you have a list for him, Jack, be sure to text it first thing. Luke'll deliver my pottery to my booth and bring me home."

"Probably wants to rub that poll in my face, with Avery there too," Jack said. "And—"

"No, Uncle Jack," Ale interjected. "I just took a peek. Poll's closed—you and Miss Jillian won!"

"Get out!" He held up his hand to high-five the kid—then Jillian. "Thought for sure Luke was gonna have the ladies swoonin' and gettin' votes in his favor. Times two whenever Avery chimed in."

"Well, you did sort of pull out all the stops," Wyatt said. "That menu was sensational. And the colossal run-in at the end sealed the deal, in my opinion. It happens so unexpectedly with you two that viewers can't help but find it as endearing as it is humorous."

"Long as it's not somethin' that's gonna scald us," Jack commented. "We'll have to be mindful from here on out not to be in the same vicinity when we've got a hot pot walkin'."

Jillian felt another sting as she reminded Jack, "We only have tomorrow's show left."

"Right," he said with a nod. And a tinge of regret.

More than a tinge.

"Well, boys, it's time to get ready for bed," Wyatt said. "Go on up with Nana, and we'll put away the game."

Wyatt and Mateo finished their wine and stored the box in an armoire before bidding Jillian and Jack good night.

"Apparently, I know how to clear a room," Jillian lamented.

"Just wanted to give us some privacy. Without it being blatantly obvious that we'd be headin' up to my room shortly."

"Ollie has to go out."

"Don't you worry about that, honey. Drink your wine."

Jack took care of the dog. Jillian watched them go, thinking a rugged man on a horse was a fine sight, but one tending to a woman's small pet? That was a vision to warm her to the core.

Unfortunately, a chill set in a minute later.

This particular man caring for a baby would likely be the ultimate in soul-stealing moments.

It was an image Jillian knew she shouldn't allow into her head. Absolutely not.

Yet it lodged there anyway.

She imagined he'd been at Wyatt's beck and call when the twins were younger, after he'd come home from SPU, and Mateo was off at an auction or in town.

Jillian knew in her heart that Jack would love being able to lend a hand—and bond with his nephews.

All this was in his nature, as she'd mentioned earlier when they'd discussed how important it was for him to be downstairs, on time, in the morning to get everyone's day started.

His compassionate, paternal presence was as strong as his sexually commanding one.

Which made it all the more painful for Jillian to consider that he might not pursue that complete package, if he thought there was a chance for something more between the two of them.

Jillian needed to set him straight about that. She was going back to her home, her greenhouse, her business. Sunday afternoon, she'd be on the road to Austin. There was nothing that could change those plans, not even Jack. She had to manage her planting cycles and create more inventory. No other option existed when she had transactions hanging in the balance.

She couldn't shake the melancholy even as Jack scooped up Ollie and moved toward the stairs, inclining his head in that direction for Jillian to accompany them.

She still had her wine and took the glass with her, needing it.

On the third floor, those extra doors mocked her.

When they were in Jack's suite, she decided she had to give him the rest of her story.

Without preamble, she said, "I was pregnant once, Jack."

Chapter Fourteen

He stopped unbuttoning his shirt, midway down the flap.

Jack's gaze met hers.

She took a deep drink, swallowed, and said, "I didn't know it. I found out when I came out of the coma. The baby was about six weeks." That'd been a shocker, as much as the extent of the injuries she'd sustained—along with the fact that she'd pulled through. "The doctor informed Scott of this. Another reason he bailed."

"You were going to have his baby—*and he* left *you?*"

"To be fair, he didn't know until—"

"There's no 'to be fair' to be had here, Jillian." Fury laced his tone. "A man who walks away from the mother of his child when she's—"

"Jack. There was no child. It was six weeks. And then it was gone."

His gaze narrowed.

Okay, truth be told, it wasn't as simple as she let on.

It was dark and terrifying. Excruciating.

She set aside her wine. Rested her hands on his forearms that were now folded across his chest as he clearly fought to keep his anger in check. Unsuccessfully.

"Jack. I . . ."

This was an agonizing admission to make, but it had to be done. He had to fully understand that Jillian Parks wasn't the woman from college that he so desperately wanted her to be. Yes, she'd made exceptional strides with her recovery, even just in the last few days. But there was a permanent alteration she had to ensure registered in his mind.

"Scott and I wanted a family," she said. "Sooner, rather than later, so we weren't always careful. We agreed if it happened, it was meant to be."

"You wanted a family." He groaned. "Jesus, Jillian. You had the potential for everything and ended up with—"

"Nothing. Yes."

Her heart constricted, like a big fist squeezing it, unrelenting. So it was difficult to breathe.

She said, "I didn't even have a place to live when I got out of the hospital, because Scott had packed up our rental and moved. But that's not what I'm getting at."

She tried to suck in a stream of air. It was choppy at best.

"Jillian, honey, why don't you sit down?" His distress rivaled his angst.

"Jack, I want you to hear me. Really listen to me. I can't have children. Not a shred of hope. There was too much internal damage from the trampling."

"Jillian, there are alternatives to—"

"I wanted my own babies, Jack. And now . . . I don't want any. I can't even fathom it."

His jaw clenched. He scrutinized her expression as he attempted to digest her words.

"I no longer want marriage and kids, Jack. As you said, I held all that potential in my hands at one point. But it clearly, clearly was not and *is not* meant to be."

Pain burned the backs of her eyes. Her throat tightened. Emotion roiled through her.

Jack still didn't speak. That told Jillian she truly had needed to get this notion into his head, not let his heart misguide him into believing there was a future here.

"I didn't lie this morning," she assured him. "I choked on a sentiment I'd never considered expressing again. But I did tell you exactly how I feel about you. It just doesn't go beyond that. The words. *We* don't go beyond the words."

Now his jaw was a steel cage. He backed away from her. Her arms fell to her sides.

He raked a hand through his hair. Shook his head. Speared her with a penetrating gaze and said, "You're back to dictatin' what my life should be, Jilly."

"That's not my intention, Jack. I'm telling you what *my* life is. Where I stand impacts you. And when I'm gone, you have to accept that I won't be coming back. Much as I'd love to, it'd be too complicated. Too painful for us. Too confusing for your family. Too much of an impediment to you moving on."

"Because that's what you want for me. To move on."

"It's the sensible thing, Jack. The only way for us to survive—" Her voice cracked. Tears popped onto the rims of her eyes. She whispered, "*This.*"

She bit back a sob. Whirled around and picked up Ollie, taking him to the door.

"Jillian, wait."

The feeling of his torment, like shards down her spine, caused her to stop.

"I can't make a choice," he said. "I can't choose between you and the ranch. I *can't* leave here."

She heard the sheer torture in his voice.

He more quietly averred, "I *won't* leave here."

She spun back around. "Jack, never in a million years would I even *hint* at that."

"I know. That's the problem, Jilly. It's all up to you—to transplant yourself, your entire existence. *Here.*"

She gaped.

He continued. "It's what I want. It is absolutely, one hundred percent what I want." He dragged a hand down his face. His eyes misted. "And it is absolutely, one hundred percent what I can't ask you to do."

"Jack." She set Ollie on the sofa and walked into his arms.

She wept on his shoulder as he held her tight.

He burrowed his face in her hair and whispered, "I don't want anyone else, Jillian. I'm not gonna love anyone else. I've already learned that. So stop pushin' me in that direction."

Jillian could cry a river.

"Stay the night," he murmured. "Just lie in my bed with me."

She'd tried to sever any possibilities between them. Yet he clung to the vestiges.

She did too.

For now.

◆　◆　◆

A woman's tears were nothing new to Jack.

He'd caught his mom holding back hers on more occasions than he could count after his dad died. He'd also stumbled upon her full breakdowns a time or two. More than that. It gutted him every time he'd see so much as a tremor through her hands when a memory took her back in time or something that someone said or did made her think of her husband.

He'd also dealt with Wyatt's heartbreaks when the boyfriend du jour didn't turn out to be the love of her life—because she wasn't looking in her own backyard. Specifically, the stables where Mateo had started working when he was a teen.

And for the love of God, Riley had been destroyed by every stray animal that had wandered onto the ranch that was too sick or injured not to put down or was handed back to its rightful owner when located. The horses, in particular, were her emotional downfall. She loved them all like they were her own. And when one was sold off or had reached its final days, she'd go straight to Jack and bawl her eyes out.

Thus, Jack was well versed in all things traumatizing when it came to feminine feelings.

Didn't mean he was anesthetized. Particularly now. With Jillian.

Because this was personal. It involved *him*.

Worse, he comprehended that one of the—if not *the*—prickliest topics was that everything she'd asserted Jack should have was everything she'd given up on. No longer desired.

Marriage and family.

Were these different circumstances, Jack would do his damnedest to persuade her otherwise.

But now knowing all she'd been through, he could understand how her best chance at recovering from what she'd lost was to cut the dream from her psyche. That was the bigger picture she'd painted when she'd said she wasn't meant for a happily ever after.

She'd solidified that in her soul.

With every fiber of his being, Jack wanted to disrupt that wavelength. Reset her. Reprogram her. Whatever "reclamation" term was most appropriate and applicable in this case, he wanted to employ it.

But in the end, where Jillian stood her ground and planted her flag was up to Jillian.

He'd be a hypocrite not to recognize that, given he'd taken the same stance with her regarding his own future.

He was in dire need of consulting Wyatt or his mom in these foreign matters of the heart, but he was still holding Jillian. Keeping her upright as her legs quaked.

Though that became more of a challenge as her entire body started to tremble. He swept her into his arms and carried her to the bed. He rid her of her boots. Removed his as well.

He stretched out on the duvet, and she curled into him.

He stroked her hair with one hand. His other arm was around her shoulders.

Jack had always had something worthwhile to say to Brett or Wyatt or Riley.

But with Jillian, he had to accept that he couldn't inadvertently, or even directly, insert his own wants and desires into the narrative in a desperate attempt to sway her.

That wasn't how he'd play this hand he'd been dealt.

If he and Jillian found common ground, it'd be because she'd made the conscientious decision to be with him—a full concession on her part.

It was a wretched resolution. Not one he was content with, obviously. But one he had to tolerate.

She cried a bit more. He reached for the box of tissues on the nightstand and started pulling sheets for her.

"I'm sorry," she said and sniffled. "Truly, I am, Jack."

He surmised that was intended as a blanket apology. For their predicament as much as for the tears.

"Jilly, you're not to blame. Maybe you thought you worked through the most difficult phase of your therapy—trying to be around people again. But your personal tragedy and how it's changed your viewpoints will always be a crucial component as you proceed. And I have to somehow reconcile in my mind that there's a wall between us that I can't scale."

She sighed, her breath blowing against his collarbone.

His shirt was drenched and still stained from their earlier incident in the kitchen. As was hers. He thought of getting them out of their clothes, but he couldn't budge with her nestled alongside him, hiccupping and sniffling. So he continued to hold her. Until her breathing was less staccato and more measured. Until she was asleep.

Jack stared up at the ceiling fan, watching the blades rotate.

He combed through every thought that he deemed logical. And plenty that were irrational.

A useless endeavor, but slumber eluded him until the wee hours.

Naturally, he was awake at five. He didn't want to rouse Jillian, so he made a compromise. He pulled his phone from his pocket and one-hand texted his sister to tell her to start without him.

Jillian would feel guilty he'd made the decision, but Jack couldn't bring himself to disturb her. He didn't fall back asleep. Just cataloged everything about her that he was going to miss when she was gone.

Jesus, that was fucking depressing as hell.

So he cut that cord and instead mentally ran through some of the things he needed to accomplish today before they prepped and did their final show. They'd have to visit the butcher for the proteins Jillian had requested. No need to stop by the farmers' market since they'd efficiently purchased produce for two days.

Garrett had already contacted Whit Tatum, and that live stream segment was locked in.

Now Jack had to wonder how he and Jillian would interact with each other after this grueling, private episode.

Actually, he was concerned as to whether she'd even want to do this last show. He might have to get Avery to fill in for her.

When Jillian eventually stirred, it was close to seven.

Her eyes were puffy and bloodshot as she gazed at him.

"You're still here," she murmured.

"Didn't feel like movin'."

"Your arm must be asleep."

"Ah, that's what that odd sensation is," he quietly joked.

"Jack." She sat up. "Why aren't you downstairs? Sun's already up."

"Oh, Jillian." He grunted. "Darlin', I'm gonna stop pretendin' I'm the be-all, end-all around here."

She winced. "But you sort of are, Jack. This ranch doesn't run itself."

"No, it does not."

"Come on," she said as she threw her legs over the side of the bed. "There's pancakes to flip and eggs to scramble."

"You're not goin' anywhere lookin' like that, Jilly. Take a glimpse in the mirror. Tell me what you need, and I'll get it for you."

She sighed. But hauled herself up and padded to the bathroom. Only to return a minute later. "Eye drops, eye compress, more tissues, my tote that's in the kitchen. Wyatt's clothes are in there, but I also brought a spare outfit."

"I'm on it." He had his phone in hand again.

Jillian sank onto a sofa. Ollie scampered over.

Jack said, "I'll take him, and Ale will feed him."

"How are you going to explain where I am?"

"I'm not. Let 'em figure it out on their own."

She snickered. "Wyatt's convinced the boys won't have a clue."

"Fine by me."

He got himself cleaned up and changed. Then he headed out with the dog, passing Wyatt along the way.

"Rough night," he simply said.

"Is she okay?"

"It's basically a breakup, Wyatt."

She sucked in a breath. "Jack."

"We're apples and oranges." He referred to a notion he'd had from the time Jillian had arrived on the ranch.

Wyatt's brow furrowed. "Are *you* okay?"

"Nope. Not by a long shot."

He sauntered off.

◆ ◆ ◆

Jillian showered and then went into the bedroom, finding the bag Wyatt had left for her.

She dealt with her eyes first, reclining slightly on the bed for ten minutes with the cool mask on. When it no longer felt as though someone had poked forks into her eyeballs, she returned to the bathroom and did her hair and makeup. She dressed and prayed she wasn't a dead ringer for the most miserable woman on the planet. But suspected she was.

The fact of the matter was that Jillian couldn't bring herself to put all her eggs in one basket again. And at that, she didn't really have eggs to contribute.

"Terrible joke," she mumbled and left the suite.

She gave herself a pep talk in hopes of perking up before she joined everyone. But the second she hit the landing downstairs, a burst of laughter echoed through the hall, coming from the direction of the breakfast table.

Jillian smiled.

Despite how massively disconcerting her night with Jack had turned out to be, Jillian got a shot of joy as she listened to the banter in the kitchen. The scents also seeped toward her, and she inhaled deeply.

Euphoria consumed her—even as she rounded the corner and found Jack topping off eggs Benedict with hollandaise sauce, cracked pepper, bacon crumbles, and grilled asparagus (that wasn't shriveled). She'd anticipated the sight of him would send her into another crying jag. Instead, she stifled a dreamy sigh.

He grinned. Like he knew.

And that easily, they fell into their groove as Jillian delivered the platter to the table and then arranged a grapefruit anise salad and roasted rosemary baby potatoes on another serving plate, with an additional heaping of applewood bacon.

Hunt brought waffles and berries. Wyatt told Ale to stop playing with the dog, wash his hands, and eat.

Brett and Chance had evidently gone into town already. Mateo sat on one side of the boys, Wyatt on the other. Garrett and Tuck were present as well, and Jillian recalled they were testing the outdoor speakers that had been repaired and remounted.

Avery came in from the courtyard, carrying a tray with what smelled like barbacoa.

Jillian gave him a grateful smile and said, "I was hoping to get some of that."

"Traitor," Jack joked.

"Well, I didn't get to try yours," she placated him. "That was a call-in show."

She took the seat next to Jack. The conversation remained animated as they ate.

Mateo kidded Jack, saying, "You were slackin' off this mornin'. Sleepin' in?"

"Had some stuff to attend to. Thanks for gettin' the potatoes goin'."

"Guessing Wyatt is responsible for the salad," Jillian said.

"Straight from your cookbook."

"Aunt Brett's missin' out," Avery commented.

"Luke'll feed her," Jack replied. "Give that woman a breakfast burrito, and she's fueled till late afternoon."

"She'll need to be, considering how busy she was yesterday," Wyatt added.

They talked about the festival, and Jillian got a sufficient accounting of the lively atmosphere, the vendors, the melding of aromas from the various restaurants, the arts and crafts, the clothes. An entire mecca along Main Street, bookended by stages with bands and dance floors.

Ale had footage to show her, but Jillian drew the line there. She didn't need to see the crowd that came from several counties. That'd for sure trigger her.

Jack was quick to catch on and diverted Ale's attention. Wyatt pitched in as well, telling him to finish up so he could take Ollie outside to play.

Jillian was grateful. And took deep breaths.

This was one more indication that being here wasn't a long-term option. Jillian was still in that bits-and-bites phase.

She and Wyatt did the dishes while Jack and Mateo retired to Jack's office to discuss cattle branding, and Avery went back to the bunkhouse to prep lunch for the cowboys.

Jillian said, "Thanks for rescuing me again with the eye-care products."

"My pleasure," Wyatt told her. "Just sorry you and Jack are goin' through a troublesome time."

"We really didn't think this through."

"Mm, I'm not so sure that's true on his end. Subconsciously, at least."

Jillian shook her head. "I should have told him my situation when he suggested I come out here. Maybe my subconscious got the best of me, too, and I thought . . . somehow I could contain my feelings. I mean, I've been skilled at it these last few years. But then I take one look at the hunky cowboy and . . . all bets are off."

"Not all," Wyatt quietly pointed out.

"You're right. I can see past him to know what's doable . . . and what's not."

Wyatt set aside her hand towel. "I can't say one way or the other because I don't know the whole situation. Jack hasn't shared it with me, Jillian. What I do know is what I see with my own two eyes. And that, my friend, is something significant." Those eyes glistened. "All I want for Jack is his happiness. That's wrapped around the ranch, certainly. But I also wish for someone in his life."

"I want all that for him, too, Wyatt." Emotion churned within her. "I'm just . . . not the answer."

"And I'm not gonna press."

"Thank you."

"I have to get Hunt to his soccer match. He'll be back for the filmin'."

"He's super helpful."

"Not only does he idolize Jack, but he really wants to learn barbecue."

Ouch, Jillian thought.

As wonderful as it was that Jack had a nephew who might want to go on the circuit with him, it was also disheartening that Jack didn't have a son to share that experience with, like he had with his dad.

Stop.

Jillian had to release all that from her brain.

She and Jack had covered the pertinent details. They knew precisely where the chips had fallen.

That was that.

Yes, easier said than done. But she had to move forward as well. Starting with her podcast.

Jack joined her at the guesthouse, and they chatted about the different types of smokers and their individual purpose, as a follow-on to the previous day's fantastically prepared chickens.

Jillian's stats were glorious to see, and she knew her audience was enjoying Jack cohosting with her.

Later, they went into town. Jillian was relieved the butcher was off the main drag and there was limited foot traffic. She was also pleased by the specialty cuts they received. So much so, she nearly bounced her way down the sidewalk.

"This is perfect for a finale," she told Jack.

When they were in the kitchen again, Jillian laid out ingredients for her mint sauce, her lemon tahini sauce, and her spicy mustard.

Jack wanted whipped mash, baby artichokes, and a charred radicchio and arugula salad with cherries and parmesan.

"A-plus for healthy choices, Jack." She impulsively kissed him.

Jack gazed down at her. "We're still doin' that, darlin'?"

"I'd say it's a new habit I should break, but . . . you're irresistible, remember?"

"Wasn't complainin'. Just makin' sure we stay on the same page."

"Right."

He kissed her forehead and said, "Let's prep."

Not long afterward, Hunt came in as Garrett and Tuck were setting up.

"What can I do?" he eagerly asked.

Jillian assigned him the task of selecting the best dishes for their presentation, and that was akin to calling him king for the day. Hunt went right to work.

"He's never gonna want to perform grunt duty for me again," Jack said.

"Of course he will. He wants to learn everything he can from you."

"In a couple years, we'll let him assist Avery. But things move pretty quick down there at the bunkhouse, 'cuz those cowboys need to get fed and get on their horses."

"But what a great way for him to pick up different techniques." She hadn't planned to bring this up or make any correlations, yet she couldn't help but say, "A total fusion of your expertise and Avery's. That's got 'award winner' written all over it."

"Yeah, Uncle Jack. I'll have more trophies than you!" Hunt declared. "And my own belt buckle."

"I do not doubt that," Jack told his nephew. "For the moment, though, try to stay focused on what Miss Jillian needs."

"I'm on it!"

Hunter also ensured the pots and pans were available.

Jack said, "I've got a surprise for Miss Jillian in the fridge, boy. Grab me the dutch oven in there."

He did as requested and put it on the island, lifting the lid.

Jillian's hands flew into the air, fisting and shaking. Enthusiastically. "Avery set me up with dinner rolls!"

"He started the rising process for ya. Just follow his directions for the last bit of cookin'."

That enthusiasm died on the vine. "Oh, geez . . . this could be disastrous."

"Foolproof, I promise."

"Ha, ha. That'll make me the fool if I screw this up."

"I have faith," Jack assured her.

Garrett counted them in, and Jack gave his intro, then said, "Shout-out to all of you who weighed in on our poll yesterday and the comments you posted. Jillian and I were honored to take the cake. But it was a close call. Luke and Avery served up some fiery fajitas, and trust me when I say those cowboys know what they're doin' with a grill."

"Which means we're stepping up our game today, to be worthy of that win," Jillian chimed in. Then explained the menu.

All went smoothly. Shockingly so. The comedy of errors came with the two of them expecting a blunder, but when it didn't happen, they were taken aback and joked about it.

The audiences were even more lively, perhaps because it was the final joint show. Or perhaps Jack and Jillian had made the special editions interactive enough to keep everyone engaged when there weren't any bloopers.

Regardless, they had the numbers that proved they were much more than a one-hit wonder. Or a one-week wonder, as it were.

Whit Tatum's performance to close out the segment was an absolute gem, and Mindy went on and on about the raving comments. Garrett had news himself.

"Y'all have the station manager dancin' in circles with the surge in ratin's," he said. "Jack, you get your fifteen-minute slot from here on out."

"Hot damn," he said as he gave himself a quick round of applause. "I can bring in Avery from time to time. Hunt too."

"Thursday's a school day," Wyatt reminded him.

"Not durin' the summer!" Hunt blurted.

"Point taken," his mother conceded.

They all continued their usual postproduction routine. Later, Jack walked Jillian and Ollie to the guesthouse.

She took his hand at the door, silently inviting him in.

They didn't waste any time. They went straight to her room. Jack slipped off her lavender cardigan and pulled the tank over her head. She helped him out of his shirt. When every stitch of clothing was heaped on the floor, Jack guided her onto the mattress.

He kept that certain amount of space between them, as usual, but tonight . . . that wasn't what Jillian wanted.

She pulled him closer.

"Jilly, I'll crush you."

"I want your weight on me, Jack. I want to feel your skin and your muscles. Your heat. I want to be completely surrounded by you."

He groaned. "Darlin', that's a dangerous game to play."

"No games, Jack. I want you to make love to me. And I want every inch of you covering me."

He eased into her slick depths and whispered, "It's like you're anticipatin' me."

"Just thinking of you being inside me gets me wet."

"Let's make you wetter."

They moved together, Jack maintaining a measured pace he gradually increased as the insistency and tension mounted between them.

Jillian slung her leg over the small of his back. He angled her hip. Drove farther into her.

Her fingers curled into his biceps. His fingers brushed away strands of hair at her temple.

He kissed her sweetly. Then heatedly.

Then he stared into her eyes and pumped steadily.

"That's exactly what I want," she murmured. "Over and over."

Chapter Fifteen

Jillian lost count of the orgasms.

She lost track of time too.

She and Jack only got so much sleep. Then sunrays were peeking through the windows, and she felt the most wretched sensation in the pit of her stomach.

Neither she nor Jack moved for what felt like a small eternity.

Unfortunately, it was inconceivable to stay in their sexy cocoon. Ollie needed attention. And the day had to get underway.

Jack was filming earlier than usual at the festival. Jillian had to pack.

At the door, he said, "I'll be back before you leave."

"Maybe . . . I should just go." Emotion burned through her.

He shook his head. "Not till I'm back. Promise me."

She knew that'd only make it more painful for both of them.

She nodded anyway.

Jack left, and Jillian gazed down at Ollie, weepily saying, "All those country music songs about the rodeo god breaking the woman's heart because he'd rather be on a horse—or getting thrown from one—and here I am being the heartbreaker."

Ollie yipped.

"Yeah, I know. You want food." She knelt down and twirled the end of his ear. "Come on, little man."

Around ten, Jillian was packed and ready to go. Only thing she was missing was the tote bag she'd left in Jack's suite.

So she took Ollie to the main house and was just climbing the stairs when she heard a new voice.

An exuberant voice.

"Jillian Parks, in the flesh!"

Jillian spun around. And sort of froze in place as she stared at a stunning redhead with Jack's blue eyes and Wyatt's radiant smile.

"Riley Reed," Jillian mused. "Wow. Jack did *not* prepare me for you."

"Said I was some annoying li'l sister who tagged along every chance she got?"

"No. Said you were a lightning rod," Jillian corrected. "He just failed to say you warrant supermodel status."

"Don't I wish. Anyway, it is so good to meet you!" She gave Jillian a tight squeeze, taking her by surprise. Then she released Jillian and stepped back. "You're even prettier in person. And oh, my God! The sparks that fly when you and Jack are on screen!"

"He's currently at the street festival," Jillian informed her. "In fact, everyone is, except Avery."

"That's because he'll never let the cowboys fend for themselves."

"I believe that to be true. Runs in the family."

"Indeed. Jack worries no one can make their own oatmeal."

Jillian's heart swelled. "That's actually one of his most adorable traits."

"Trust me, no one minds." Riley winked.

And here we go again with the Reed charisma.

Riley suddenly noticed the pup and bent at the waist to scratch behind his ear. "Who do we have here?"

"Ollie. He'll happily show you his belly in exchange for rubs."

"Is that so?"

"Give her the meerkat, circus clown."

Riley started with a gentle stroking of his stomach, and that was all the encouragement Ollie needed to ham it up.

"Good Lord, he's the absolute cutest!" Riley stood and said, "Fair warnin', I fall in love with every animal on this property. Can't help myself."

"Oh, well, we were just leaving. I forgot something in Jack's room and—"

"Ahhh, did you now?" Riley wagged her brows. "So all that wicked chemistry kept things hot off camera too?"

Finally, the blush returned. Perhaps because this was a new Reed she was dealing with. Or maybe it was because Jillian was inching closer to leaving this place. And that seemed odd, when—if she searched her feelings—what she really wanted was to spend more time with Jack.

Moot, of course.

She skipped over that and Riley's comment.

"I'll just grab my bag and be on my way," she said.

"Wait! I've gotten no time with you! Have lunch with me at Luke's," Riley implored.

"Actually, bad idea. His cantina is right in the thick of things with the street festival."

"Perfect location. We can check that out too."

Jillian rolled her eyes. Might as well tackle this elephant in the room before it sat on her.

"Thing is, Riley, I don't do crowds. I had an accident years ago and developed ochlo—"

"Enochlophobia."

Jillian's head whipped back. "Jack told you?"

"No, it's what Whit Tatum was initially diagnosed with because of his stage fright issues. He'd been lost in a crowd once when he was a kid, and his therapist thought that was the problem. Turns out . . . he just fuckin' has stage fright. Good ol' fashion stage fright."

"So he solved his problem with a YouTube channel. Genius. And by the way, those songs you write for him are spectacular."

"He's one of my favorite clients. Anyway, we don't have to worry about the festival crowd." She pulled her cell from a trendy bag that was looped around her forearm and hit a button. Two seconds later . . . "Luke, Ry. You at your booth or at the restaurant? Restaurant, perfect. Make me and Jillian some fajitas?" She added a "pretty please" pout he couldn't see but which resonated in her voice. "We're on our way."

She disconnected and told Jillian, "Cantina's not open yet. And at that, he says the place has been empty because everyone's eatin' on the street."

"I did tell him I'd stop by before I left town."

"There you go!"

Lightning rod, indeed.

Jillian collected her tote with her wallet inside. Riley offered to drive and told her to bring Ollie along.

Jack's youngest sister chatted incessantly on the way into Serrano, and Jillian loved that—took the pressure off her. Plus, it helped Jillian to get to know her, since Riley was already quite familiar with her, having watched all the joint shows.

"Jack on his own is entertainin'," Riley said. "But the two of you together is like a firecracker and a lit fuse!"

"We did have a few explosive moments that could have gone either way . . ."

"They were all fabulous. And the comments—*phew*. Some of them bordered on risqué." She laughed. "Hell, the majority of them did. I can't believe Wyatt let Ale read any of 'em. Then again, anything not techie goes right over that boy's head."

"That's sort of what we've been banking on."

They reached town, and Riley took one of the reserved spots in the cantina's parking lot.

They left the vehicle and rounded the corner toward the entrance. Were almost there when a woman let out a loud shriek.

Jillian's pulse jumped.

"Daisy Johnston, what are you losin' it over?" Riley called out as the woman across the street dropped a dress she'd had in her hand and started searching frantically about her. "Somethin's up. I went to high school with her."

They crossed to the other sidewalk as Daisy yanked her phone from her purse. She told Riley, "I turned my back for one second, and Colin Grady is suddenly gone! I'm his nanny!"

Jillian's spirits plummeted. She scanned the immediate area as Daisy got the sheriff's office on the line.

Riley connected with Luke again, saying, "Call your people manning your booth and tell 'em to be on the lookout for Colin Grady—he's run amok."

Daisy was explaining what the boy was wearing. Riley relayed the info to Luke.

Jillian caught sight of the little boy in his jeans, boots, and blue-and-white flannel shirt. He couldn't have been more than four. And he headed right into the crowd, ducking under a skirted table on the perimeter and then vanishing.

"Colin's over there." Jillian pointed. She passed the leash to Daisy. "Do *not* let go of him!"

"I swear!"

Jillian was on the move in an instant, running toward the entrance to the festival. She barreled through, Riley close behind her, crying out her name.

"Excuse me!" Jillian yelled as she pushed past the throng. "Excuse me. Sorry—small child on the loose! Everyone look out for him!" She wound her way around tight conglomerations and plowed through the larger ones, her heart pounding, her ears ringing, her eyes blurring. "Colin!"

She spied him winding through long legs and booted feet, then stumbling and nearly falling.

Terror struck her. If he hit the ground, those feet would trample him. The crowd was thick, and it was difficult to see the kid every time he maneuvered this way or that.

Jillian continued to dodge and weave, her pulse pounding in her veins.

"Jillian!" Riley reached her and gestured toward a break in the booths—another entrance. "Force him toward me!" Riley twisted and shoved and worked her way to the spot she'd indicated.

Jillian kept up her pace, banging into people and apologizing. Her head started to spin, but her eye was on the prize. She caught up to Colin and corralled him toward Riley, who wrangled the kid and hoisted him up and out of the activity. Jillian followed.

"Oh, my God," Riley breathlessly said as she held the kid in her arms. "Fuckin' hate cardio."

"Makes two of us." Jillian bent over and placed her hands on her thighs. She was out of breath too, but it wasn't solely due to physical exertion.

She straightened. Riley gasped.

"Jesus Christ, you're as pale as a ghost!"

"Lightheaded too. That's a problem." Jillian swayed. Her heart felt as though it might erupt from her chest. Her vision was still cross-eyed.

Riley got back on the phone. "Luke, we're around the corner—come get us!"

Riley stuffed her cell in her pocket, apparently having left her handbag with Daisy. She gripped Jillian's arm and dragged her farther from the festivities.

"Just breathe, Jillian."

"Trying."

Luke came running from the opposite end of the block and immediately wrapped an arm around Jillian's waist, tugging her to him for support.

"Is Colin all right?" he asked his sister.

"Little bugger led us on a wild goose chase."

Luke got Jillian inside the cantina and into a chair. He poured water for her and Riley. Then called Jack.

It was all a bit of a clusterfuck in her mind because she couldn't think or see straight.

But then the door opened, and Jack strutted in.

Jillian's eyes locked with his. Her axis righted.

She watched him move stealthily toward her, concern etched on his ruggedly handsome face.

Something about his broad shoulders and his reassuring presence calmed her. Soothed her.

He yanked out a chair and sat in front of her, clasping her hands in his.

Jillian was still dazed and yet . . . strangely riveted.

"She went after Colin in that crowd," Riley explained. "Like, didn't even think twice about it."

Daisy had followed them into the cantina and said, "She saved his life, Jack. This is all my fault for lookin' away. I am so sorry." She was crying, so Riley kept Colin in her arms. Luke took Ollie's leash.

"Jilly," Jack said in his low, intimate tone. "Darlin', blink if you can hear me."

She laughed.

Not really. It was more of a squawk.

"That's a start," he said. He cupped her face with his hands and stared into her eyes. "You knew better than to do that."

"I shouldn't have brought her here," Riley contended. "I'm so sorry, Jack. Jillian. I thought it'd be perfect with no one in the restaurant."

Jillian finally spoke. "You're not to blame." Her voice was raspy. "I wanted to come. And, Jack . . ." She pulled in thin, stuttering strands of oxygen. "I just . . . I *had* to go after Colin. I saw him, and all I could think was that once he was entrenched, anything could happen to him."

"That's a fact, Jillian. People aren't glancin' down at their feet. Their checkin' out demos, yakkin' it up, shootin' videos, drinkin' their beers."

"He's just so small." She nearly choked on the words.

Jack's hands fell away, and he reached for her water glass. "Drink this. Little sips."

She did as instructed.

The sheriff arrived to ensure all was well.

Jack said, "I'll take Jillian back to the ranch." He helped her up. "You should rest, honey."

"I'll be fine. I just need some air." Not necessarily true. She quaked from head to toe.

Jack got her to his truck, and she closed her eyes and tried to black out her mind. Ollie sat in her lap, licking her bare arm, and that was comforting. Except, the dark and twisty part of her brain imagined what it would be like to lose him in a throng of people. Jillian couldn't fathom it. The jostling and the kicking were real to her, and tiny Ollie would never survive. Just as she'd feared about Colin.

A sob tore from her throat.

She'd come so damn far this week. Only to have her last day turn into her worst nightmare.

A sign. A warning she should heed.

Jillian wasn't ready for a full immersion into society. Memorial Day weekend bashes. Fifty-guest reunions. Street festivals.

She wanted to shatter her box. She truly did.

And in many respects, she had. Just not entirely. And following today's harrowing experience, she could use a few new sessions with her therapist.

This was so much that Jack didn't need to deal with.

No, he wasn't like Scott. He wasn't interested in taking the easy way out, walking away from her.

Jillian needed the reprieve.

When they reached the guesthouse, she was out of the truck before Jack could come get her. She put Ollie on the ground and braced a hand against the door to steady herself.

Jack rested an elbow on the hood, not getting too close.

"It's not a setback," she quietly said. "You're not a threat to me, Jack Reed."

"You're still pale, Jilly. And holdin' back tears."

"I don't want to cry, Jack. I want to acknowledge that I still have a ways to go with my reclamation. And the best place for me right now is Seattle."

Talk about a knife to the heart. They weren't words she wanted to say. But Jillian had to accept the reality of the situation—and it went beyond today's incident.

She and Jack had remained at their impasse.

She was out of supplies.

She had a crop to harvest.

The sand had run out of their hourglass.

"This sucks," he grumbled.

She let out a pained laugh. "It really does."

"This is not how I wanted us to part, Jilly."

"Me, either, Jack. But life doesn't always turn out the way we want it to, does it?"

His teeth gritted.

She sighed. "What happened in town doesn't spoil our week together, Jack."

"It'll be the primary thing you think about when you look back on this."

She shoved away from her spot and joined him at his. She gazed up at him and said, "Trust me when I say, cowboy, there are plenty of high points I'll hold close." She swept her lips over his. And murmured, "I meant it when I told you this was the best week of my life. Because of you."

His eyes shut for a moment. Then he said, "Darlin', I just don't know how to say goodbye."

"Then don't say it."

Her arms wound around his neck.

He held her tight. And whispered, "I love you, Jillian Parks."

"This is all my fault," Riley dramatically, remorsefully, wailed as she plopped into a chair next to Jack on the patio. She reached for the decanter of bourbon and refreshed his glass, sipping from it first. "Jillian left the ranch because I took her into town, and it freaked her out. Swear to God, Jack, I checked with Luke first, and there was no one—"

"It's not your fault, Ry." He reclaimed his glass and took a deep drink. "Jillian was plannin' to leave today. This afternoon. She just took off a little earlier than scheduled."

"How could you let her drive when she was so shook up?"

"Was I supposed to hold her hostage?" he grumpily retorted.

"Maybe."

He gave a half snort. "Ry, for one, once she was alone in her SUV—in her comfort zone—she would calm further down. Two . . . the woman needs to get back to her own life. Maybe I could have convinced her to stay another day or more. But that episode at the festival was a catalyst to get her focused on returnin' home. And the thing of it is, Ry, that's where she has to be right now. She has responsibilities too. They can't be discounted."

"I understand that. Though—"

"Honey, she never once let on about how stressful it is to have all those orders, hundreds of 'em, waitin' to be filled and having her hands tied because she'd run out of inventory. Not to mention all the requests for autographed books. She has her own career, Riley. And it's her *livelihood*," he punctuated. "So."

He drained the glass.

Riley gave him another refill. And said, "Maybe, tonight, you let the rest of us pick up the slack, Jack. Take your horse out. Go fishin', whatever. Play hooky."

"Much as I appreciate the bye, Ry, none of that would keep my mind off Jillian. I'd rather concentrate on cookin'. So lemme finish this glass, and I'll fire up the grill."

His week didn't get any better. The only good thing Jack could say about that was he had myriad obligations to tend to. Bills to pay, balance sheets to reconcile, cattle to herd. He spent his nights working and reworking his menus for the holiday event. That occupied quite a bit of his time, considering he was planning to host from ten to ten on Saturday, from noon to nine on Sunday, and from eleven to five on Monday.

His tickets were nearly sold out, and the station manager committed to buying whatever was left over to give away as promos. Considering they didn't come cheap, Jack had a nice budget for the food and supplies. He was also getting a cut from the beer and wine distributors and his affiliate programs. Garrett had secured advertisers, sponsorships, and endorsements as well. All in all, Jack stood to net a huge chunk of change, even after paying servers and insurance and miscellaneous other fees.

All he had to do was stay the course.

Not drown in thoughts of Jillian.

On Thursday, Jillian pulled into her drive, relief washing over her.

For one thing, she and Ollie had made it safely home, sans any triggering incidents. If anything, the trip had gotten a bit boring outside Texas.

She entered the house, and the relief dissipated.

She stood in the small foyer waiting for the sound of boisterous voices and laughter to slam into her. Willing the decadent aromas of southwestern food and barbecue to waft on the air.

But it was quiet in her quaint home. The only scent came from the lavender air freshener plugged into an outlet that she'd forgotten to remove before she'd left.

Ollie sat at her feet and stared up at her, his soulful eyes seeming full of confusion. She might have been imagining that. But probably not.

Jillian shut the door behind them, planning to unload in the morning since it was past nine and she was weary from the day's long journey.

She texted Jack to tell him she'd arrived because he'd asked that she do so. Then she got Ollie set up, and she took a sleeping pill, as she'd done every night since leaving the ranch.

She'd given them up some time ago, despite her insomnia. But she hadn't wanted to fall asleep at the wheel, given the lengthy stretches on the road.

As she and Ollie crawled under the covers, she realized that slumber had not eluded her at the ranch—unless Jack intentionally kept her up. Even at that, he was the early riser while she stayed in bed.

She tried to push thoughts of him from her mind, which only happened when the meds kicked in.

The next few weeks were dedicated to her chilies and her orders. Her downstairs kitchen was filled with a peppery aroma that still wasn't comparable to Jack's, but it was much less bland than during the first couple of days after she'd returned home. She batched, packaged, and shipped. Tended to her plants. Repeated the process. She was grateful for the spike in sales that continued to impress her. She recorded her podcast with more flair geared toward outdoor cooking. She gave up some trade secrets in her paid newsletter—and saw an increase in subscribers.

Mindy called her via video one day to say, "You have nibbles on endorsing some products, and I've been compiling a list of potential advertisers for your newsletter, blog, and podcast."

"I never wanted to clutter my blog with ads. Too annoying to navigate, just to get to the ingredients or the cooking instructions."

"Point taken. Let me shoot you some numbers, though. Might have you singing a different tune."

"I'll look, but I'll have to be judicious."

"More streams of revenue, Jillian. You can build a bigger greenhouse."

She groaned. "This may come as a shock, but I kind of have my hands full. I'm also testing hybrids for next year's line."

"So ambitious. Listen, capitalizing on the success of those shows with Jack is paramount. So take a peek at what I'm suggesting, and we'll talk."

"Of course."

"On to the personal stuff. How are you?"

"You ask me that every day."

"BFFs do that."

Jillian smiled. "Thank you. I'm getting better. Therapy was a smart move. We still haven't figured out why I'm compelled to charge into a crowd to save someone, but I'm more settled. Thinking of going to the farmers' market tomorrow to drop off my products to my third-party vendor, instead of having my courier do it. Eventually, I'll drive into the city to deliver to the restaurants I contract with. And someday . . . I'll get on a ferry."

"I'm sorry? Ferry like a boat, or fairy with wings?"

"Ha, ha. I used to love to spend the day around Puget Sound. I don't believe I'll ever go to another concert in my lifetime, or any sort of festival. No packed bars or movie theaters. But there are other activities around here that I can partake in. Slowly."

"Hmm," Mindy ambiguously mused.

"Hmm, what?"

"Well, I'm a little worried you'd be doing this alone."

"Ollie will be with me," she countered.

"You know what I'm saying, Jillian."

"No six-foot-something strapping cowboy to protect me?"

"I'm not inferring you require protection. He wasn't there at the street fair when you saved a kid's life."

"Potentially saved a kid's life. And that doesn't matter. He was there when I needed him the most. It was surreal, Mindy. He came through the cantina door, and I fixated solely on him and . . . that was it. I was still shaking, but I could function. I could speak. I could breathe. Simply by being close to him."

"Walked right into that one, girlfriend," Mindy murmured, her voice tinged with emotion, her eyes misting.

Jillian stared at her. "Setting me up to see what I'm missing out on doesn't change things, Min."

"Ooh, I have a nickname now," she more perkily said, to lighten the mood.

"My dad called me Jills."

"Look at us, bonding all fifth grade–like. Next thing you know, we'll be painting our toenails the same color."

With a laugh, Jillian said, "I draw the line at s'mores and sleepovers."

"Since I don't live in the same city . . ."

"We're a perfect match."

"And we both have a lot of work to do. I'll call you tomorrow."

"I look forward to it."

They disconnected.

Jillian sipped hot tea from her favorite "You had me at *Woof*" mug and let this new sense of camaraderie seep through her. But she fell shy of allowing more thoughts of Jack to swirl in her brain. She couldn't afford to get mired.

So she washed her cup and went to the greenhouse to complete another harvesting.

She gazed at the bare spots in her gardens and frowned.

She'd been contemplating new hybrids for weeks. Yet she hadn't planted any new crops.

Granted, she had an ample supply for her current product line. But if she didn't start growing soon, she'd have difficulty launching her next line.

Another week passed, and she hadn't committed to what her new specialty seeds would be. Nothing tasted right when she sampled rehydrated powders as her betas. The scents were off. Combinations that should inherently blend and offer their own unique twist fell flat.

Or were too sharp. Too salty. Too . . . unbalanced.

A day later, Jillian was in the bathroom when she noticed she was spotting. The pink tinge on the toilet paper made her roll her eyes.

"I have a UTI, and the infection is throwing off my taste buds," she surmised.

At least she now had an explanation as to why she couldn't tolerate any of her mixes.

She called her gynecologist's office and was in the next morning, hating to leave Ollie behind for the first time but having no other choice.

She also wasn't pleased with the earful she got from Dr. Delany while she was in stirrups.

"You haven't been here in over two years, Jillian," the physician said.

"Didn't really see the point. My Paps were always normal, and I endured extensive studying of my vagina when I was in the hospital."

"I'm well aware," she said. "I did the studying. Not an excuse."

Jillian gave the mea culpa face. "How much longer?"

"I want your urine test results before I let you go."

Her brow crooked.

"To confirm if this truly is a urinary tract infection. But also . . ."

Jillian sat up as the doctor shifted away and stripped off her gloves. Washed her hands.

"Also, what?"

"You've healed remarkably well, Jillian. So much more than I could have anticipated. Perhaps if I'd seen you more frequently—particularly over the last year—I might be a little more prepared for this."

"Prepared for *what*?" she asked, slightly panicked. "Did I grow a second uterus?"

Dr. Delany laughed. "No, not at all. But your single uterus, and everything surrounding it, have really come along."

"I'm sorry . . . come along? Is there a technical term we should be using?"

"Just wait."

A minute or two later, her PA knocked on the door and then entered, handing the doctor a sheet of paper, then leaving.

Dr. Delany scanned the results, shook her head, and then gave Jillian an incredulous look. That quickly morphed into an apologetic one.

"I am sooo perplexed," Jillian muttered, her anxiety mounting.

"It's just . . . again, had I seen you recently . . ." She paused, as though needing to collect her thoughts. Then said, "I'm not reprimanding you, Jillian, I know how emotionally painful subjecting yourself to all of these exams can be. However, I would have noted that the scar tissue I saw and the endometriosis I expected, as well as other impacts from the trampling, have repaired themselves. You've healed, Jillian."

"I don't really know what that means."

"Aside from being a breakthrough case study . . . I'm telling you that your reproductive system has literally bounced back." She handed over the piece of paper. "Congratulations. You're pregnant."

Chapter Sixteen

The tears wouldn't stop.

Of course they wouldn't.

Dr. Delany personally drove Jillian home. Her PA followed in Jillian's SUV.

Once they left, she set up a call with her therapist. But that wouldn't happen till later in the day. Maybe by then, Jillian would have her breath back and could make sense of all this.

Dr. Delany had stuck with layman's terms at first. Until Jillian just couldn't accept that she was some sort of miracle patient and needed words that went beyond her comprehension so that she didn't really have to *comprehend* what was being said to her.

Mindy made her promised video call, and Jillian ignored it at first.

But they were friends now.

So she connected.

"Jesus H. Christ!" Mindy blurted the second she saw Jillian's bloodshot and weepy eyes. "What's happened?"

Jillian synopsized in a fractured voice.

Mindy blinked. Numerous times. She remained in BFF mode as she said, "This is astounding!"

"How so?" Jillian wailed.

"Well, clearly it's the cowboy's baby. And clearly, you're in love with the cowboy. Who's in love with you. So . . . clearly—"

"If you say that one more time—"

"Right, okay. So, point being . . . maybe there's a reason why you haven't replanted your greenhouse, why you can't decide on hybrids, why you—"

"Oh. My. God. Mindy!"

"So, no Min today? I see how you are. Knocked up and already feisty."

Jillian gaped.

Mindy snickered. "Please. Much as I know this is a scientific and physiological matter, I'm more inclined to embrace the idea of divine intervention."

"This isn't a joke, Mindy. I'm. Pregnant."

Delightfully so? Heartbreakingly so?

She couldn't decide.

"No, it is not a joke, Jillian. It's a cosmic phenomenon. Vindication for everything you lost. For everything Jack never got to dream of because he had a ranch to rescue when he was only nineteen years old."

A fresh wave of tears hit Jillian.

Mindy continued. "Jills. When you told me your story after we first started working together and you wouldn't consider any live promos, you told me that you and Scott had wanted a family and if it happened, it was meant to be. Then something seriously tragic happened, and he disappeared. Willingly so. Because he wasn't the right one for you— and that wasn't the time for you to start a family. But now . . . ? You've healed, Jillian."

Jillian stared at her. Sniffled. Reached for a tissue and dabbed at all the wetness while she let Mindy's connotation sink in.

Though Mindy prompted her further. "You went to Texas. And, sure, maybe the motivation was marketing your products. But really, deep down . . . wasn't it all about the cowboy? From the very beginning?"

◆ ◆ ◆

Jack didn't like some of the setting. Yes, he'd approved it weeks ago, but today?

He glanced around the elongated outdoor kitchen, the primary part of the L having been added to so that there was seating for twenty-four. Beyond that space were two dozen round tables on the event lawn, which sat ten each—because all Jack's tickets had sold and the station had offered him twice the face value to allow for another fifty people.

There were numerous carving, appetizer, and salad stations. Later on, they'd roll out dessert carts.

For now, Jack stared at the counter in front of him and just . . . couldn't get on board with how big it was. How was he supposed to make eye contact and interact with this multitude of people while remaining in the frame? Certainly, there were more cameras. Not just Tuck's and Ale's. Garrett had brought in the morning TV show crew. Helpful, but still.

The people who'd paid premium rates for this up-close-and-personal experience would expect Jack's attention. Difficult to give when he was busy cooking. And that'd be going on all day.

Avery and Luke were there to prep meats with him, even keeping an eye on the lockers that were filled with ribs and brisket, as well as lamb and pork shoulders that had been smoking overnight.

Brett, Wyatt, and Riley were in charge of salads and sides. Hunt ran around like a chicken with his head cut off to get everyone everything they needed. Chance and the cowboys had set the tables, chairs, and umbrellas, and were unloading the dining and flatware supplies, lining trash bins, filling ice buckets, laying out the dance floor in front of the stage where the first band was warming up.

Hired staff manned the food stations, and servers were ready to pour water, bus tables, see to any request.

It was all coming together perfectly, and yet Jack felt . . . off.

Catching on to his consternation, his mom asked, "Somethin' we're missin', Jack?"

"Yeah. Jillian."

But that was moot. So they opened the gates to the TRIPLE R for the shuttle buses they'd arranged, which provided round-trip rides from town to the ranch and back, so no one was drinking and driving, and to limit vehicle traffic on site.

They got the show on the road.

It was an electrifying day, without doubt. So much merriment and dancing and good times. They didn't run out of food, though came close. The weather held at a beautiful eighty-two degrees. The blips were minimal, unnoticeable by most.

Only problem was . . .

Wyatt said, "Your comments are about ninety percent the same." She sank into a sofa cushion next to him in the living room that night, while the cowboys reset the event lawn for the next day, and the cleaning crew Jack had contracted did the rest of the work.

He sipped bourbon and asked, "What's the prevailing topic?"

"Where's Jillian?"

Jack groaned. "Big surprise."

He didn't elaborate. Just thanked Wyatt for her help and went upstairs to his suite.

He showered and tried to relax, since they were doing this all over again tomorrow. He convinced himself it'd be a better day. Once the seats had been filled, he'd been too busy to obsess over anything other than serving up food and witty commentary.

Luckily, he'd had Luke and Avery to fill in gaps for him. And the cameras had cut away to the guests and the bands, the people dancing. So the spotlight wasn't on him at all times. Still, twelve hours of entertaining wore him out.

Didn't take much for him to crash. Only to be up and at it again first thing in the morning.

The prep was a close repeat, just with some different food selections to keep things interesting.

The cameras had just started rolling when someone posed that million-dollar question that had blown up his feed yesterday.

"Hey, where's Jillian, anyway?"

Jack felt the dagger to his heart. Thankfully, he was tending to the chicken on the long cowboy grill, his back to the counter so no one could see his pained expression. Or hear his grunt.

He'd forever kick himself for suggesting she come to the ranch for those joint shows in the first place . . . except he'd loved having her here. Even if only for one short week.

He removed breasts and leg quarters slathered with his BBQ sauces, charred just right, and carried the sheet pan to his workstation in front of the production crew so they had prime shots of his end result and his demonstration of slicing into the juicy meat.

His mind wasn't totally on the poultry, though.

He was never getting over this woman. No doubt about it.

Jack said to Hunt, "Get me some tongs, will ya?"

"Sure, Uncle Jack. But . . ." His jaw dropped.

"Sooner rather than later, Hunt. We have people to serve."

"It's just . . ." His eyes widened. As did his grin.

"Looks like you've got yourself another winner there, Jack."

The feminine voice came from behind him.

His heart nearly stopped.

Hunt nearly fell off his stool.

Jack set aside his knife. Braced himself for a moment with his hands curling around the edge of the counter as emotion flooded his veins.

Then he stripped off his gloves, tossed them aside, and turned.

Jillian stood at the opposite end of the outdoor kitchen, in the opening.

So many feelings slammed into Jack at once, he couldn't speak. Couldn't even come up with a coherent thought.

The backs of his eyes burned. His throat tightened.

Goddamn, she was so pretty. And smiling sweetly. Though her eyes misted.

Her voice quavered as she asked, "Mind if I join you?"

"Ah, shit," he mumbled. More emotion crashed over him.

But the corner of his mouth lifted.

He said, "Darlin', if you don't, I fear complete anarchy with this group."

"Can't have that." She closed the gap between them. And threw her arms around him.

He held her tight, murmuring, "Jesus, woman. If you're not back for good, you're gonna be the death of me."

"I flew here to get to you, Jack. Granted, on a semiprivate jet with its own terminal that Mindy booked for me. But I flew, Jack," she repeated. "To get to you."

"Jillian, every day without you feels like an anvil on my soul."

"Turns out, I'm not interested in living without you, Jack. Can't even plant my own crops. Something kept telling me not to."

"I don't understand any of that."

"I'll explain later."

At the moment, the crowd was going wild with applause and cheers. Jillian's tears wet his skin, and he shed a few too.

He didn't want to let her go. Even when Garrett discreetly prompted him with the clearing of his throat, and the catcalls became a bit more lascivious.

Finally, he released her. Turned from the cameras and the guests, briefly, to compose himself. Then he dialed up the charm, saying, "Y'all know she can't resist me. How about it, Jilly? Wanna *Rub It In* with me?"

"We still talkin' about barbecue, Jack?" she flirted.

And that put them right back on track.

The rest of the afternoon flowed spectacularly into a lively evening.

Mindy and Ollie were in tow, but the former was preoccupied by Garrett, and the latter was taken care of by Ale as the production wound down.

Jack and Jillian found some privacy down by the river. They sat on the swing and tried to catch their breath from the bustling day.

Eventually, he glanced at her and said, "I want you forever, Jillian. Not just a week. Not just a holiday weekend. *Forever.*"

"That's actually quite convenient, cowboy."

His gaze narrowed.

She snuggled up to him and murmured, "Because I want you too. And according to Mindy, there's some cosmic force that's dying to bring us together. Permanently." She paused, then more seriously added, "I believe it's attempting to restore my faith in humanity while making me a medical industry example, while also giving me back hopes and dreams I'd lost."

"You make my head spin, darlin'," he confessed, not sure what she was saying.

She kissed his cheek. And whispered, "I'm pregnant, Jack."

◆ ◆ ◆

Jillian awaited his response.

And waited.

She felt all his muscles go rigid.

He didn't seem to be breathing.

He stared out at the river, his jaw doing its ritual grinding.

"Jack, blink if you can hear me."

"Not funny, Jilly."

"It was sort of funny." He'd said the same to her at the cantina. "And besides . . . I need a reaction."

"You mean besides the one where my heart is leapin' from my chest?"

She twined her arm around his and squeezed. "I'm quite familiar with the feeling. Imagine my surprise. I was told never to expect kids. I took that to mean I could never *have* kids. Turns out, according to my gyno, those are two very different things."

"But—"

"The prognosis was dire, yes. My body fought back, I guess. I don't know." She shrugged. "Patients who are told they'll never walk again prove their doctors and physical therapists wrong. So I'll be another medical wonder under scrutiny and written up in journals—but who cares about all of that? Jack, I'm going to have a baby."

"No, Jillian." He unraveled from her. Turned to face her. And amended, "*We're* going to have a baby."

"Well . . . I didn't want to be presumptuous or anything," she told him as new tears streamed down her cheeks.

He gazed at her. Intently. And asked, "You've made this decision?" She nodded.

"But you didn't want this," he reminded her. "No marriage. No kids."

"Jack . . . I based an entire belief system—for six years—on a horrific freak accident that left me alone and broken. But I resurfaced. And then I came here. And . . ." She swallowed down a lump of emotion. "Yes, the street festival incident threw me. That's really no surprise. I wasn't ready to be in that kind of environment. Even with the BBQ event today, I knew to stay within the confines of that L-shaped kitchen and keep all the people on the other side of the counter. But, Jack. I love the ranch. I love your family. I love you. And . . . we successfully conceived!"

He grinned through his own emotion—she saw it in his eyes, and it moved her. He swept his hand through her hair and kissed her the way only Jack Reed could.

Then he said, "Marry me, Jilly. Be my wife, the mother of my children, the owner of my heart and soul."

"Yes, Jack. If you promise all the same," she said. "You know, only in the masculine sense."

He chuckled. "Deal, darlin'." He pulled her to him and kissed her again.

Giving Jillian back everything she'd ever wanted.

Giving Jack what he deserved.

Giving them both so much more to look forward to. Together.

Acknowledgments

I have lived a full year with these characters in my head, and I'm so thrilled they're seeing the light of day. Thank you to my critique partners, including *New York Times* bestselling authors Cheyenne McCray (a queen of cowboy romances) and Erin Quinn (an expert at creating lush settings), for helping me to shape the proposal that went to my agent, Sarah E. Younger at the Nancy Yost Literary Agency. I was pleased to work with Sarah on yet another project, and she found a beautiful home for this book at Montlake. It was a pleasure to reconnect with Lauren Plude and have the opportunity to work with an amazing editor, Krista Stroever, and the rest of the team.

I'm also grateful for the words of encouragement from the judges of the Mid-Michigan Romance Writers of American 2022 Best Banter Contest regarding the two scenes that double-finaled in—and won—the competition. I'm glad you liked Jack and Jillian's witty repartee, and I hope readers will enjoy their sexy vibe too!

Book Two is in the works, and I look forward to sharing it with y'all! Hugs!

About the Author

With works ranging from contemporaries to rock star romances to romantic suspense to paranormals, Gigi Templeton is an international bestselling author. Her novels and novellas have been published under three pseudonyms by traditional publishers, including St. Martin's Press and Hachette/Forever, digital publishers such as Harlequin's Carina Press, and serialized fiction apps such as Radish Fiction and YONDER. Templeton's *Spiced Right* won the Mid-Michigan Romance Writers of America's (MMRWA's) Best Banter Contest in November 2022. She was also a finalist for the *Romantic Times* Best Book of the Year and Seal of Excellence.

Templeton lives in Arizona with her real-life hero and her rescued Maltese, and she is currently studying culinary arts and food photography. Read her blog and sign up for her newsletter at www.ggtblog.com and follow her on Facebook and Twitter @ggtbooks.